WATTERS • LEYH • PIETSCH • LAIHO

LUMBERJANES™

SINK OR SWIM

BOOM! BOX™

BOOm! BOX™

LUMBERJANES Volume Six, April 2017. Published by BOOM! Box, a division of Boom Entertainment, Inc. Lumberjanes is ™ & © 2017 Shannon Watters, Grace Ellis, Noelle Stevenson & Brooke Allen. Originally published in single magazine form as LUMBERJANES No. 21-24. ™ & © 2016 Shannon Watters, Grace Ellis, Noelle Stevenson & Brooke Allen. All rights reserved. BOOM! Box™ and the BOOM! Box logo are trademarks of Boom Entertainment, Inc., registered in various countries and categories. All characters, events, and institutions depicted herein are fictional. Any similarity between any of the names, characters, persons, events, and/or institutions in this publication to actual names, characters, and persons, whether living or dead, events, and/or institutions is unintended and purely coincidental. BOOM! Box does not read or accept unsolicited submissions of ideas, stories, or artwork.

A catalog record of this book is available from OCLC and from the BOOM! Studios website, www.boom-studios.com, on the Librarians Page.

BOOM! Studios, 5670 Wilshire Boulevard, Suite 450, Los Angeles, CA 90036-5679. Printed in China. First Printing.

ISBN: 978-1-60886-954-1, eISBN: 978-1-61398-625-7

THIS LUMBERJANES FIELD MANUAL BELONGS TO:

NAME:_____

TROOP:_____

DATE INVESTED:_____

FIELD MANUAL TABLE OF CONTENTS

LUMBERJANES
FIELD MANUAL

For the Intermediate Program

Tenth Edition • June 1984

Prepared for the

**Miss Qiunzella Thiskwin
Penniquiqul Thistle Crumpet's**
CAMP FOR 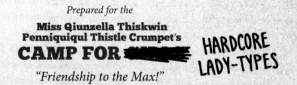 HARDCORE LADY-TYPES

"Friendship to the Max!"

A MESSAGE FROM THE LUMBERJANES HIGH COUNCIL

Miss Quinzella Thiskwin
Penniquiqul Thistle Crumpet's
Camp for
FRIENDSHIP TO THE MAX!

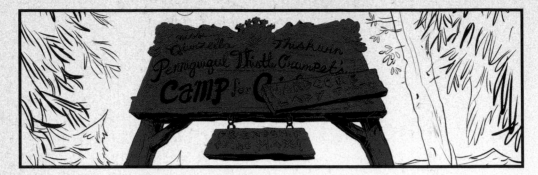

We love life. That is something that we feel is obvious in the way we present ourselves, but sometimes it is important to say these things out loud. Every life, and we mean all of them, is important and even if it hasn't quite figured out what its role is in the grand scheme of things, we believe that it will make a difference in all the lives that it touches. One of the things we want to ensure is taken to heart for each and every young camper that we have the joy of mentoring is that they know how important they are, and that they understand that even if they haven't quite figured it out yet, they will.

It was at our last gathering that we thought fondly back on our times as Lumberjanes. The camp was very different back then, and in some ways, nothing has changed. We remember running wild in the woods, learning skills that we never dreamed of, and yet can't imagine life without in in our more experienced age. We hope that every camper here sees the many opportunities that we try to offer at our camps and that each and every Lumberjane understands why we feel the lessons we want to teach are important. It might be a few years after they have left the camp before they truly realize the potential of some of the teachings they learned in the safety of our camp, but we hope that they all get to experience that moment.

To every new scout that we have joining our family, we want to welcome you to our camp. To every Lumberjane that is returning, we hope that you make this new term just as exciting, if not even more so, than the last. Each and every one of you have something unique and beautiful inside of you, and we hope that during your time at camp that you are able to share it with others. Being part of the Lumberjanes has influenced our lives in so many ways, and we are excited to see how it influences yours.

THE LUMBERJANES PLEDGE

I solemnly swear to do my best
Every day, and in all that I do,
To be brave and strong,
To be truthful and compassionate,
To be interesting and interested,
To pay attention and question
The world around me,
To think of others first,
To always help and protect my friends,
[redacted]
And to make the world a better place
For Lumberjane scouts
And for everyone else.

THEN THERE'S A LINE ABOUT GOD, OR WHATEVER

LUMBERJANES™

SINK OR SWIM

Written by
Shannon Watters
& Kat Leyh

Illustrated by
Carey Pietsch

Colors by
Maarta Laiho

Letters by
Aubrey Aiese

Cover by
Noelle Stevenson

Badges and Design by
Kelsey Dieterich
Associate Editor
Whitney Leopard
Editor
Dafna Pleban
*Special thanks to **Kelsey Pate** for giving the Lumberjanes their name.*

Created by **Shannon Watters, Grace Ellis, Noelle Stevenson & Brooke Allen**

LUMBERJANES FIELD MANUAL
CHAPTER TWENTY-ONE

Lumberjanes "Out-of-Doors" Program Field

ALL FOR KNOT BADGE

"An easy-going bonding activity."

Everyday at camp comes with its own obstacles, some of those are the same everyday issues that we face regardless of where we are. The other obstacles, the ones that surprise us, those are the problems that we need our friends for. We need our community and we need our friends to help us out of these problems. They aren't frequent, and they often show up out of the blue, but that is why we work so hard at building such a tight-knit community here at camp. As a Lumberjane, you will need to know how to respond to these kinds of problems, regardless if they are your own or if they are from another member of this camp.

The *All For Knot* badge is meant to be a bonding activity, not only between the different types of rope that your counselor has given you, but between the campers who decide to earn this badge together. The *All For Knot* badge is one of the most unique badges at this camp because this is a badge that must be earned as

a team. Every member of the team will need to show off their mastery of rope and knot tying to earn this badge.

To obtain the *All For Knot* badge, the campers must first take the basic knot tying courses that are required of all campers. They must learn mastery over rope and gain the knowledge that is needed for basic tying around camp. Rope is commonplace at camp, whether it's from pitching tents or tying boats to the dock, they can be found to have many uses. When a group of campers feels they are ready to earn the *All For Knot* badge, they will approach the appropriate counselor and start the test. Every member of the team will need to tie the knot that their counselor asks for, and if one member of the team fails to complete the task, then every member of the team fails the test. They are allowed to come back and test for the badge the following day, but may not change their team and may not take the task more than once a day.

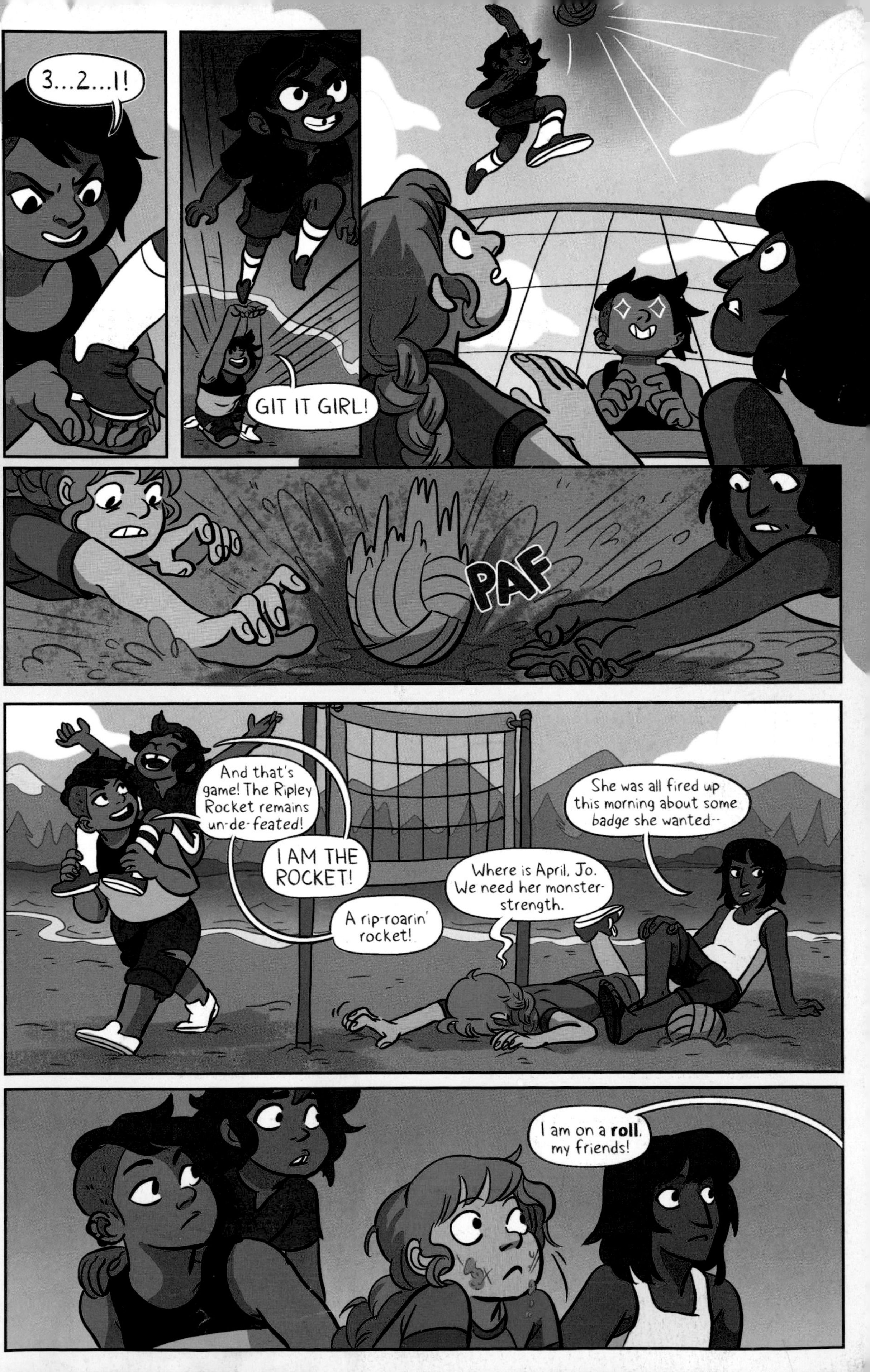
3...2...1!
GIT IT GIRL!
PAF
And that's game! The Ripley Rocket remains un-de-feated!
I AM THE ROCKET!
A rip-roarin' rocket!
Where is April, Jo. We need her monster-strength.
She was all fired up this morning about some badge she wanted--
I am on a **roll**, my friends!

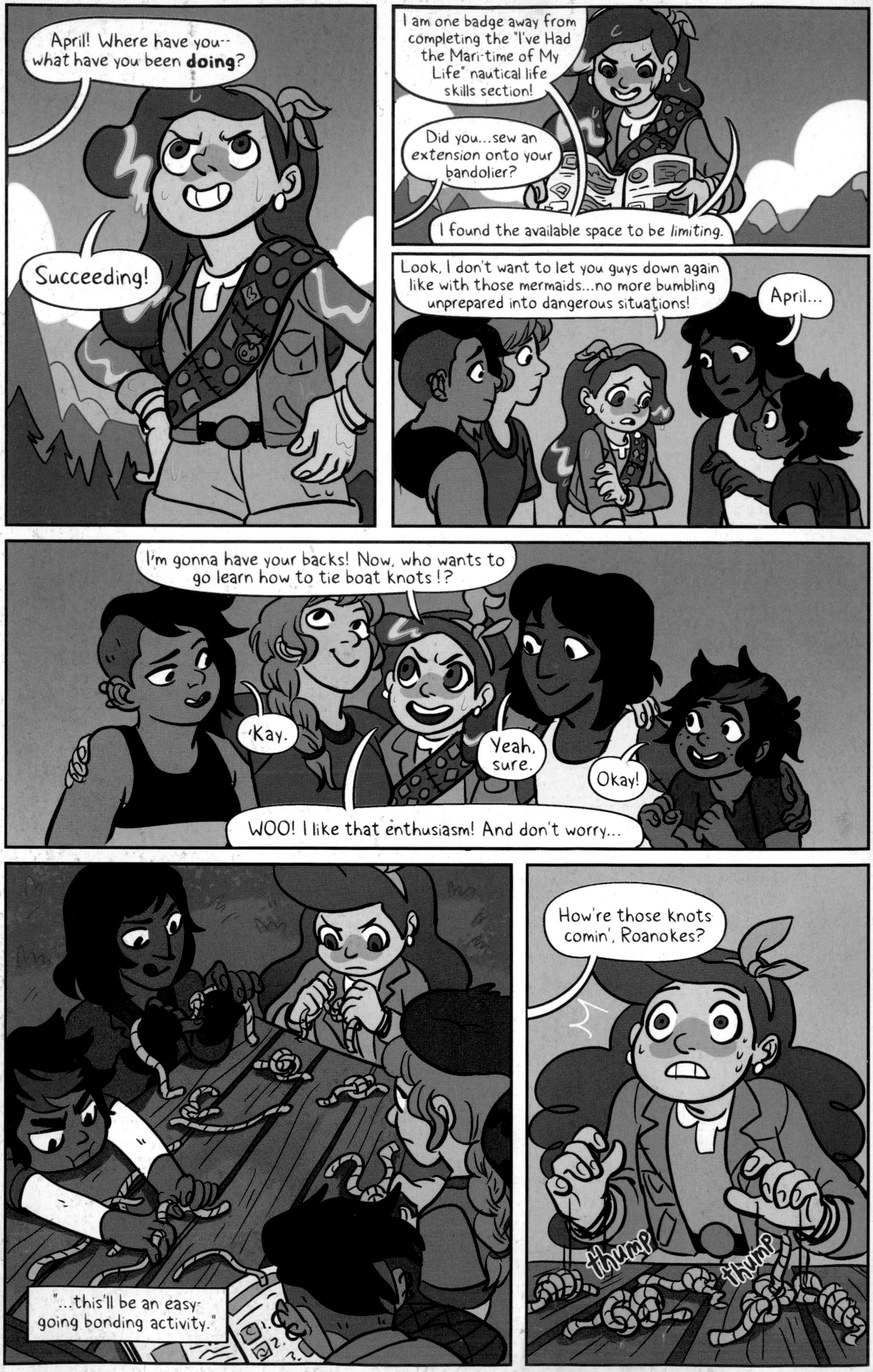
April! Where have you-- what have you been **doing**?
Succeeding!
I am one badge away from completing the "I've Had the Mari-time of My Life" nautical life skills section!
Did you...sew an extension onto your bandolier?
I found the available space to be *limiting*.
Look, I don't want to let you guys down again like with those mermaids...no more bumbling unprepared into dangerous situations!
April...
I'm gonna have your backs! Now, who wants to go learn how to tie boat knots!?
'Kay.
Yeah, sure.
Okay!
WOO! I like that enthusiasm! And don't worry...
"...this'll be an easy-going bonding activity."
How're those knots comin', Roanokes?
thump
thump

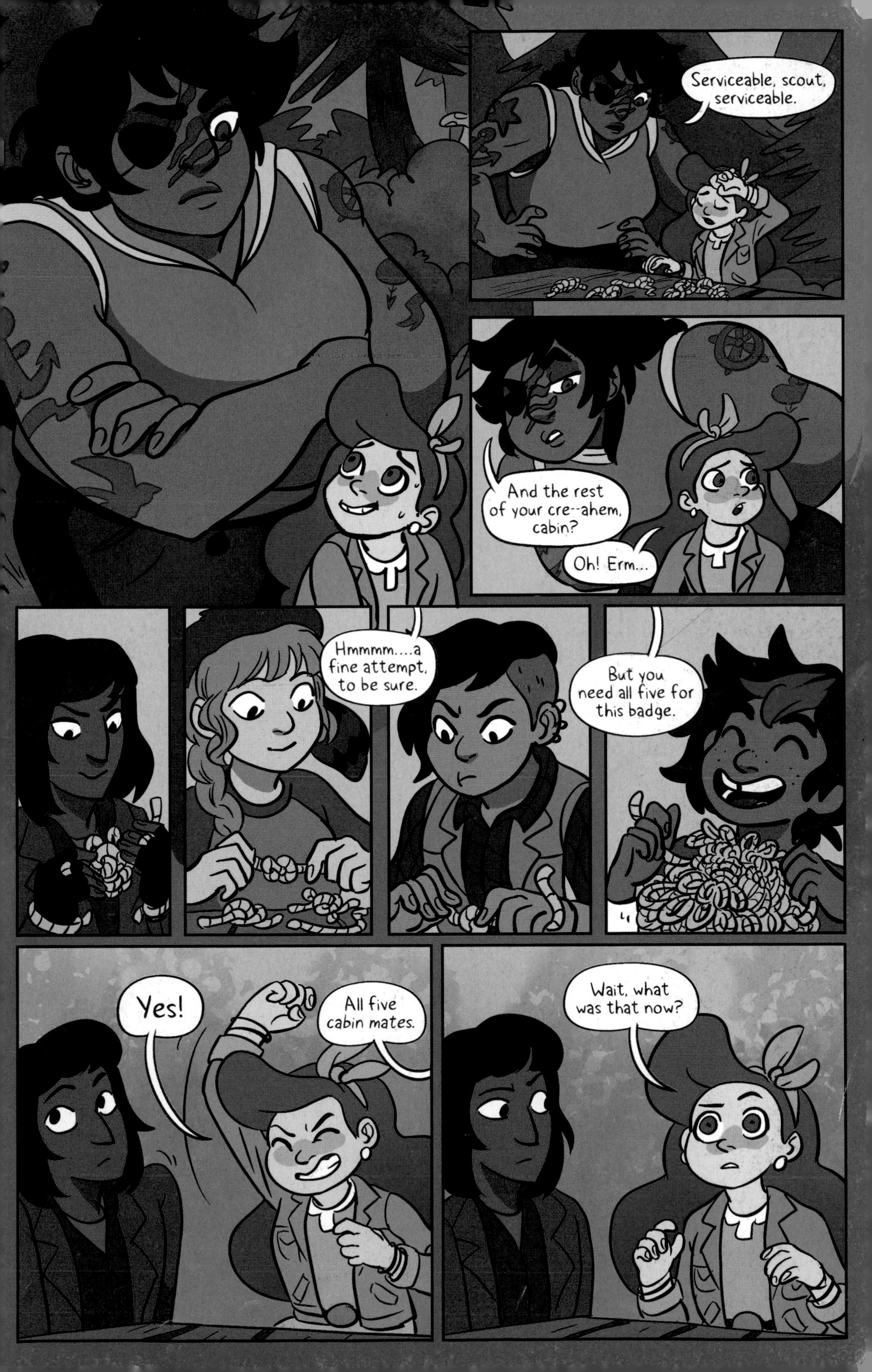
Serviceable, scout, serviceable.
And the rest of your cre--ahem, cabin?
Oh! Erm...
Hmmmm....a fine attempt, to be sure.
But you need all five for this badge.
Yes!
All five cabin mates.
Wait, what was that now?

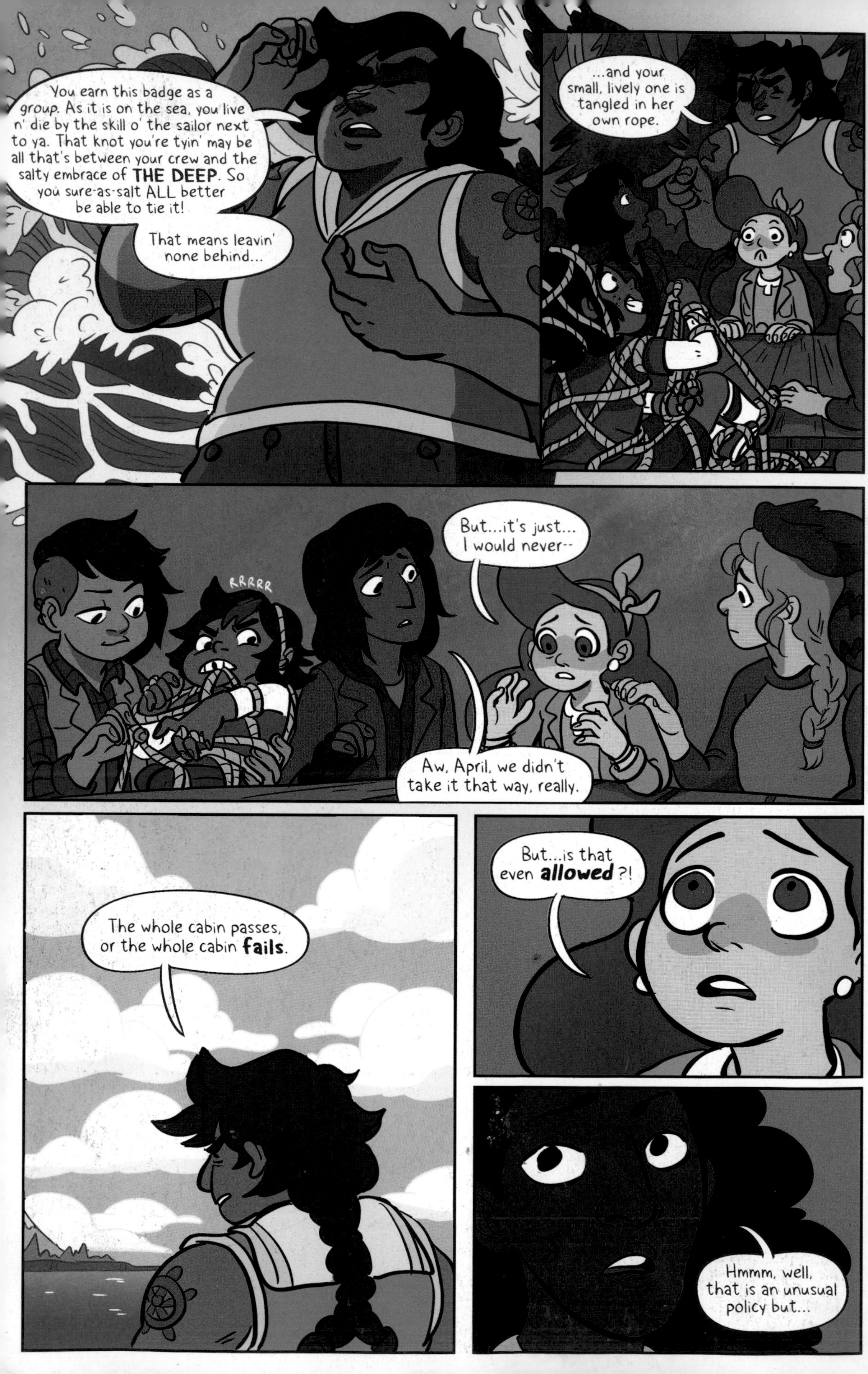

You earn this badge as a group. As it is on the sea, you live n' die by the skill o' the sailor next to ya. That knot you're tyin' may be all that's between your crew and the salty embrace of **THE DEEP**. So you sure-as-salt ALL better be able to tie it!
That means leavin' none behind...
...and your small, lively one is tangled in her own rope.
RRRRR
But...it's just... I would never--
Aw, April, we didn't take it that way, really.
The whole cabin passes, or the whole cabin **fails**.
But...is that even **allowed**?!
Hmmm, well, that is an unusual policy but...

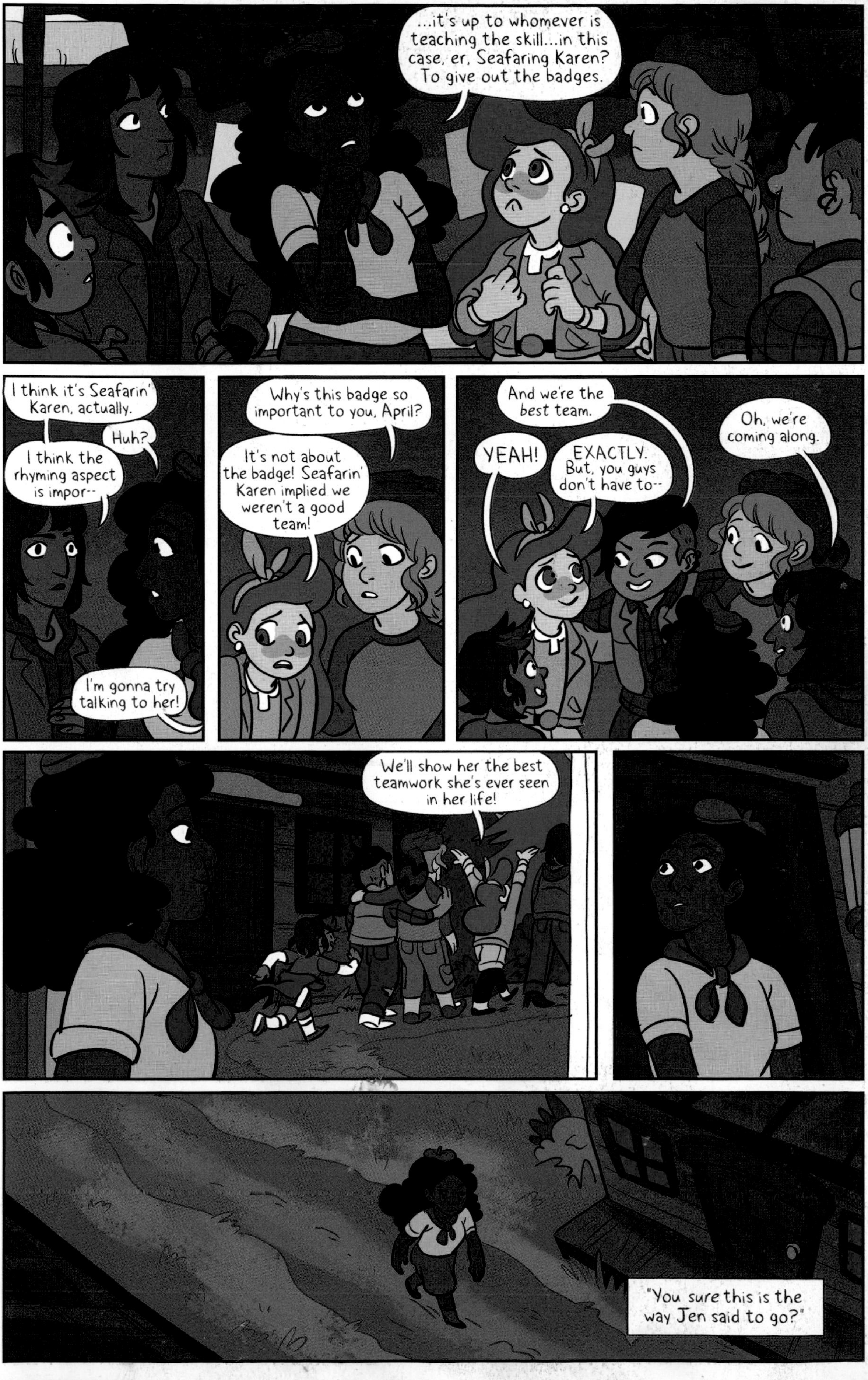
...it's up to whomever is teaching the skill...in this case, er, Seafaring Karen? To give out the badges.
I think it's Seafarin' Karen, actually.
Huh?
I think the rhyming aspect is impor--
I'm gonna try talking to her!
Why's this badge so important to you, April?
It's not about the badge! Seafarin' Karen implied we weren't a good team!
And we're the best team.
YEAH!
EXACTLY. But, you guys don't have to--
Oh, we're coming along.
We'll show her the best teamwork she's ever seen in her life!
"You sure this is the way Jen said to go?"

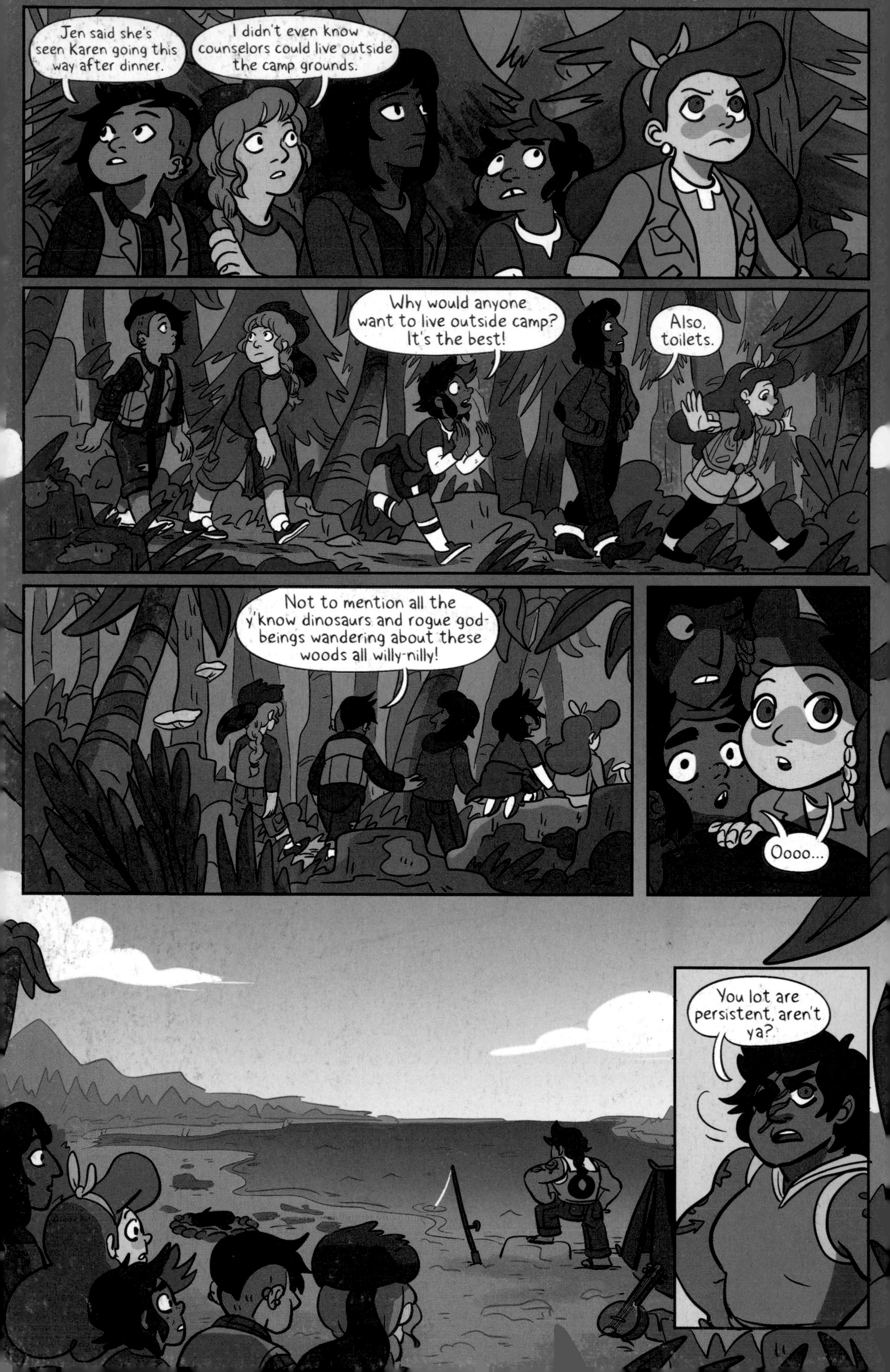
Jen said she's seen Karen going this way after dinner.
I didn't even know counselors could live outside the camp grounds.
Why would anyone want to live outside camp? It's the best!
Also, toilets.
Not to mention all the y'know dinosaurs and rogue god-beings wandering about these woods all willy-nilly!
Oooo...
You lot are persistent, aren't ya?

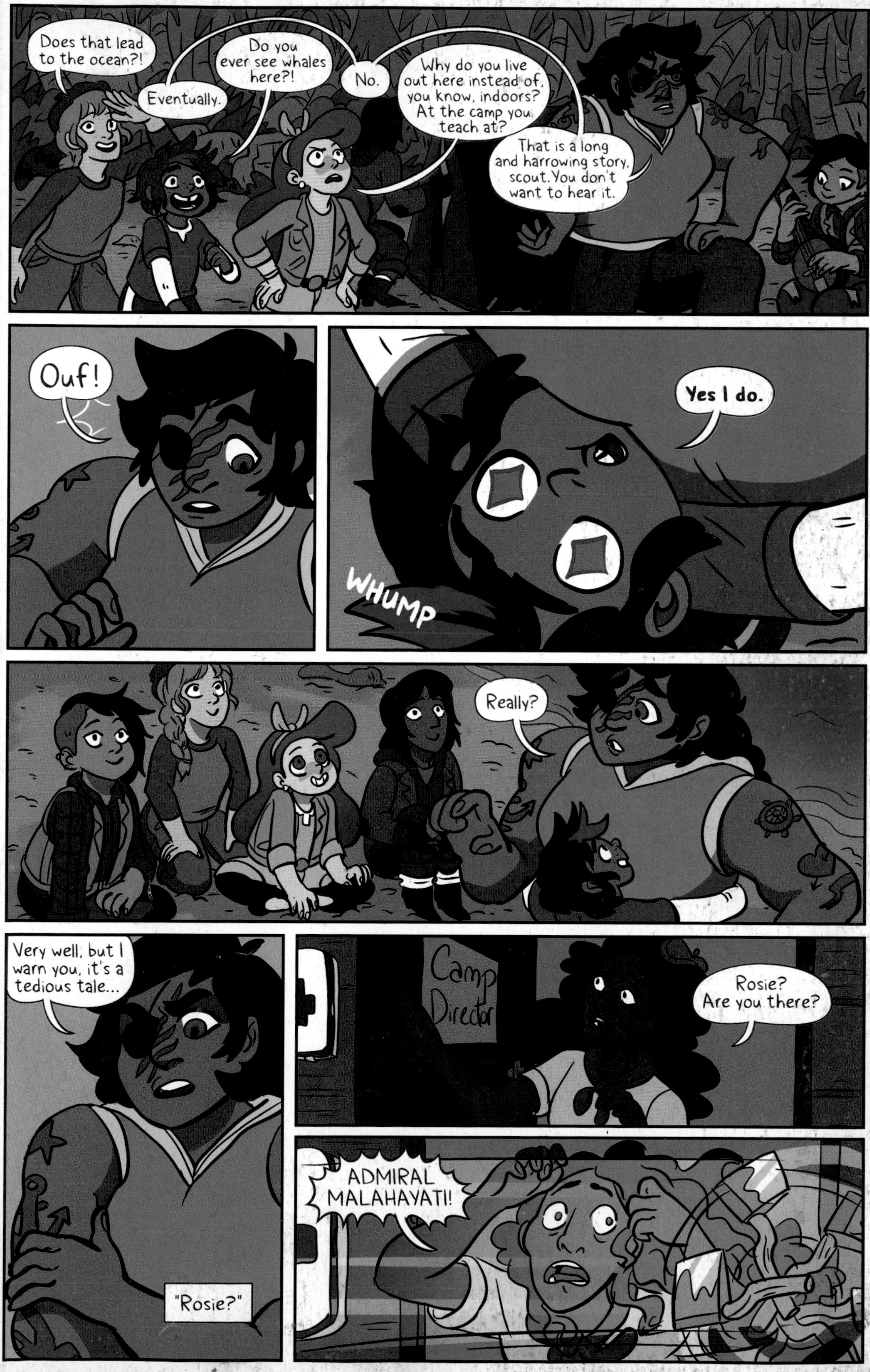

Does that lead to the ocean?!
Eventually.
Do you ever see whales here?!
No.
Why do you live out here instead of, you know, indoors? At the camp you teach at?
That is a long and harrowing story, scout. You don't want to hear it.
Ouf!
Yes I do.
WHUMP
Really?
Very well, but I warn you, it's a tedious tale...
"Rosie?"
Camp Director
Rosie? Are you there?
ADMIRAL MALAHAYATI!

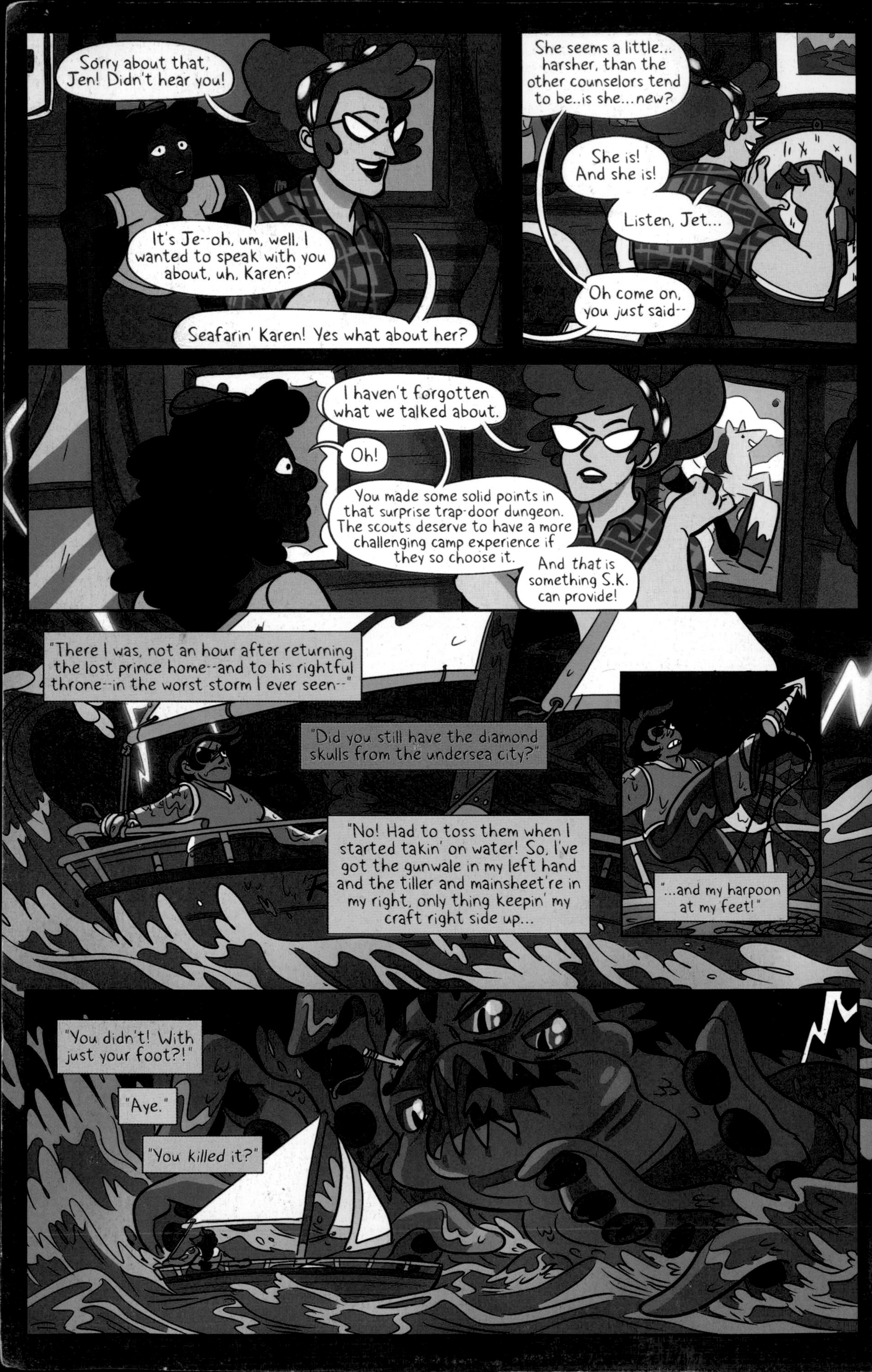
Sorry about that, Jen! Didn't hear you!
It's Je--oh, um, well, I wanted to speak with you about, uh, Karen?
Seafarin' Karen! Yes what about her?
She seems a little... harsher, than the other counselors tend to be..is she... new?
She is! And she is!
Listen, Jet...
Oh come on, you just said--
I haven't forgotten what we talked about.
Oh!
You made some solid points in that surprise trap-door dungeon. The scouts deserve to have a more challenging camp experience if they so choose it.
And that is something S.K. can provide!
"There I was, not an hour after returning the lost prince home--and to his rightful throne--in the worst storm I ever seen--"
"Did you still have the diamond skulls from the undersea city?"
"No! Had to toss them when I started takin' on water! So, I've got the gunwale in my left hand and the tiller and mainsheet're in my right, only thing keepin' my craft right side up...
"...and my harpoon at my feet!"
"You didn't! With just your foot?!"
"Aye."
"You killed it?"

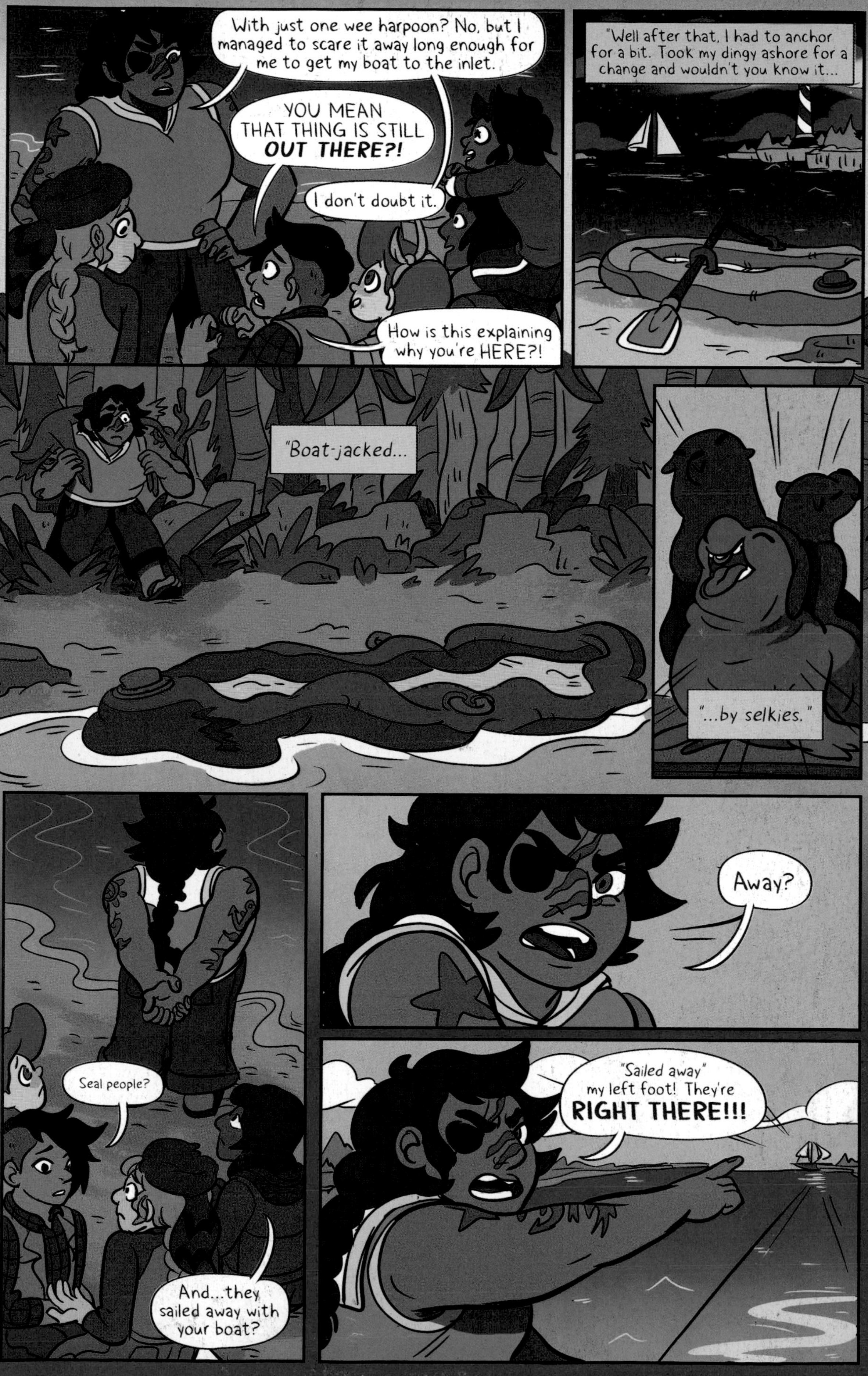
With just one wee harpoon? No, but I managed to scare it away long enough for me to get my boat to the inlet.
YOU MEAN THAT THING IS STILL **OUT THERE?!**
I don't doubt it.
How is this explaining why you're HERE?!
"Well after that, I had to anchor for a bit. Took my dingy ashore for a change and wouldn't you know it...
"Boat-jacked...
"...by selkies."
Away?
Seal people?
And...they sailed away with your boat?
"Sailed away" my left foot! They're **RIGHT THERE!!!**

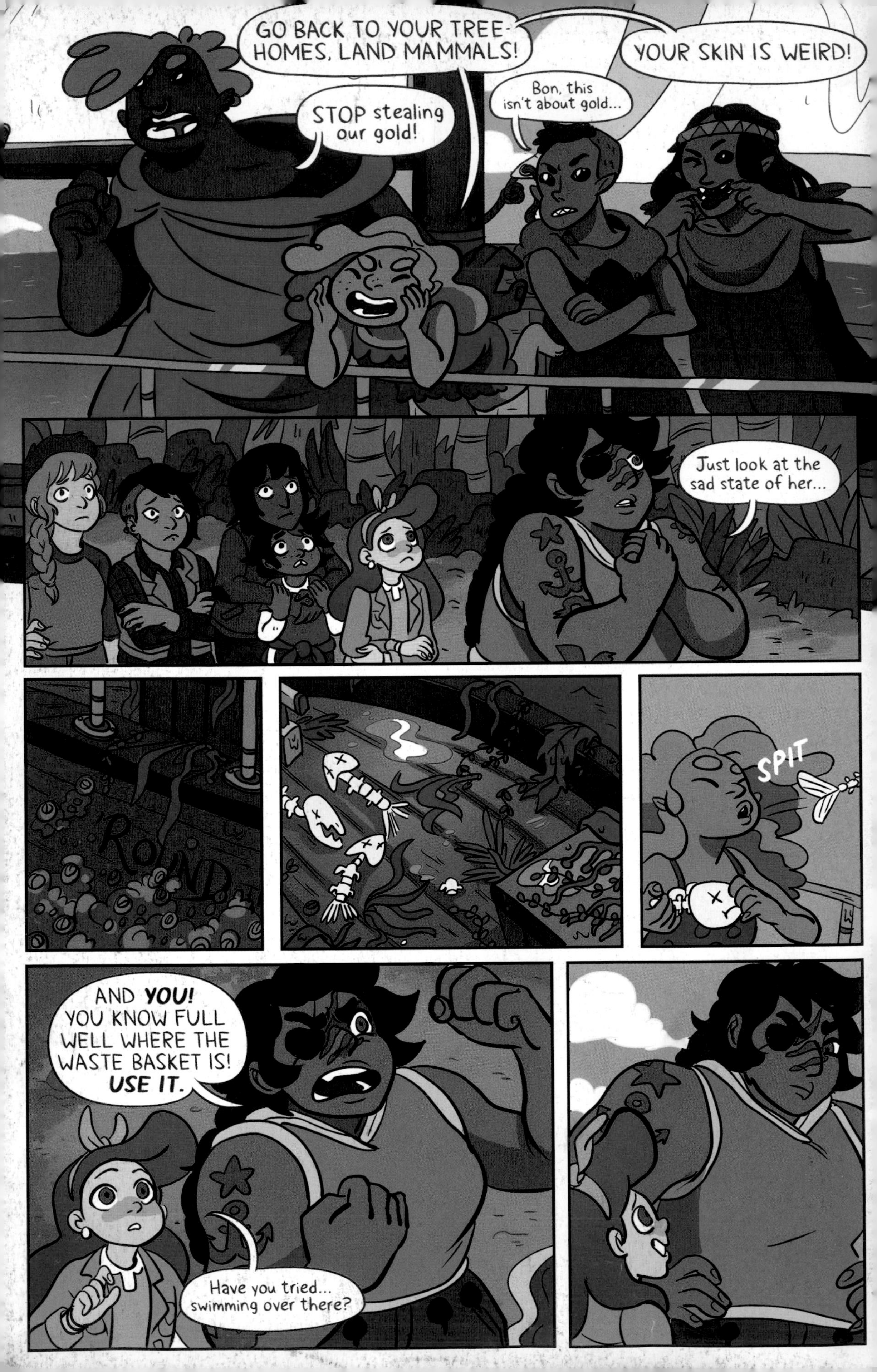
GO BACK TO YOUR TREE-HOMES, LAND MAMMALS!
YOUR SKIN IS WEIRD!
STOP stealing our gold!
Bon, this isn't about gold...
Just look at the sad state of her...
ROUND
SPIT
AND YOU! YOU KNOW FULL WELL WHERE THE WASTE BASKET IS! USE IT.
Have you tried... swimming over there?

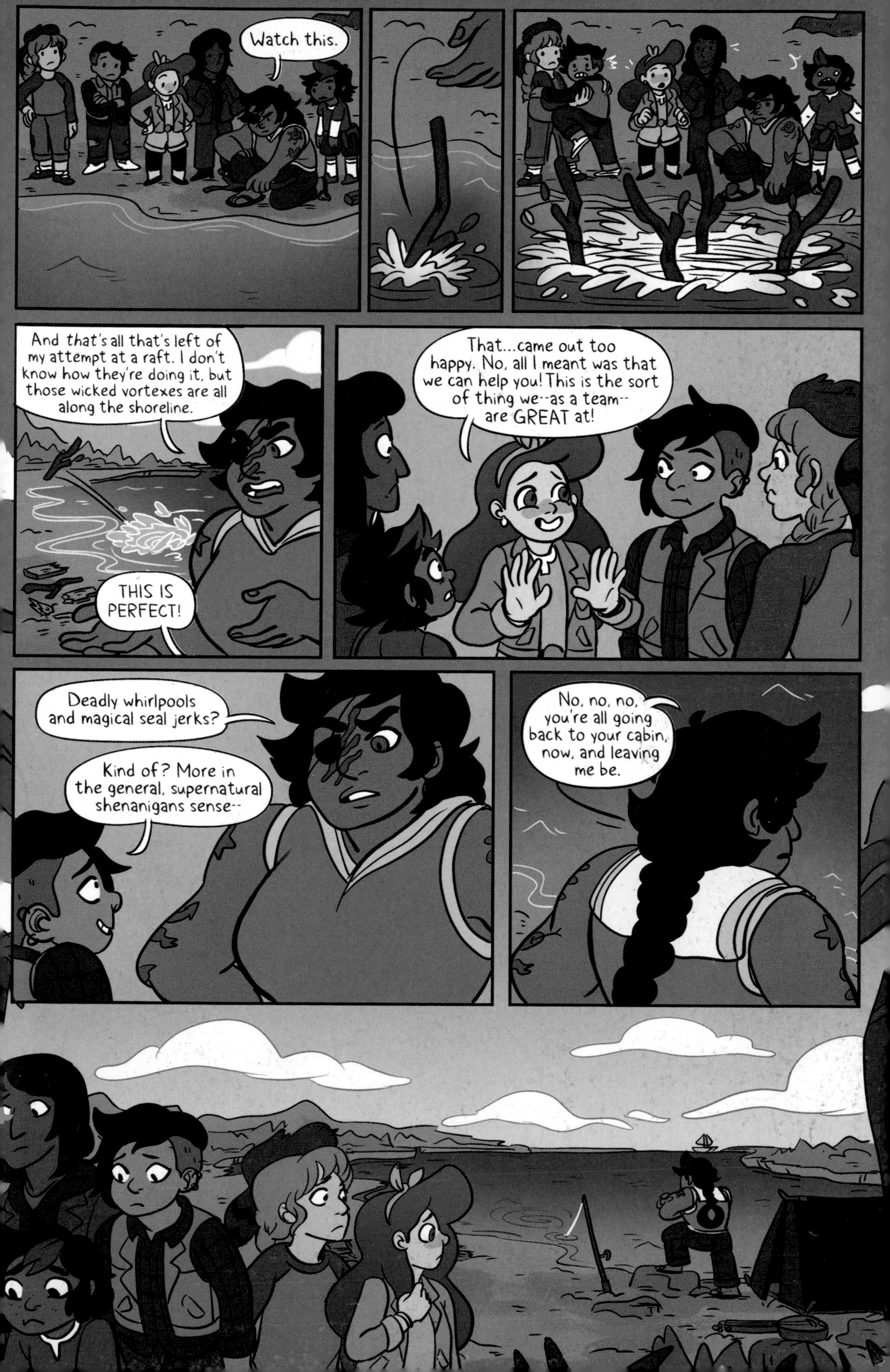
Watch this.
And that's all that's left of my attempt at a raft. I don't know how they're doing it, but those wicked vortexes are all along the shoreline.
THIS IS PERFECT!
That...came out too happy. No, all I meant was that we can help you! This is the sort of thing we--as a team--are GREAT at!
Deadly whirlpools and magical seal jerks?
Kind of? More in the general, supernatural shenanigans sense--
No, no, no, you're all going back to your cabin, now, and leaving me be.

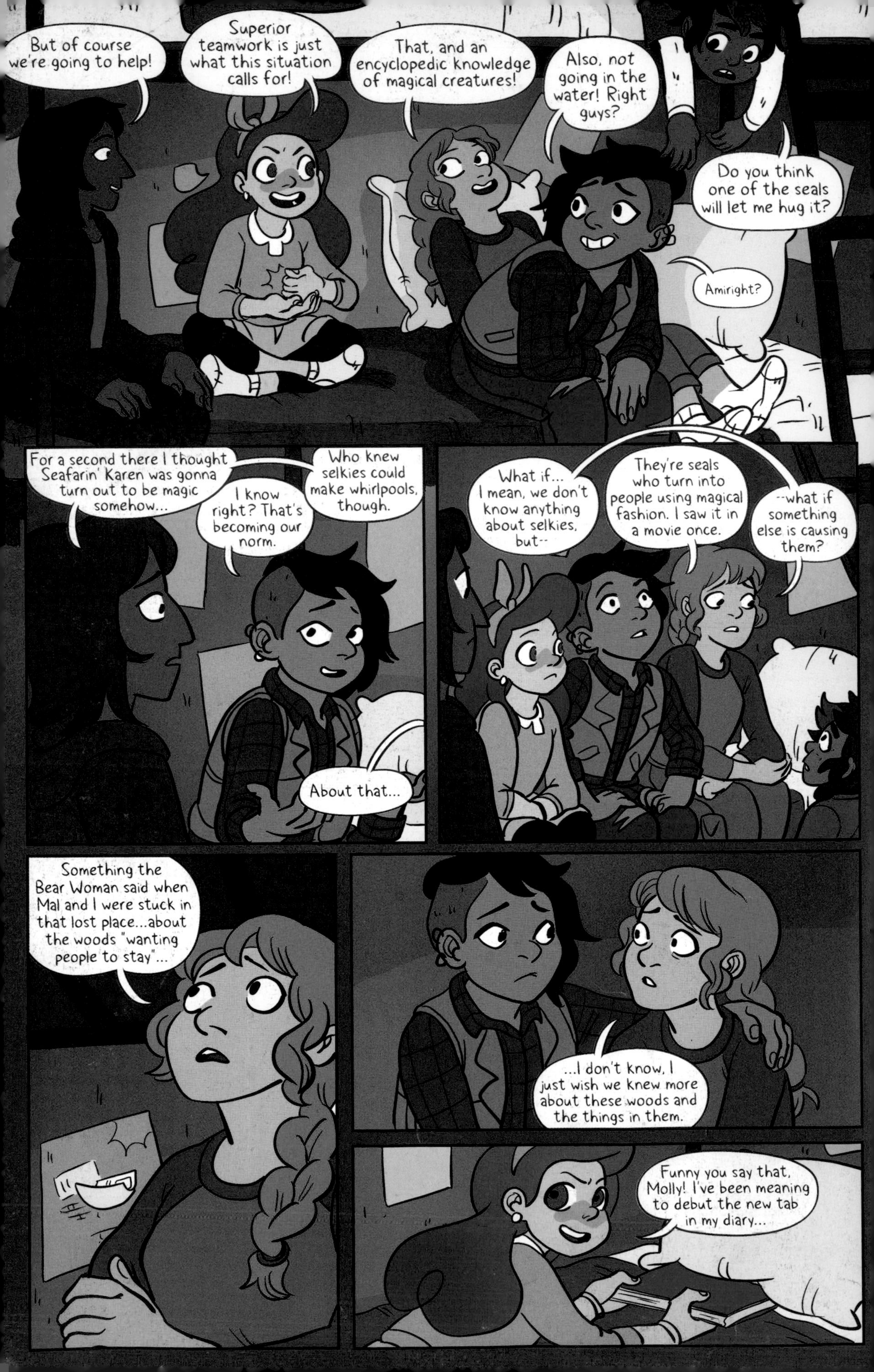
But of course we're going to help!
Superior teamwork is just what this situation calls for!
That, and an encyclopedic knowledge of magical creatures!
Also, not going in the water! Right guys?
Do you think one of the seals will let me hug it?
Amiright?
For a second there I thought Seafarin' Karen was gonna turn out to be magic somehow...
I know right? That's becoming our norm.
Who knew selkies could make whirlpools, though.
About that...
What if... I mean, we don't know anything about selkies, but--
They're seals who turn into people using magical fashion. I saw it in a movie once.
--what if something else is causing them?
Something the Bear Woman said when Mal and I were stuck in that lost place...about the woods "wanting people to stay"...
...I don't know, I just wish we knew more about these woods and the things in them.
Funny you say that, Molly! I've been meaning to debut the new tab in my diary...

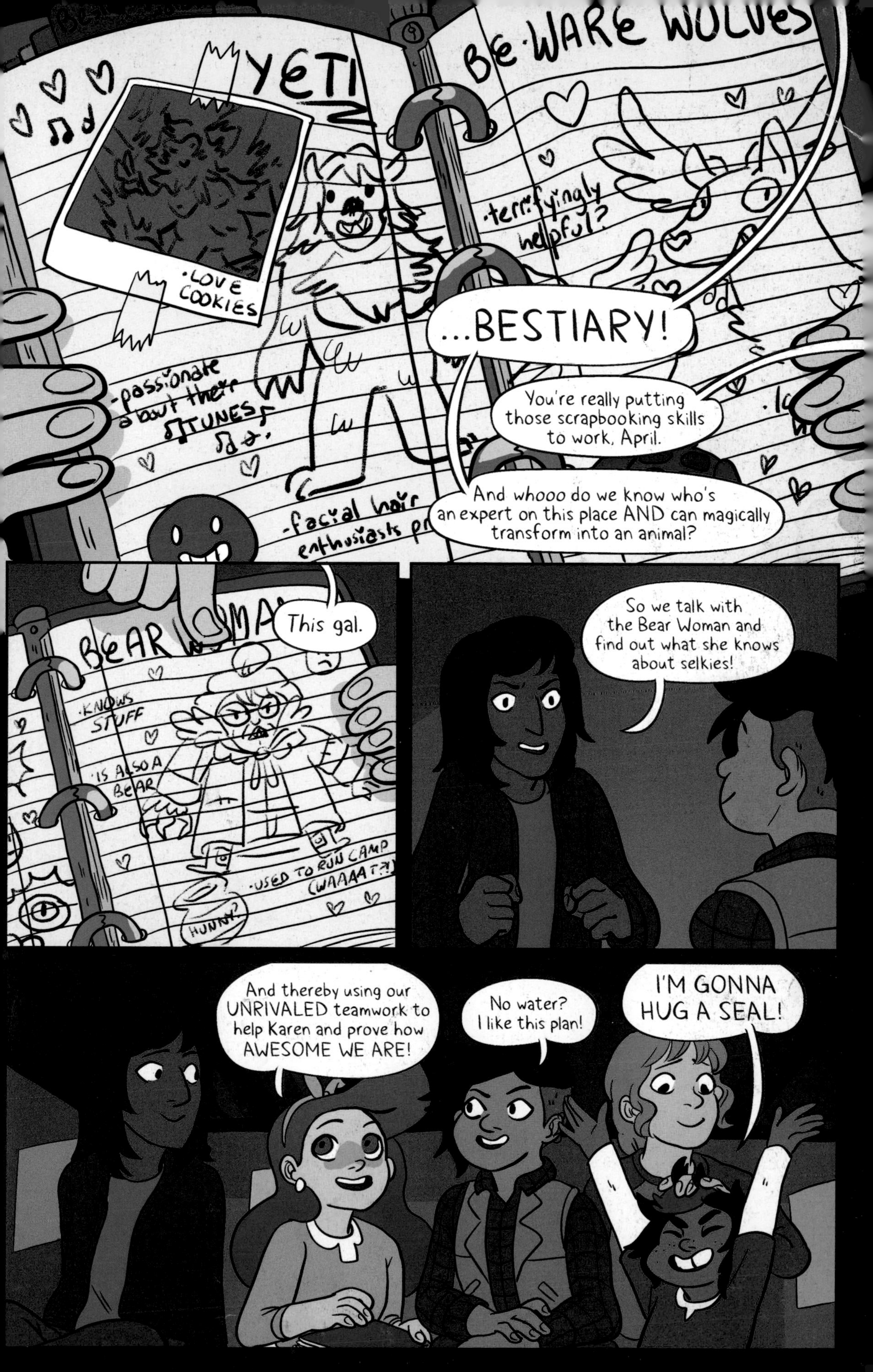
YETI
BE·WARE WOLVES
·LOVE COOKIES
-passionate about their TUNES
·terrifyingly helpful?
-facial hair enthusiasts
...BESTIARY!
You're really putting those scrapbooking skills to work, April.
And whooo do we know who's an expert on this place AND can magically transform into an animal?
BEAR
This gal.
·KNOWS STUFF
·IS ALSO A BEAR
·USED TO RUN CAMP (WAAAAT?!)
HUNNY?
So we talk with the Bear Woman and find out what she knows about selkies!
And thereby using our UNRIVALED teamwork to help Karen and prove how AWESOME WE ARE!
No water? I like this plan!
I'M GONNA HUG A SEAL!

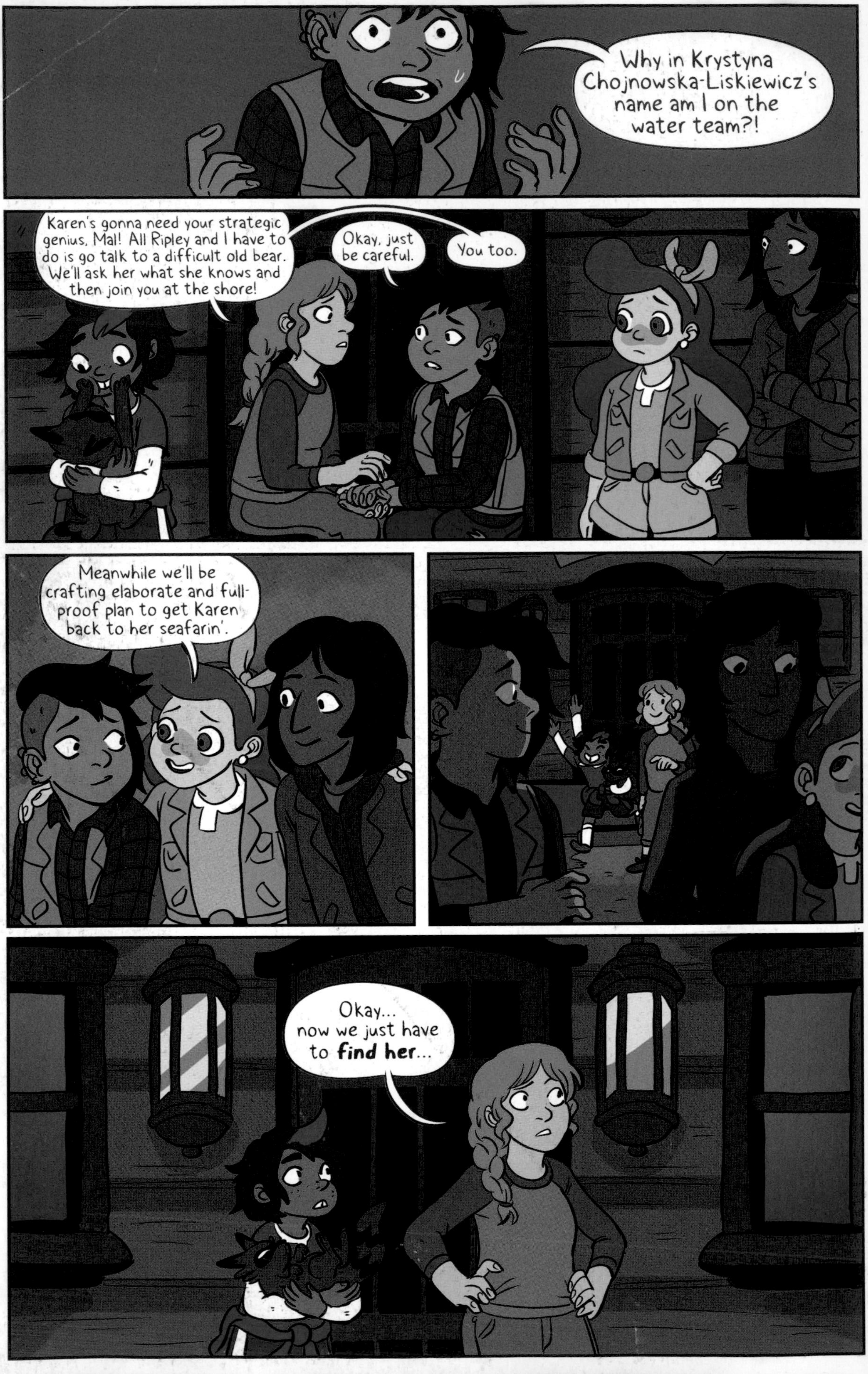
Why in Krystyna Chojnowska-Liskiewicz's name am I on the water team?!
Karen's gonna need your strategic genius, Mal! All Ripley and I have to do is go talk to a difficult old bear. We'll ask her what she knows and then join you at the shore!
Okay, just be careful.
You too.
Meanwhile we'll be crafting elaborate and full-proof plan to get Karen back to her seafarin'.
Okay... now we just have to **find her**...

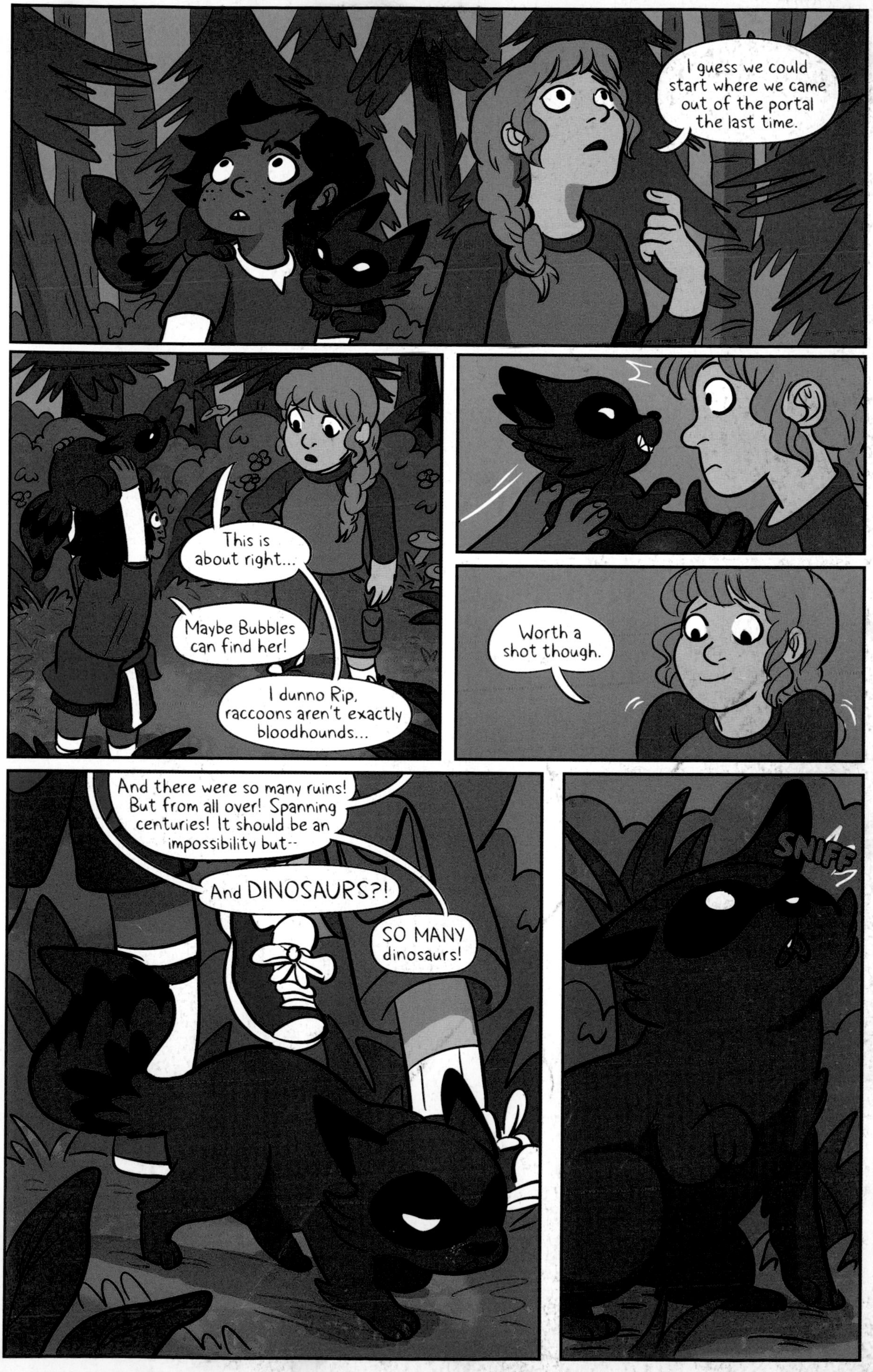
I guess we could start where we came out of the portal the last time.
This is about right...
Maybe Bubbles can find her!
I dunno Rip, raccoons aren't exactly bloodhounds...
Worth a shot though.
And there were so many ruins! But from all over! Spanning centuries! It should be an impossibility but--
And DINOSAURS?!
SO MANY dinosaurs!
SNIFF

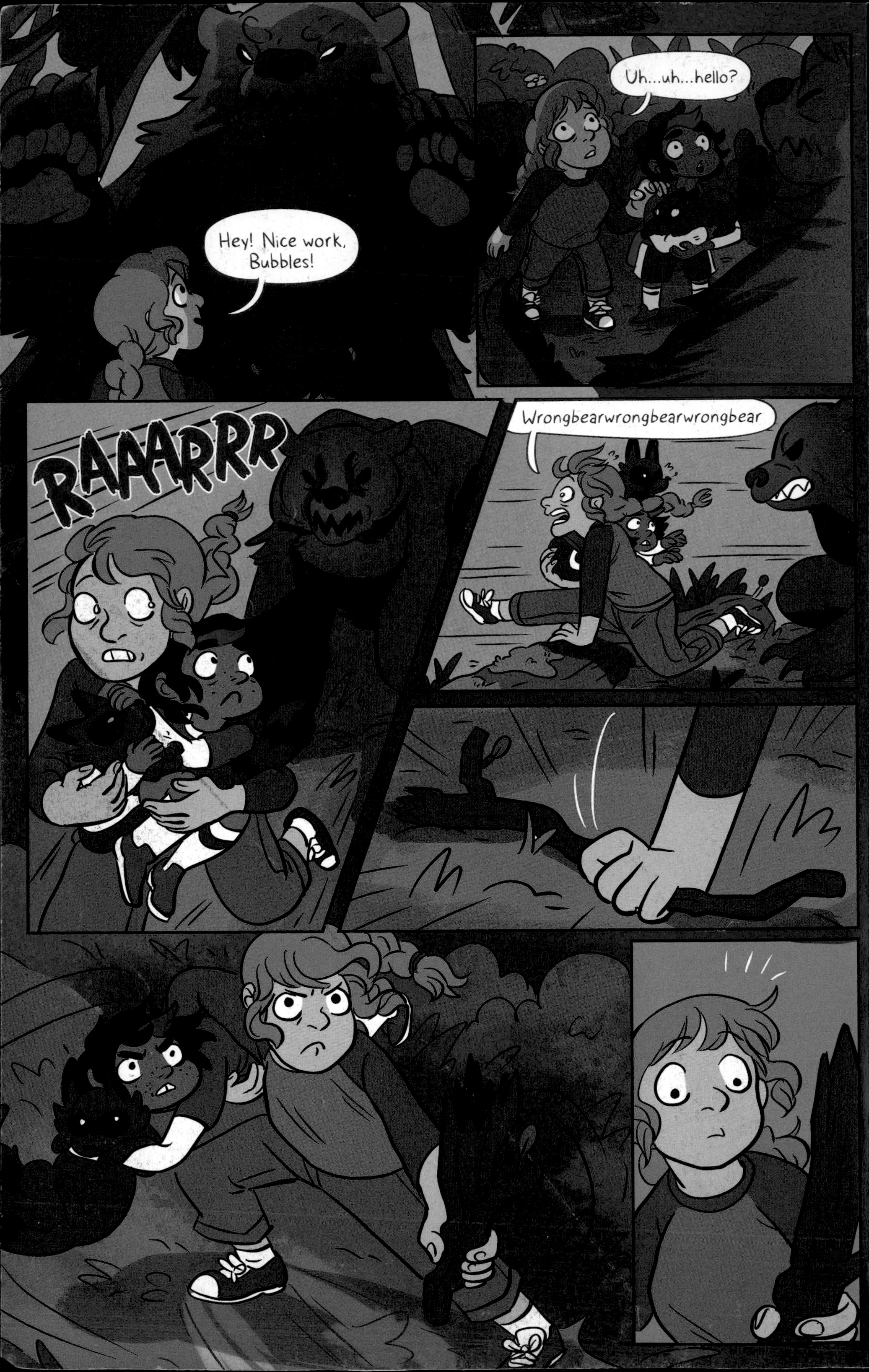
Hey! Nice work, Bubbles!
Uh...uh...hello?
RAAARRR
Wrongbearwrongbearwrongbear

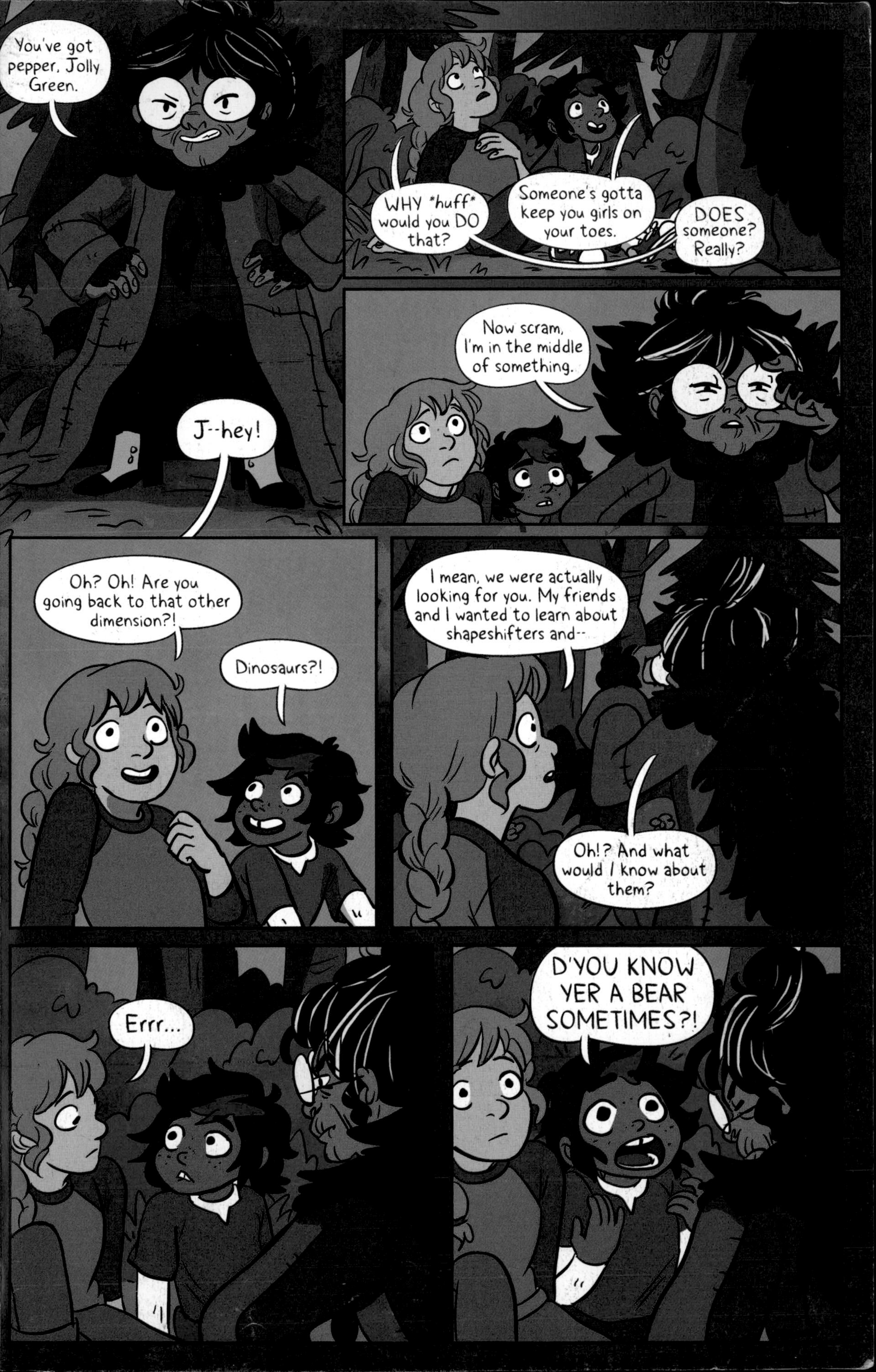
You've got pepper, Jolly Green.
WHY *huff* would you DO that?
Someone's gotta keep you girls on your toes.
DOES someone? Really?
Now scram, I'm in the middle of something.
J--hey!
Oh? Oh! Are you going back to that other dimension?!
Dinosaurs?!
I mean, we were actually looking for you. My friends and I wanted to learn about shapeshifters and--
Oh!? And what would I know about them?
Errr...
D'YOU KNOW YER A BEAR SOMETIMES?!

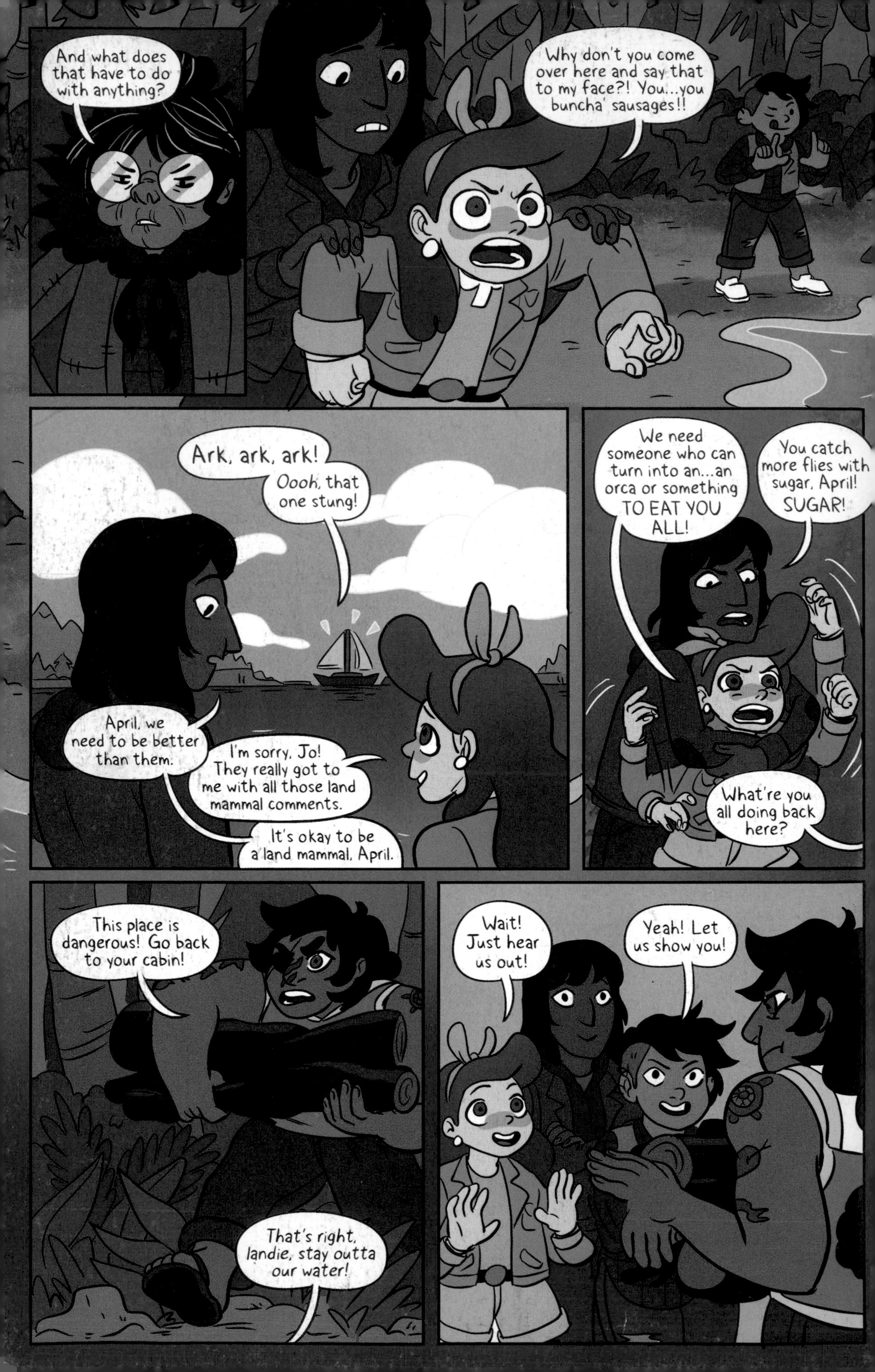
And what does that have to do with anything?
Why don't you come over here and say that to my face?! You...you buncha' sausages!!
Ark, ark, ark!
Oooh, that one stung!
April, we need to be better than them.
I'm sorry, Jo! They really got to me with all those land mammal comments.
It's okay to be a land mammal, April.
We need someone who can turn into an...an orca or something TO EAT YOU ALL!
You catch more flies with sugar, April! SUGAR!
What're you all doing back here?
This place is dangerous! Go back to your cabin!
That's right, landie, stay outta our water!
Wait! Just hear us out!
Yeah! Let us show you!

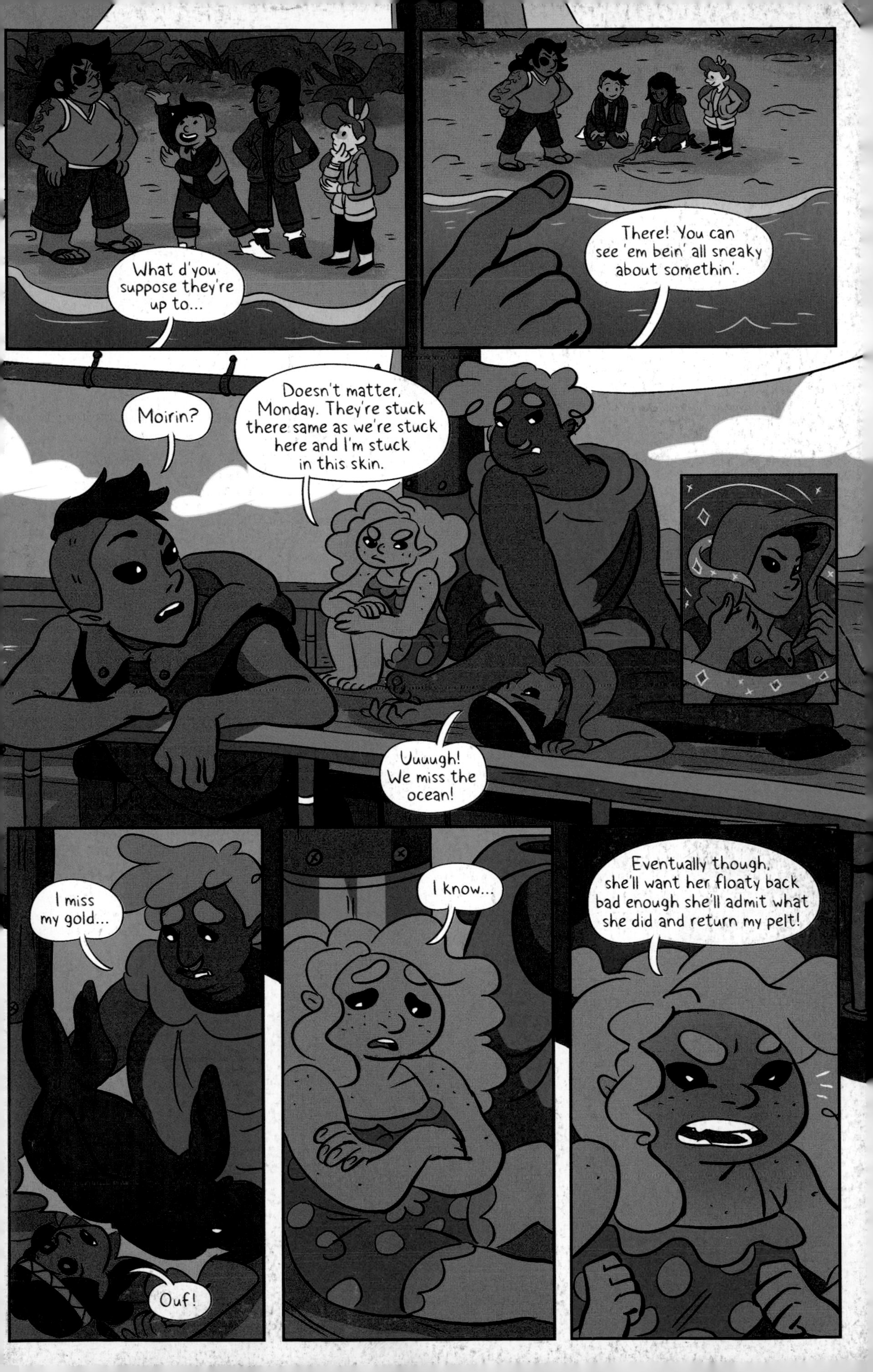
What d'you suppose they're up to...
There! You can see 'em bein' all sneaky about somethin'.
Moirin?
Doesn't matter, Monday. They're stuck there same as we're stuck here and I'm stuck in this skin.
Uuuugh! We miss the ocean!
I miss my gold...
Ouf!
I know...
Eventually though, she'll want her floaty back bad enough she'll admit what she did and return my pelt!

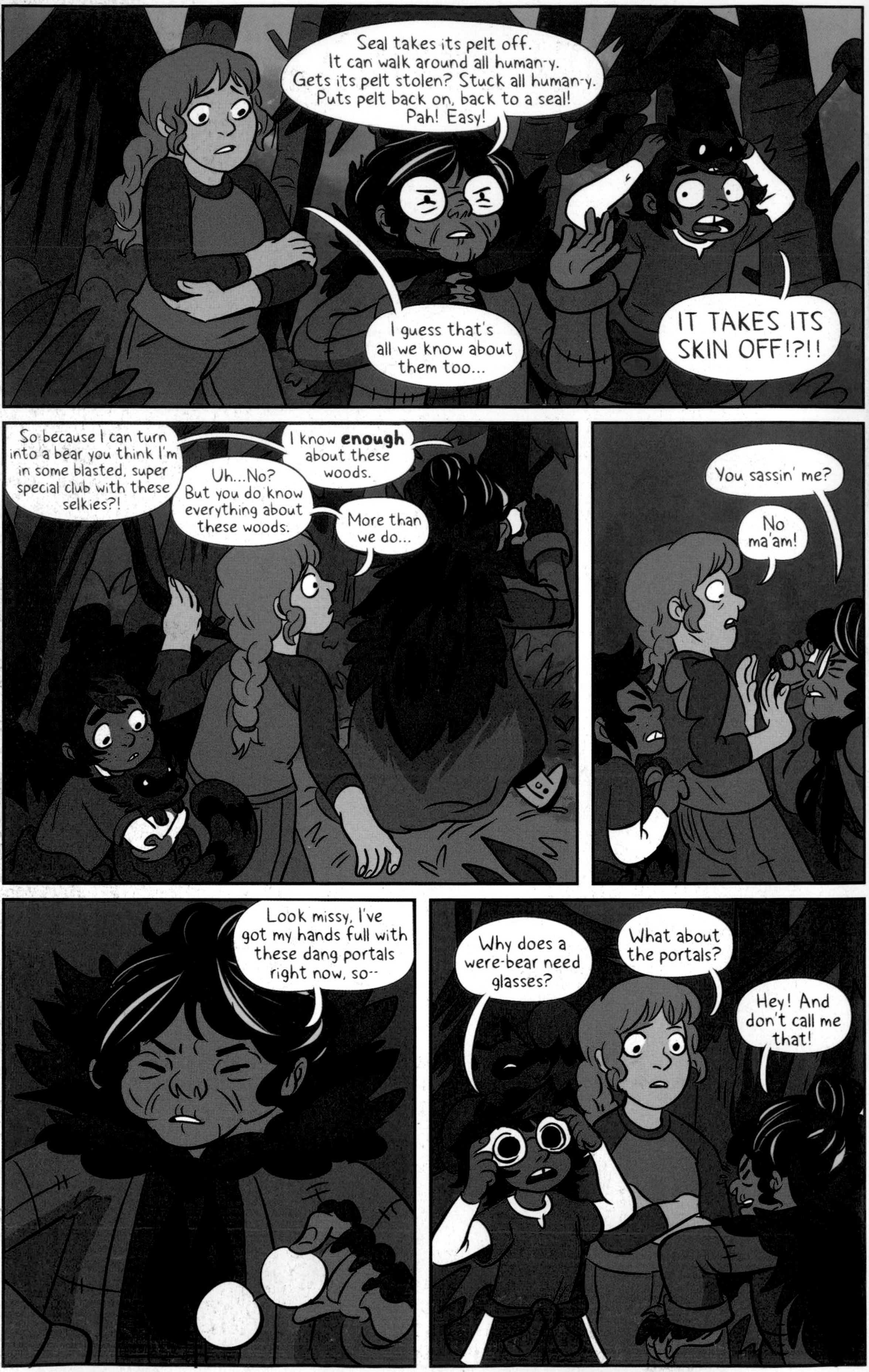
Seal takes its pelt off. It can walk around all human-y. Gets its pelt stolen? Stuck all human-y. Puts pelt back on, back to a seal! Pah! Easy!
I guess that's all we know about them too...
IT TAKES ITS SKIN OFF!?!!
So because I can turn into a bear you think I'm in some blasted, super special club with these selkies?!
Uh...No? But you do know everything about these woods.
I know **enough** about these woods.
More than we do...
You sassin' me?
No ma'am!
Look missy, I've got my hands full with these dang portals right now, so--
Why does a were-bear need glasses?
What about the portals?
Hey! And don't call me that!

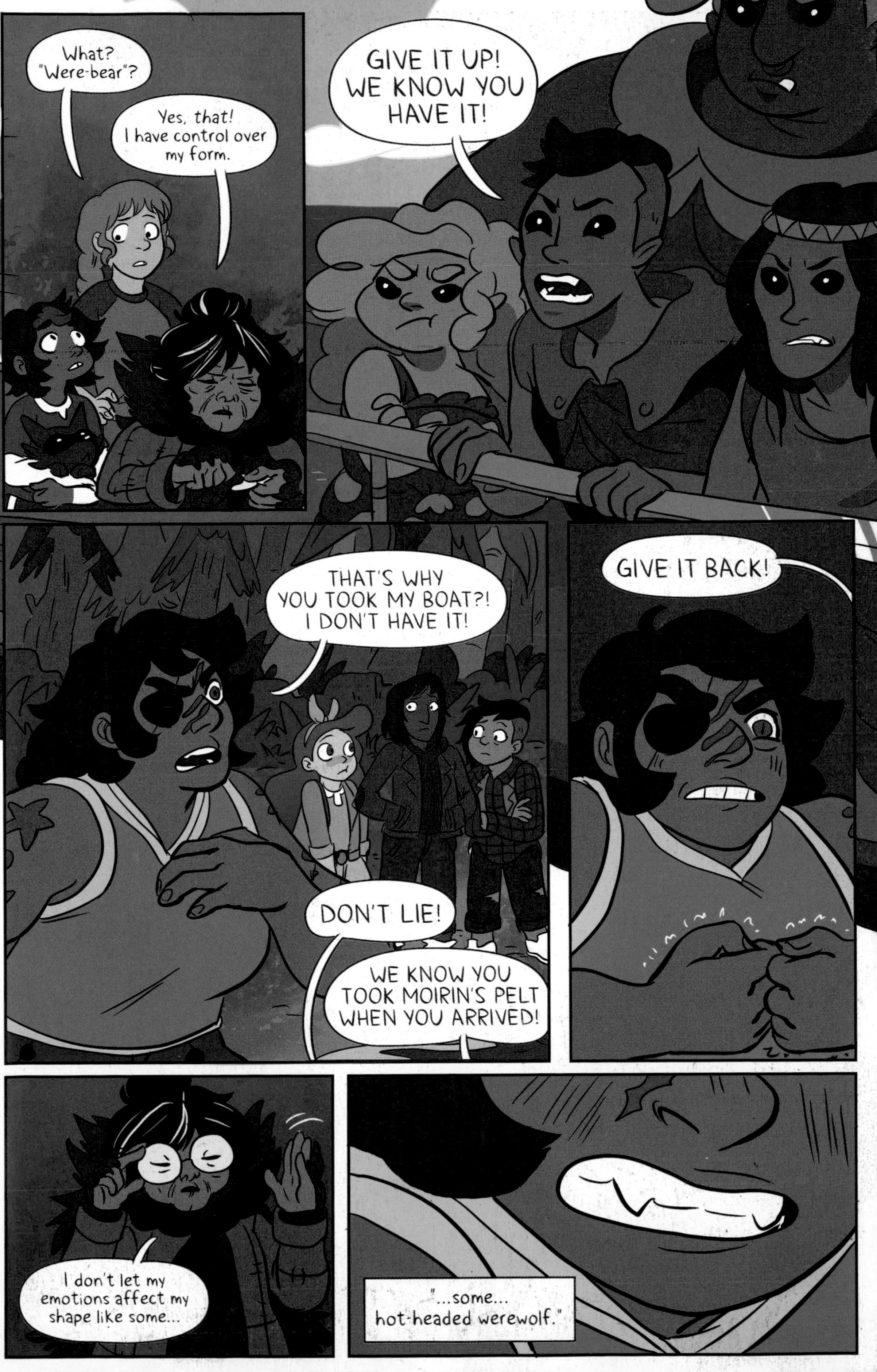
What? "Were-bear"?
Yes, that! I have control over my form.
GIVE IT UP! WE KNOW YOU HAVE IT!
THAT'S WHY YOU TOOK MY BOAT?! I DON'T HAVE IT!
DON'T LIE!
WE KNOW YOU TOOK MOIRIN'S PELT WHEN YOU ARRIVED!
GIVE IT BACK!
I don't let my emotions affect my shape like some...
"...some... hot-headed werewolf."

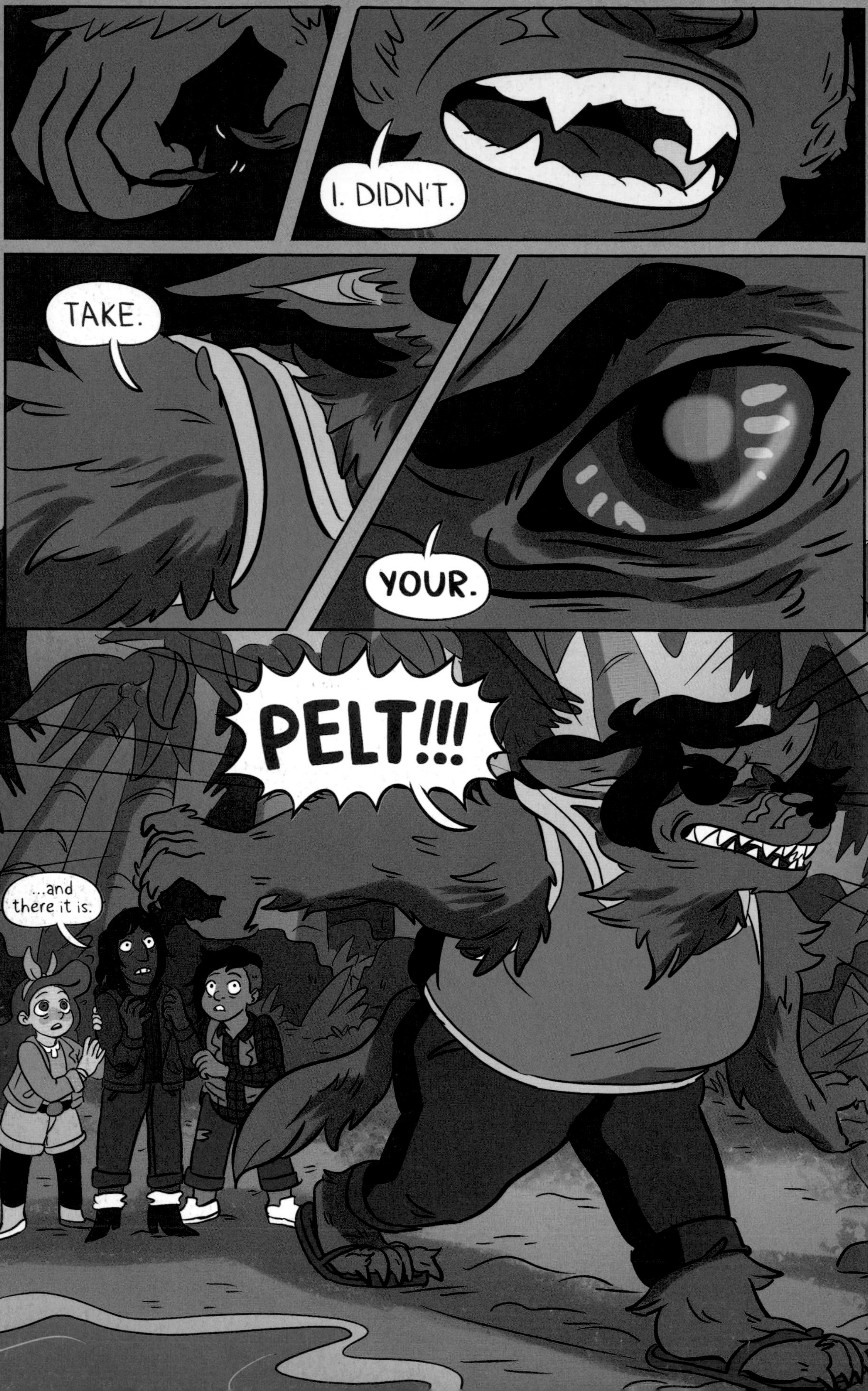
I. DIDN'T.
TAKE.
YOUR.
PELT!!!
...and there it is.

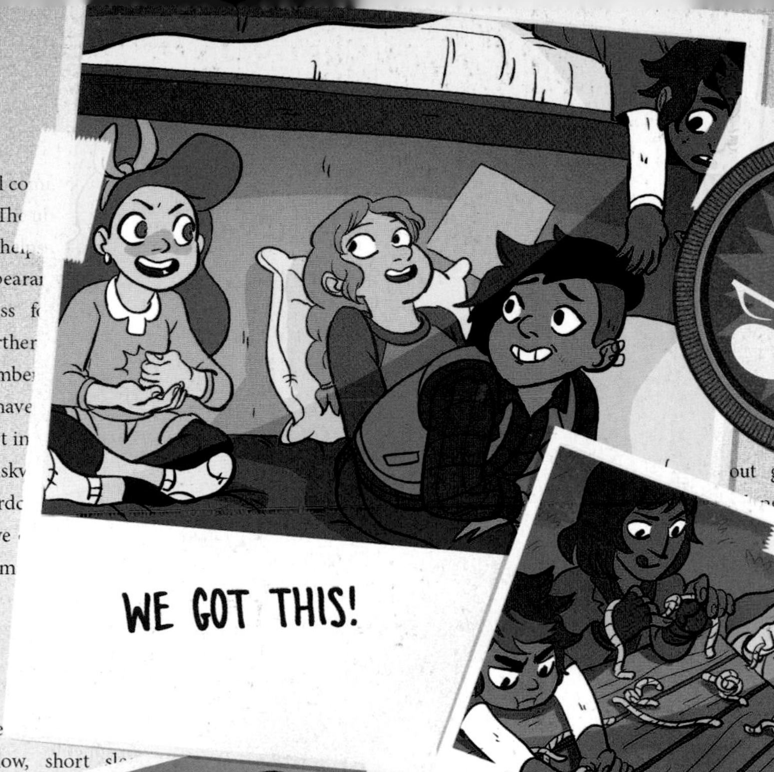
WE GOT THIS!

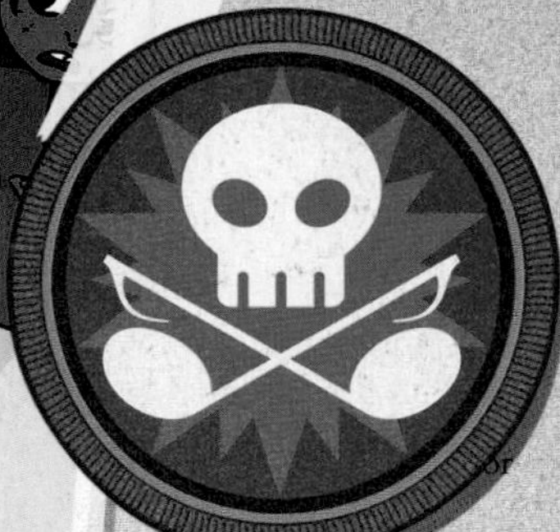

will co

Th

It he

appearar

dress f

Further

Lumbe

to have

part in

Thiskw

Hardc

have

them

out grows her uniform or

ter Lumberjane.

a she has

her

her

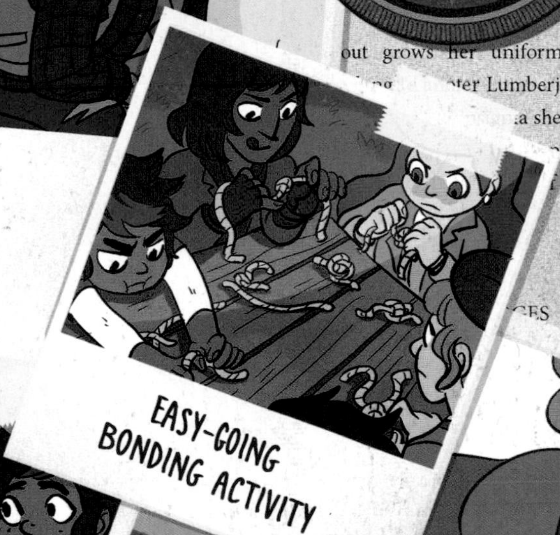
EASY-GOING
BONDING ACTIVITY

The

yellow, short sl

emb

the w

choose

slacks,

made o

out-of-do

green bere

the colla

Shoes ma

heels, rou

ings or

socks shou

with the es or wi

the uniform. Ne , bracelets, or oth do

belong with a Lumberjane uniform.

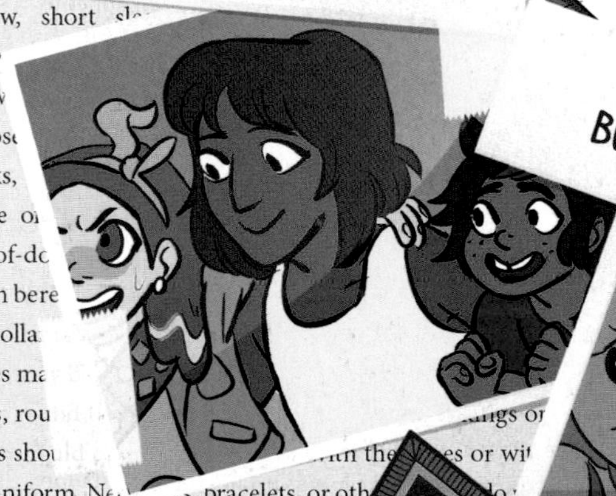

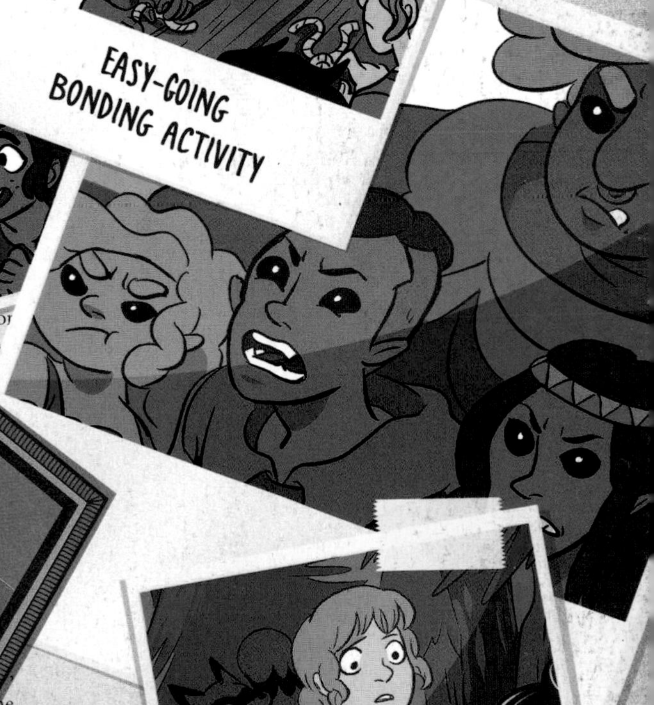

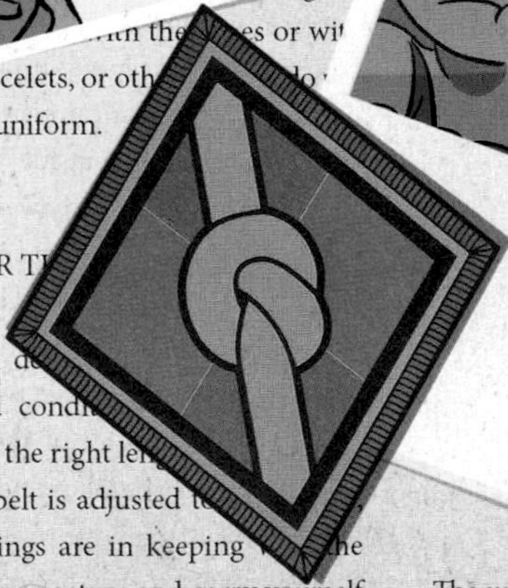

HOW TO WEAR T

To look well in a uniform d uniform be kept in good condi pressed. See that the skirt is the right le height and build, that the belt is adjusted t that your shoes and stockings are in keeping the uniform, that you watch your posture and carry yourself with dignity and grace. If the beret is removed indoors, be sure that your hair is neat and kept in place with an insonspicuous clip or ribbon. When you wear a Lumberjane uniform you are identified as a member of this organization and you should be doubly careful to conduct yourself in a way that will show everyone that courtesy and thoughtfullness are part of being a Lumberjane. People are likely to judge a whole nation by the selfishness of a few individuals, to criticize a whole family because of the misconduct of one member, and to feel unkindly toward and organization because of the

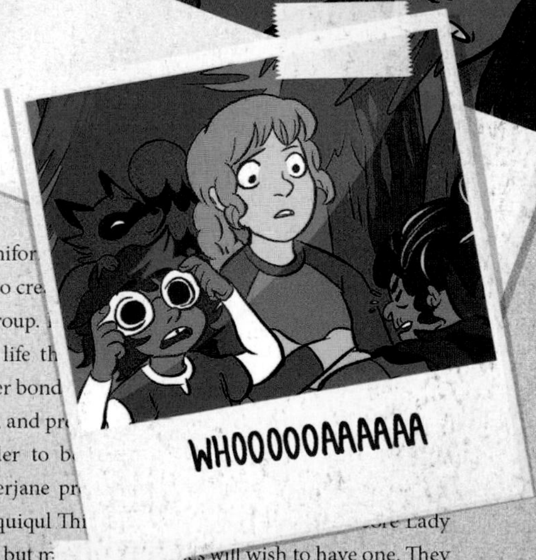
WHOOOOOAAAAAA

The unifor

helps to cre

in a group.

active life th

another bond

future, and pr

in order to b

Lumberjane pr

Penniquiqul Thi ore Lady

Types, but m es will wish to have one. They

can either bu , or make it themselves from

materials available at the trading post.

LUMBERJANES FIELD MANUAL

CHAPTER TWENTY-TWO

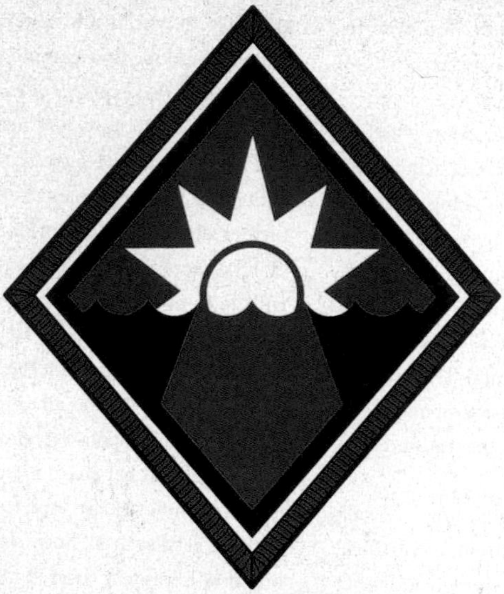

Lumberjanes "Out-of-Doors" Program Field

SEAS THE DAY BADGE

"Carp-ay Diem and all that noise."

It's important for every camper at our camp for hardcore lady-types feel like they are getting the most out of their day. If a camper is ever bored, then it's up to that camper, and the friends that they've collected at this camp, to solve the issue of their boredom by challenging themselves to something exciting and new. We pride ourselves with the challenging tasks that we have at our camp, and know that we are able to push every camper to their limits so that they grow to the best versions of themselves, no matter where they are in their lives.

Every Lumberjane will have their favorite badge when they eventually leave camp, and this is a personal favorite of some members of the High Council. The *Seas The Day* badge is about making sure you get the most you can out of every hour, minute, and second of the day. Every day that you are given is a unique opportunity for campers to change a life, whether it's the life of another camper, of a passing forest creature that they might find in the forest, or maybe the life they change is their own. Either way, the goal of this badge is for our campers to take a look at their day and understand how they can live life to the fullest before time resets itself as the sun sets. Living life to the fullest is the ground work to a happy and fulfilled life that we want every camper to have.

There are many ways to obtain the *Seas The Day* badge. The main point to the badge is the action that the camper takes to make sure they are using their day to the fullest. The *Seas The Day* badge needs a full 24 hours to complete, and in order for the camper to be eligible to receive the badge, they must start at sunrise before they begin their actions for the rest of the day. They will have two check points throughout the day: sunrise with their counselor to start off the task to earn the badge and then at dinner they must check in with their counselor again to go over every task they've completed so far.

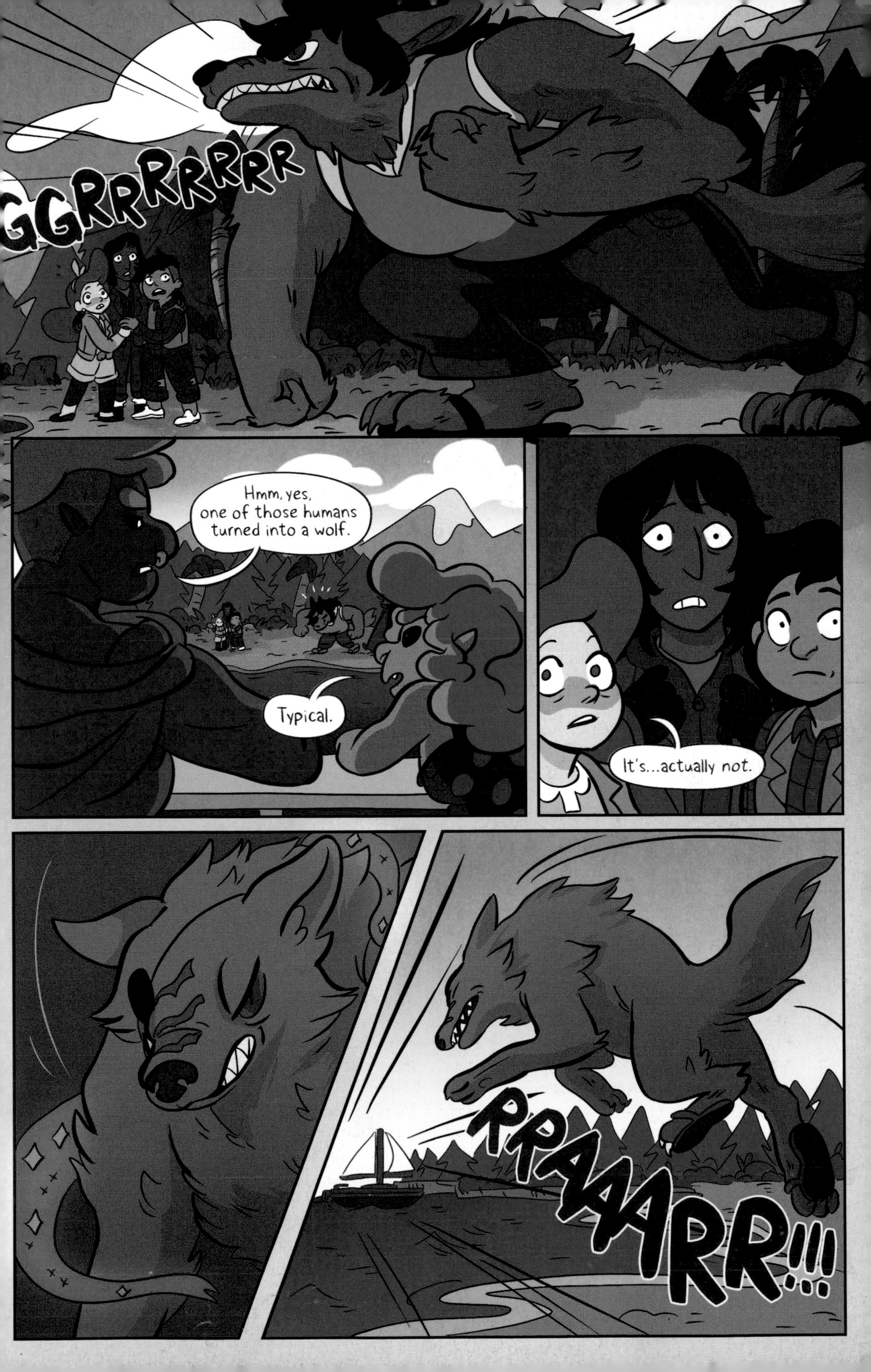
GGRRRRRRR
Hmm, yes, one of those humans turned into a wolf.
Typical.
It's...actually not.
RRAAAARR!!!

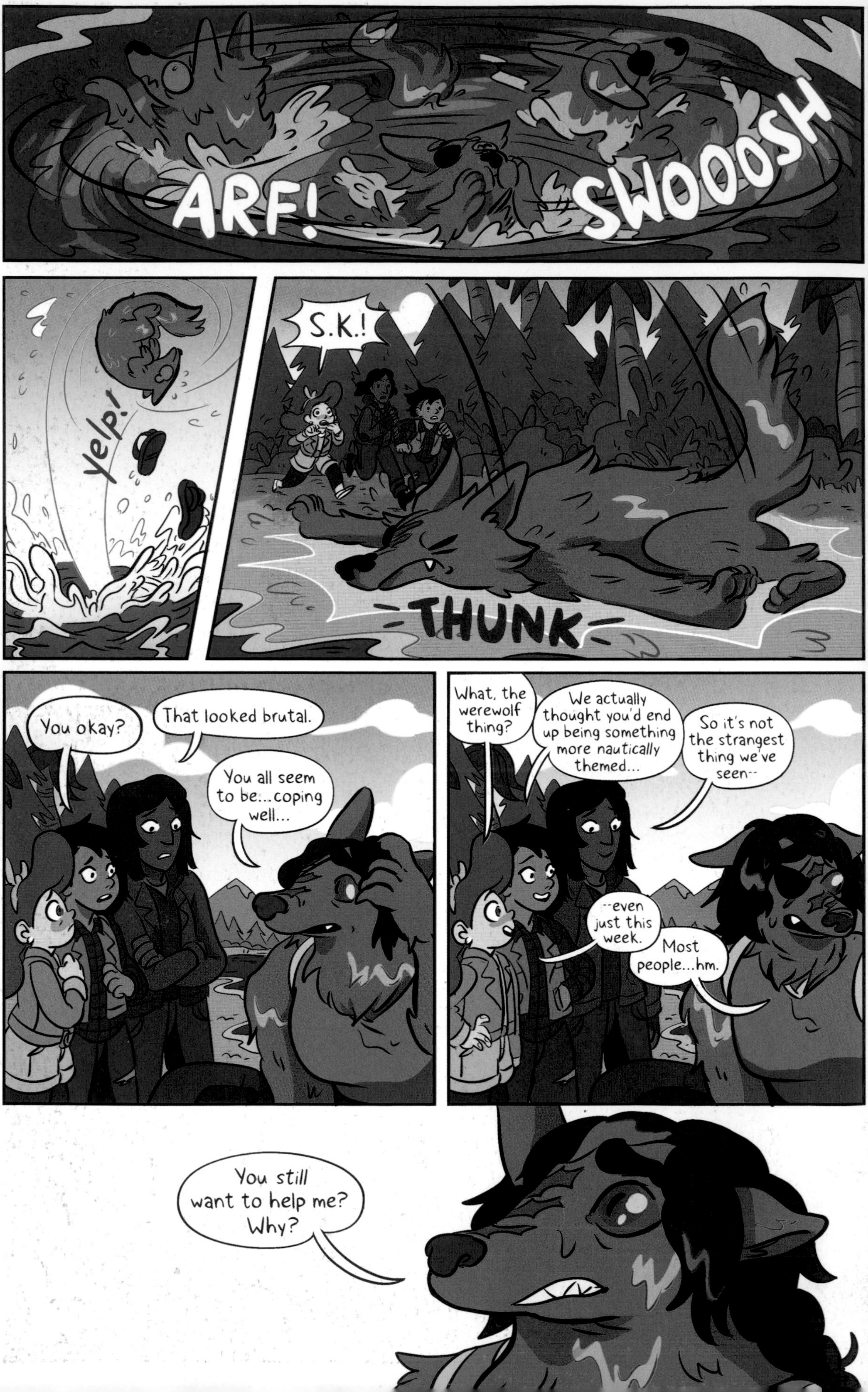
ARF!
SWOOOSH
yelp!
S.K.!
THUNK
You okay?
That looked brutal.
You all seem to be...coping well...
What, the werewolf thing?
We actually thought you'd end up being something more nautically themed...
So it's not the strangest thing we've seen--
--even just this week.
Most people...hm.
You still want to help me? Why?

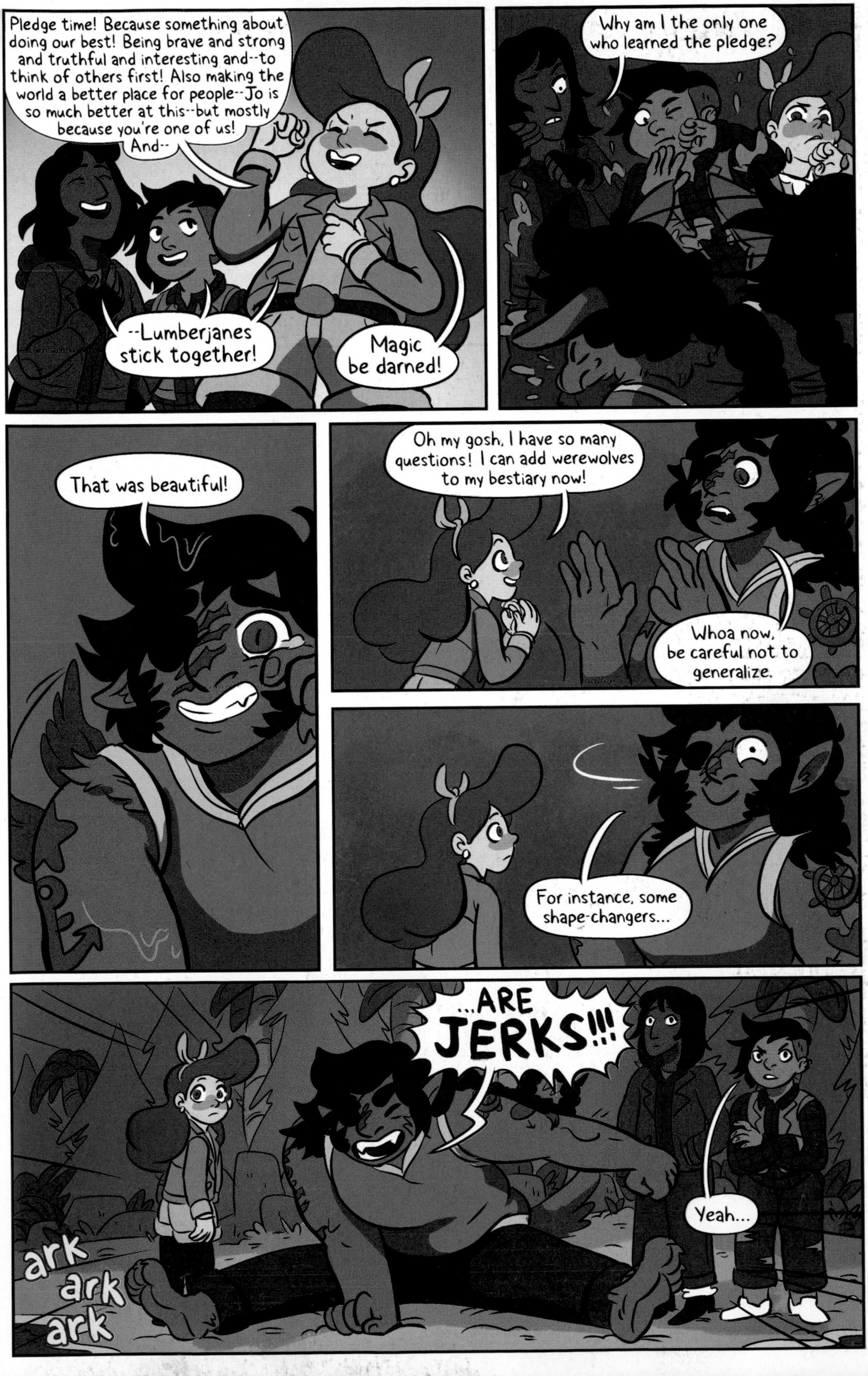
Pledge time! Because something about doing our best! Being brave and strong and truthful and interesting and--to think of others first! Also making the world a better place for people--Jo is so much better at this--but mostly because you're one of us! And--
--Lumberjanes stick together!
Magic be darned!
Why am I the only one who learned the pledge?
That was beautiful!
Oh my gosh, I have so many questions! I can add werewolves to my bestiary now!
Whoa now, be careful not to generalize.
For instance, some shape-changers...
...ARE JERKS!!!
Yeah...
ark ark ark

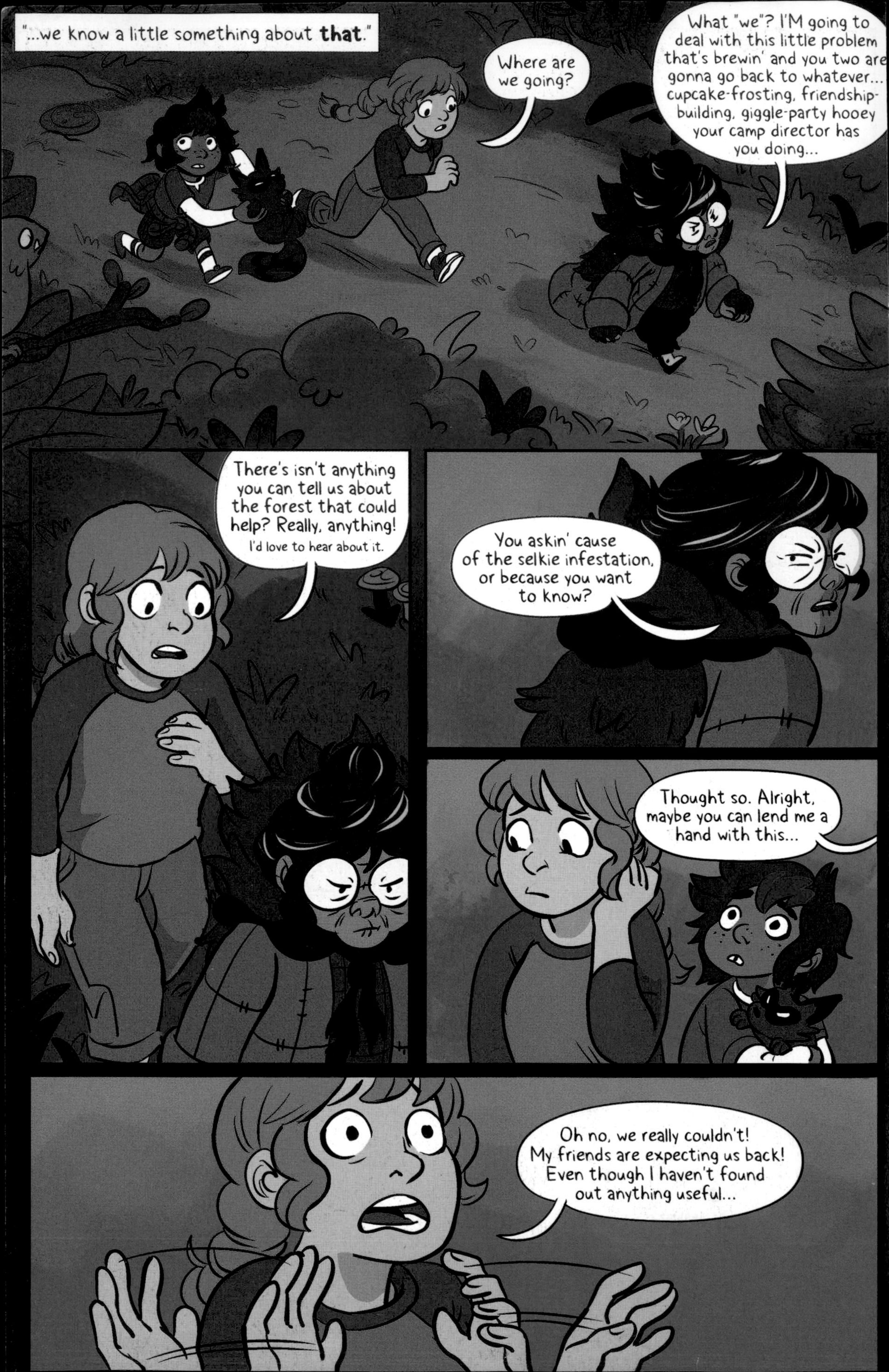
"...we know a little something about **that**."
Where are we going?
What "we"? I'M going to deal with this little problem that's brewin' and you two are gonna go back to whatever... cupcake-frosting, friendship-building, giggle-party hooey your camp director has you doing...
There's isn't anything you can tell us about the forest that could help? Really, anything! I'd love to hear about it.
You askin' cause of the selkie infestation, or because you want to know?
Thought so. Alright, maybe you can lend me a hand with this...
Oh no, we really couldn't! My friends are expecting us back! Even though I haven't found out anything useful...

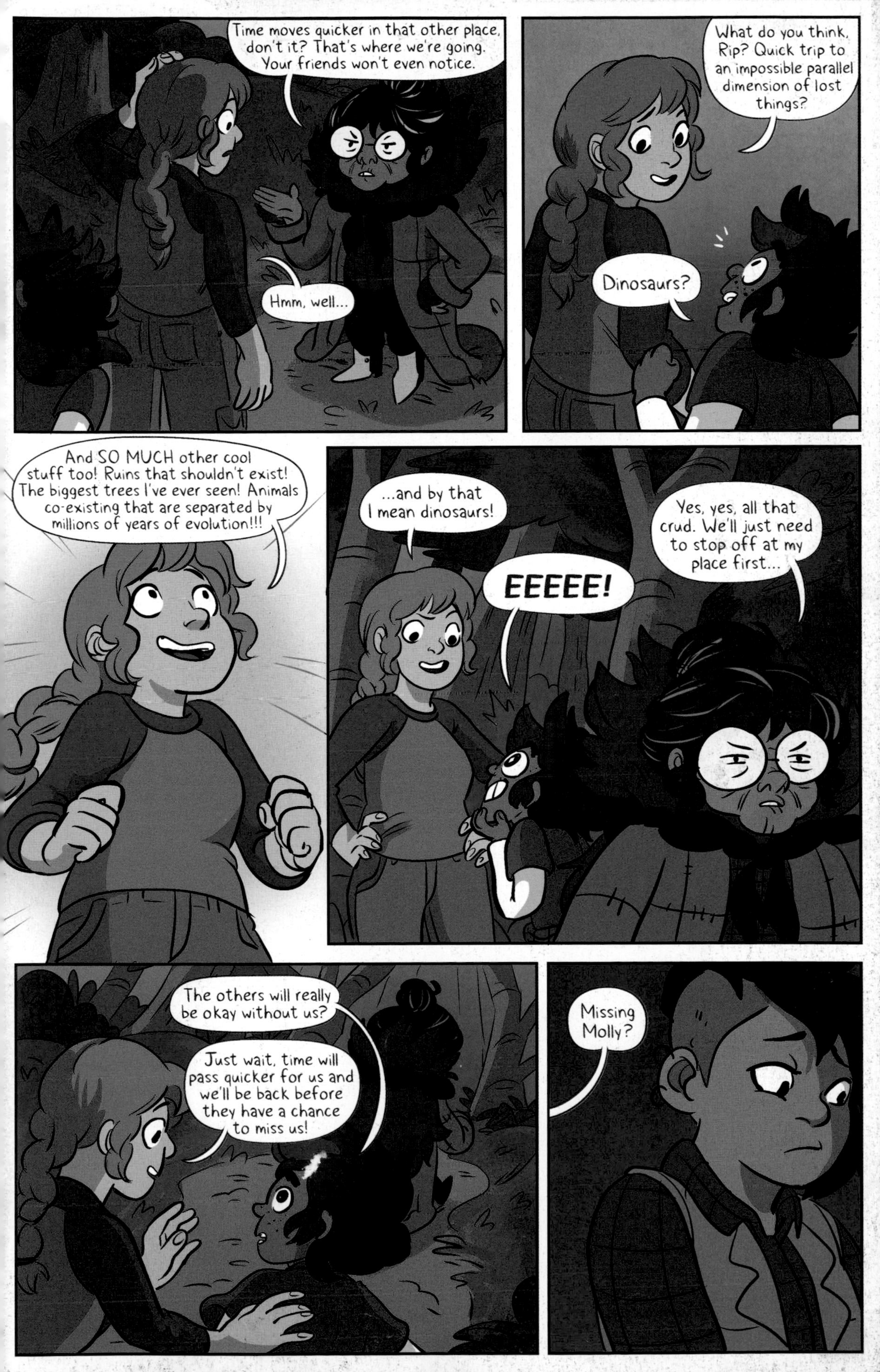
Time moves quicker in that other place, don't it? That's where we're going. Your friends won't even notice.
Hmm, well...
What do you think, Rip? Quick trip to an impossible parallel dimension of lost things?
Dinosaurs?
And SO MUCH other cool stuff too! Ruins that shouldn't exist! The biggest trees I've ever seen! Animals co-existing that are separated by millions of years of evolution!!!
...and by that I mean dinosaurs!
EEEEE!
Yes, yes, all that crud. We'll just need to stop off at my place first...
The others will really be okay without us?
Just wait, time will pass quicker for us and we'll be back before they have a chance to miss us!
Missing Molly?

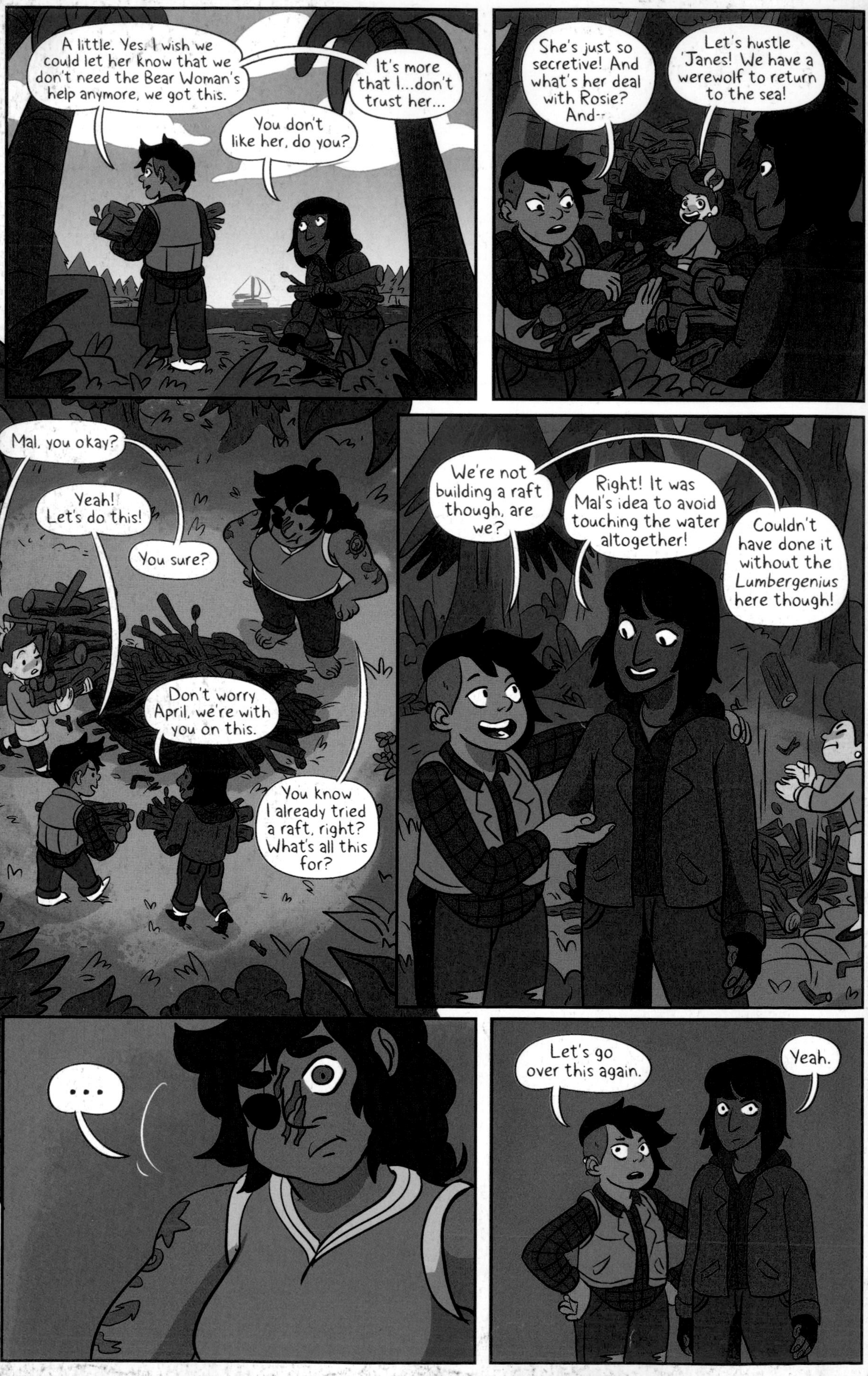
A little. Yes. I wish we could let her know that we don't need the Bear Woman's help anymore, we got this.
It's more that I...don't trust her...
You don't like her, do you?
She's just so secretive! And what's her deal with Rosie? And--
Let's hustle 'Janes! We have a werewolf to return to the sea!
Mal, you okay?
Yeah! Let's do this!
You sure?
Don't worry April, we're with you on this.
You know I already tried a raft, right? What's all this for?
We're not building a raft though, are we?
Right! It was Mal's idea to avoid touching the water altogether!
Couldn't have done it without the Lumbergenius here though!
...
Let's go over this again.
Yeah.

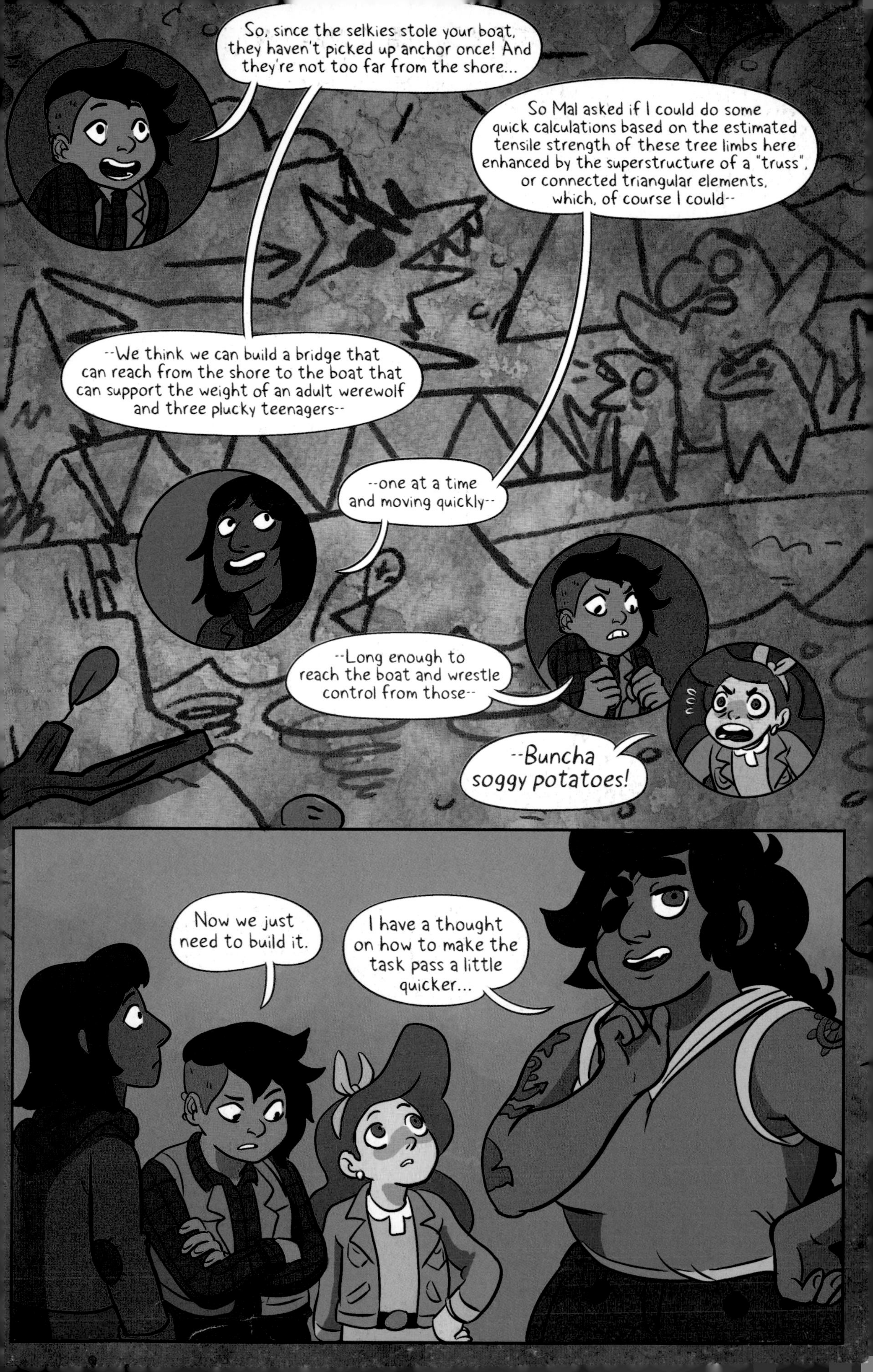
So, since the selkies stole your boat, they haven't picked up anchor once! And they're not too far from the shore...
--We think we can build a bridge that can reach from the shore to the boat that can support the weight of an adult werewolf and three plucky teenagers--
So Mal asked if I could do some quick calculations based on the estimated tensile strength of these tree limbs here enhanced by the superstructure of a "truss", or connected triangular elements, which, of course I could--
--one at a time and moving quickly--
--Long enough to reach the boat and wrestle control from those--
--Buncha soggy potatoes!
Now we just need to build it.
I have a thought on how to make the task pass a little quicker...

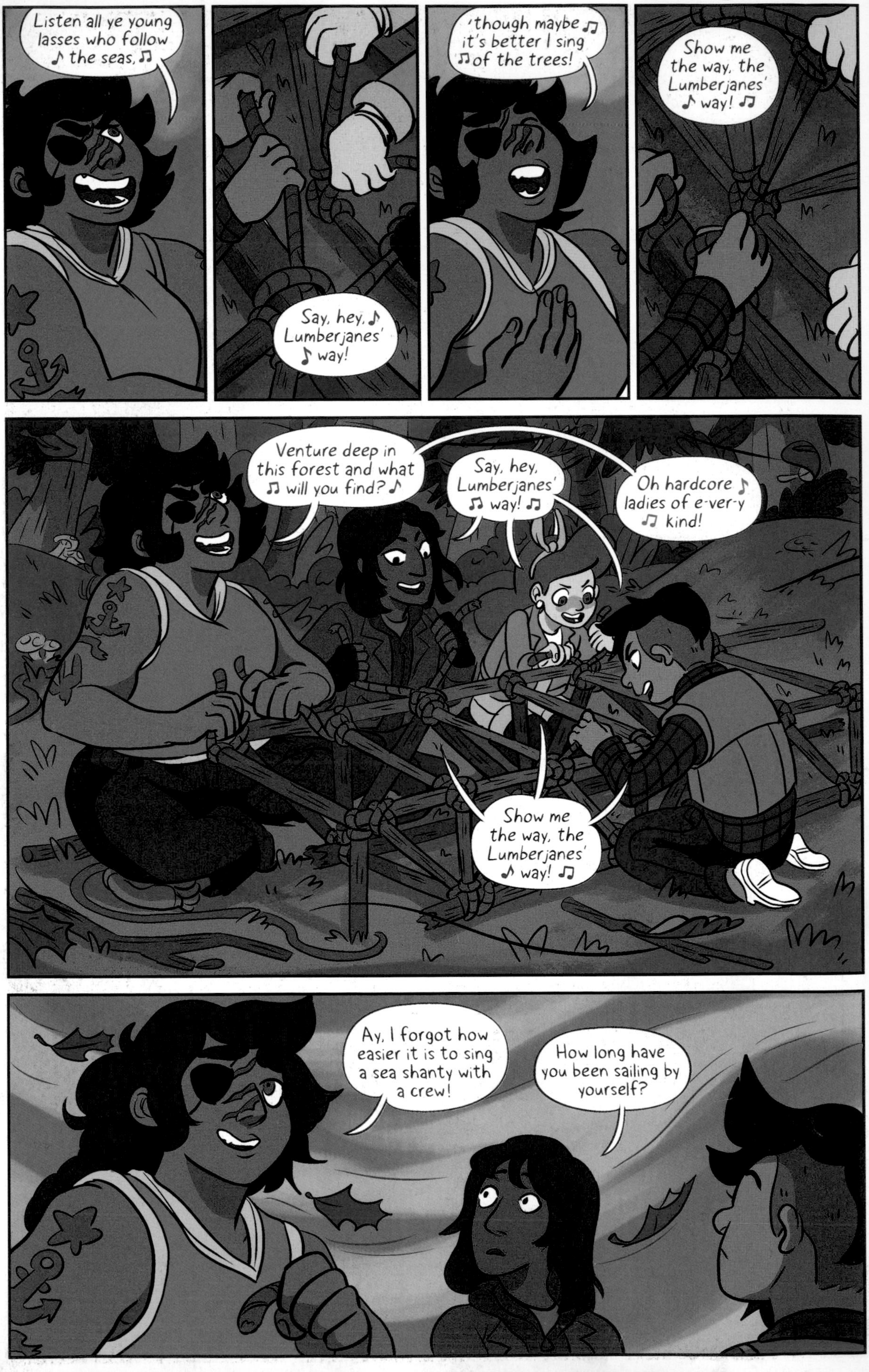

Listen all ye young lasses who follow ♪ the seas, ♫
Say, hey, ♪ Lumberjanes' ♪ way!
'though maybe ♫ it's better I sing ♫ of the trees!
Show me the way, the Lumberjanes' ♪ way! ♫
Venture deep in this forest and what ♫ will you find? ♪
Say, hey, Lumberjanes' ♫ way! ♫
Oh hardcore ♪ ladies of e-ver-y ♫ kind!
Show me the way, the Lumberjanes' ♪ way! ♫
Ay, I forgot how easier it is to sing a sea shanty with a crew!
How long have you been sailing by yourself?

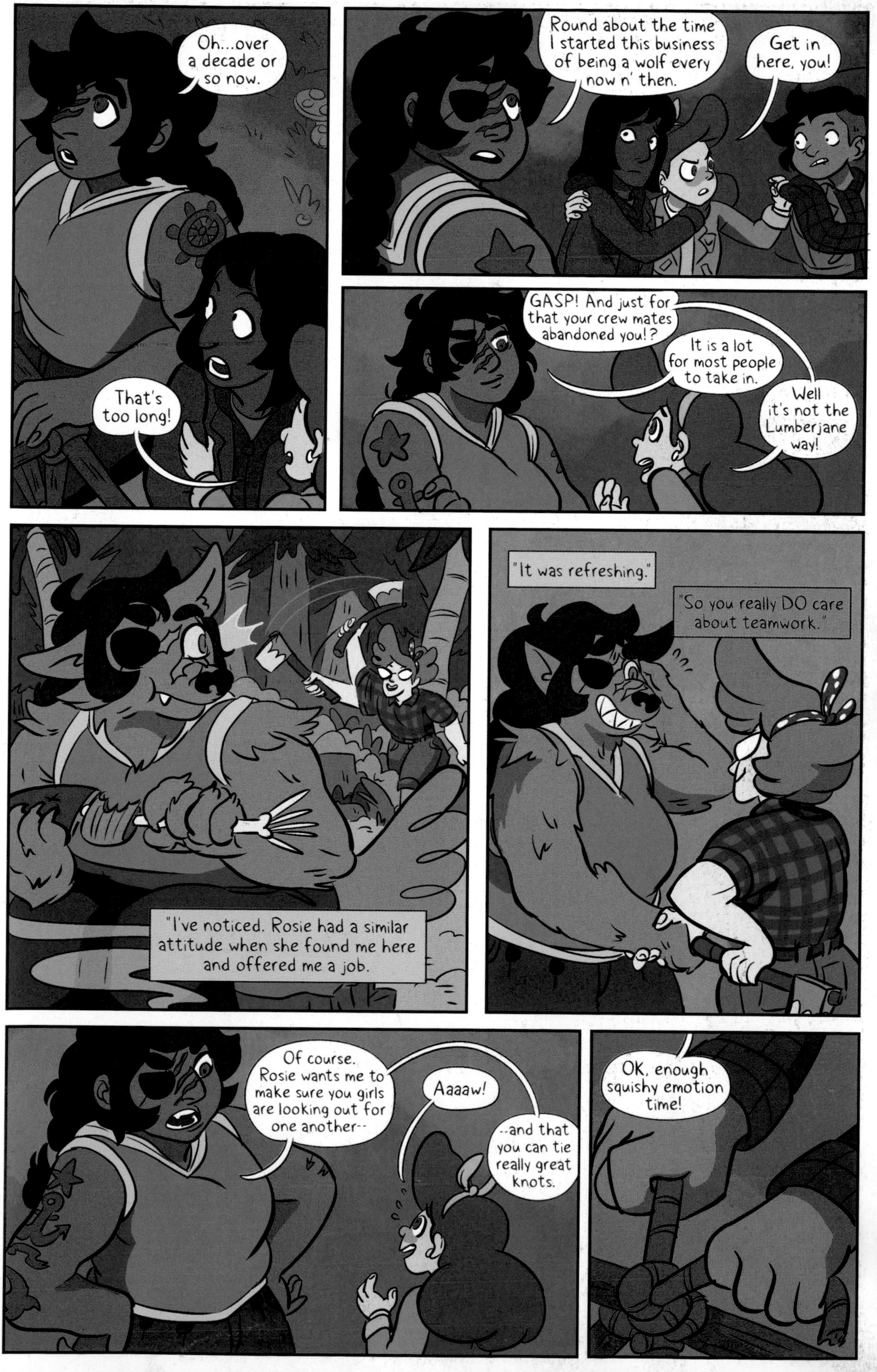
Oh...over a decade or so now.
That's too long!
Round about the time I started this business of being a wolf every now n' then.
Get in here, you!
GASP! And just for that your crew mates abandoned you!?
It is a lot for most people to take in.
Well it's not the Lumberjane way!
"It was refreshing."
"I've noticed. Rosie had a similar attitude when she found me here and offered me a job.
"So you really DO care about teamwork."
Of course. Rosie wants me to make sure you girls are looking out for one another--
Aaaaw!
--and that you can tie really great knots.
OK, enough squishy emotion time!

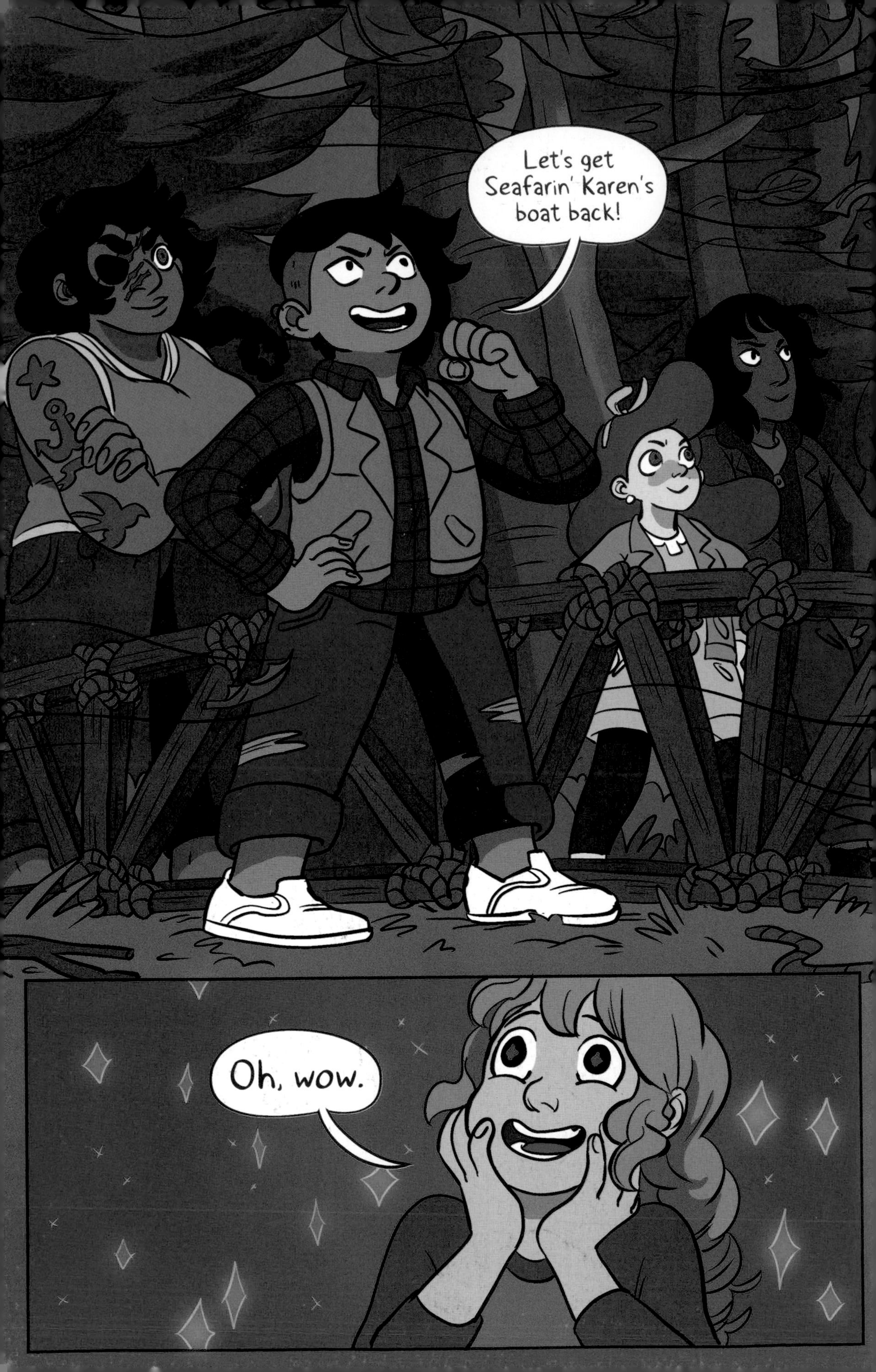
Let's get Seafarin' Karen's boat back!
Oh, wow.

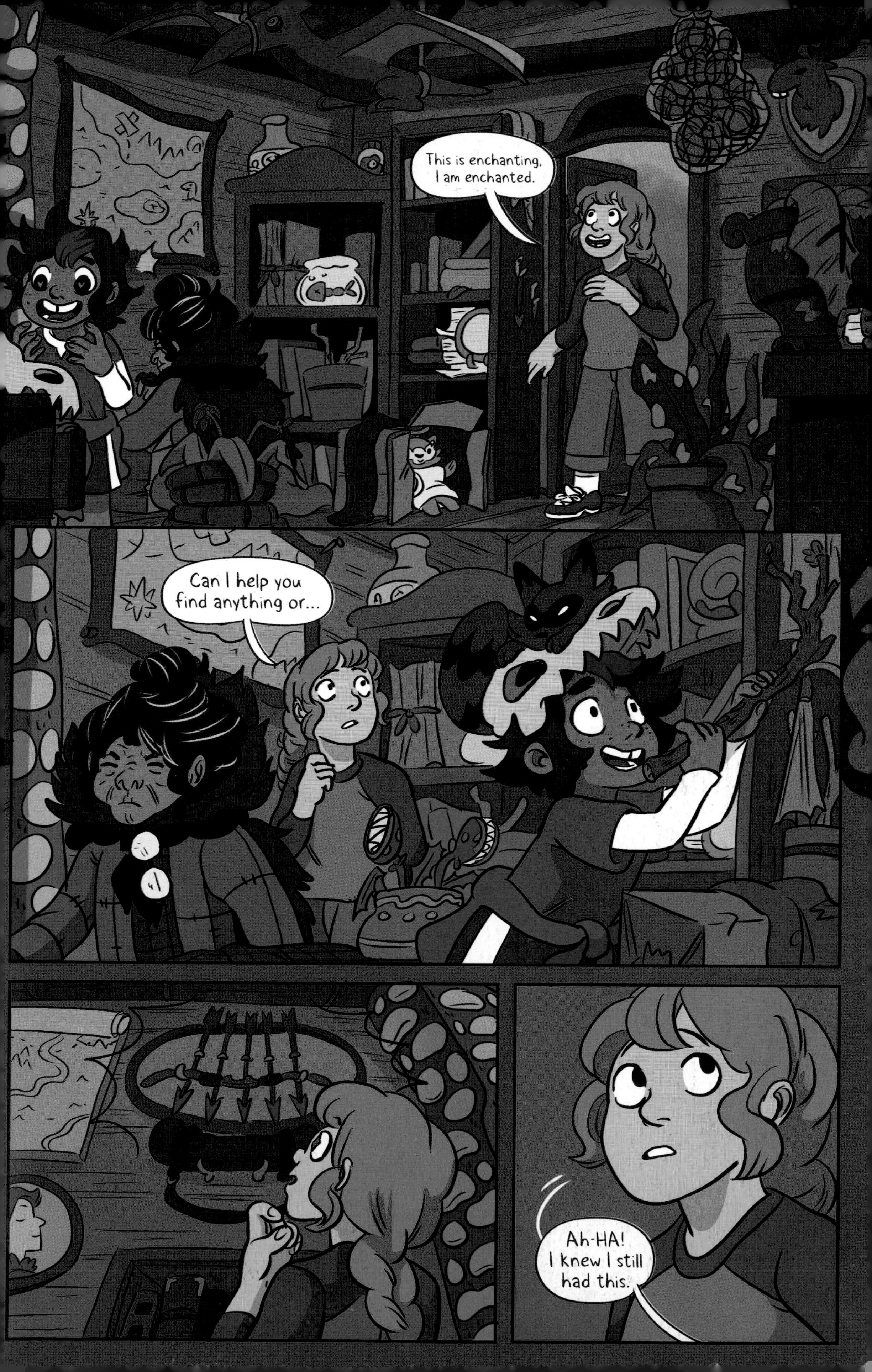

This is enchanting, I am enchanted.
Can I help you find anything or...
Ah-HA! I knew I still had this.

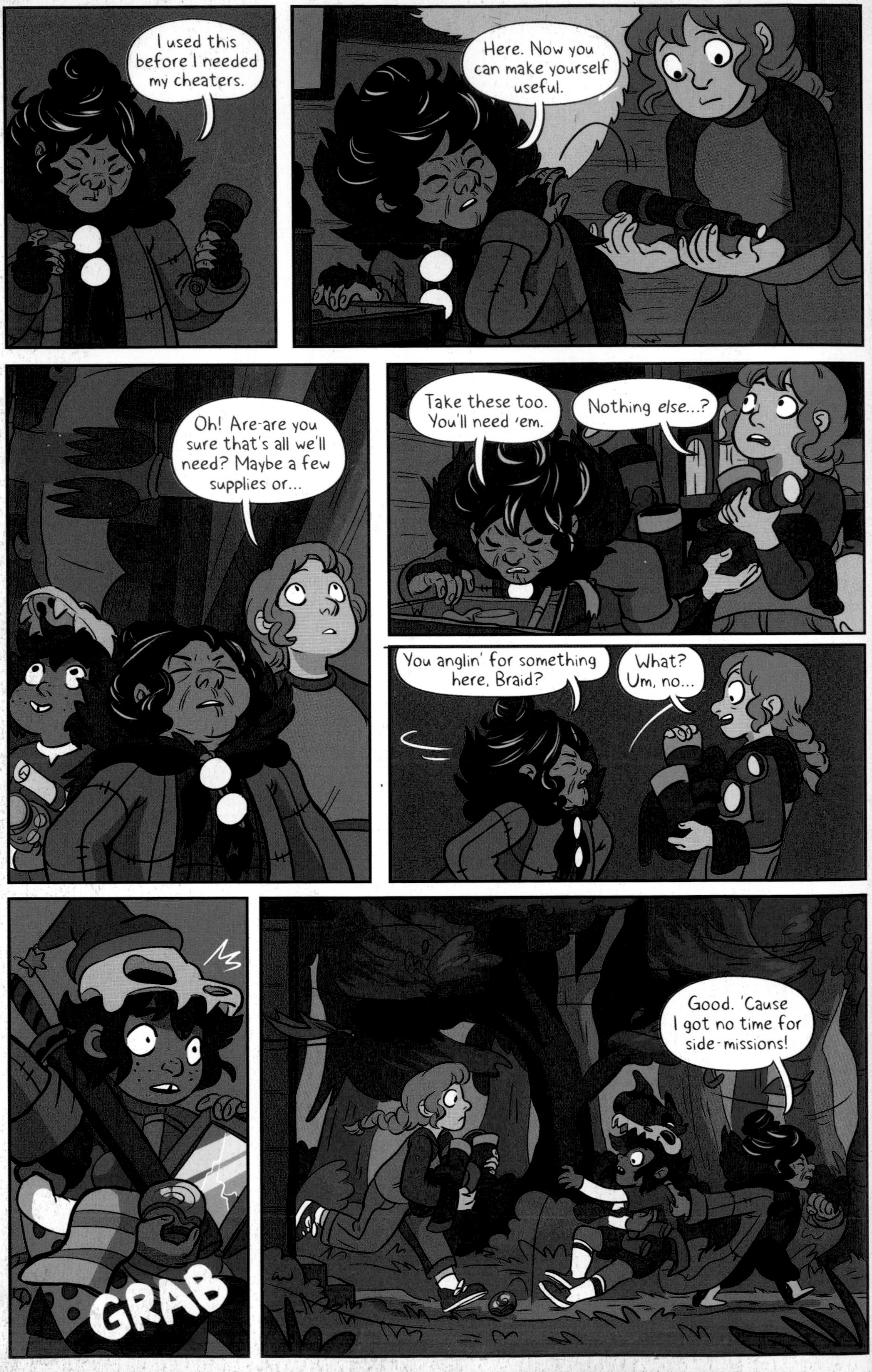
I used this before I needed my cheaters.
Here. Now you can make yourself useful.
Oh! Are-are you sure that's all we'll need? Maybe a few supplies or...
Take these too. You'll need 'em.
Nothing else...?
You anglin' for something here, Braid?
What? Um, no...
GRAB
Good. 'Cause I got no time for side-missions!

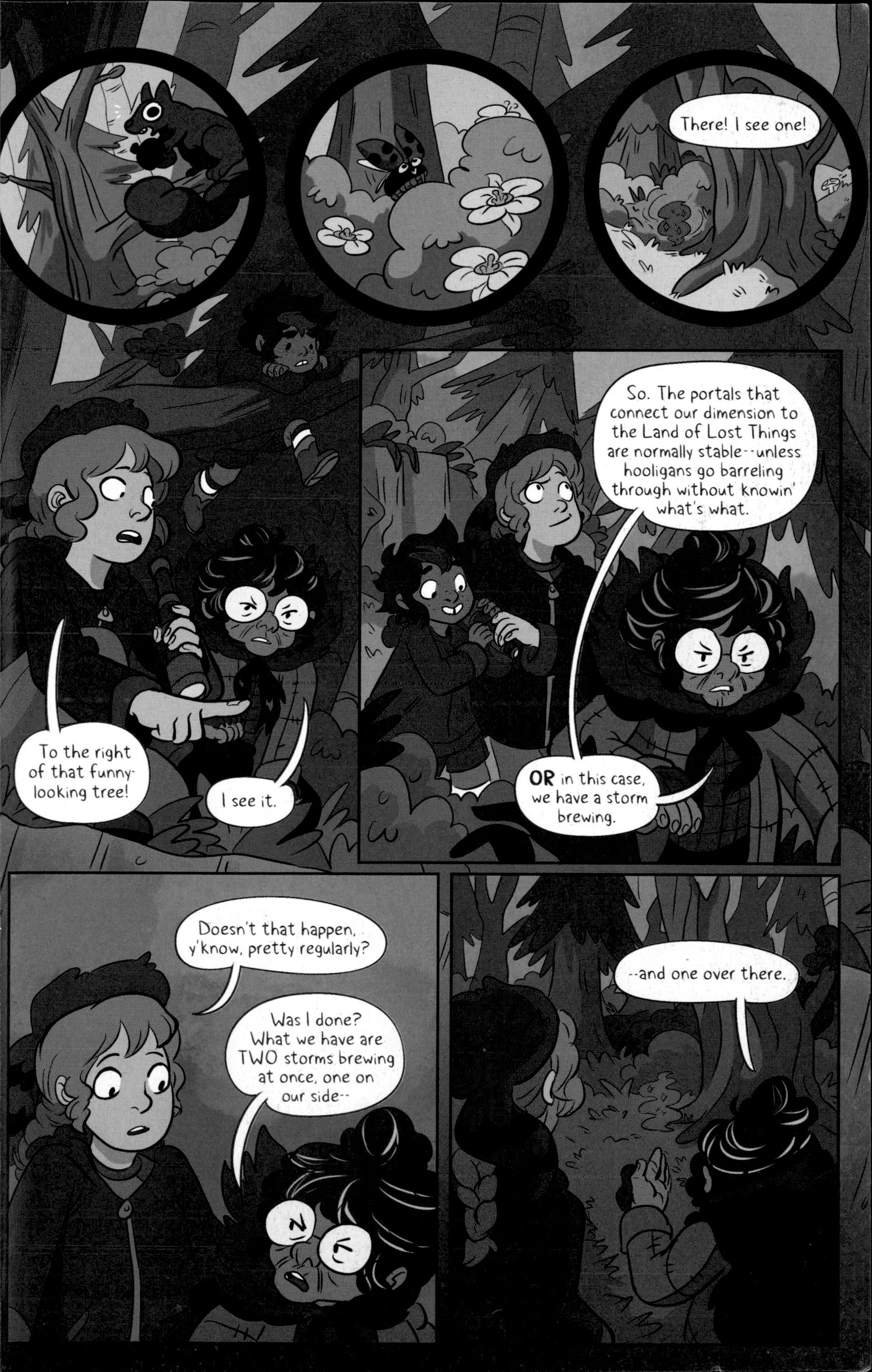
There! I see one!
To the right of that funny-looking tree!
I see it.
So. The portals that connect our dimension to the Land of Lost Things are normally stable--unless hooligans go barreling through without knowin' what's what.
OR in this case, we have a storm brewing.
Doesn't that happen, y'know, pretty regularly?
Was I done? What we have are TWO storms brewing at once, one on our side--
--and one over there.

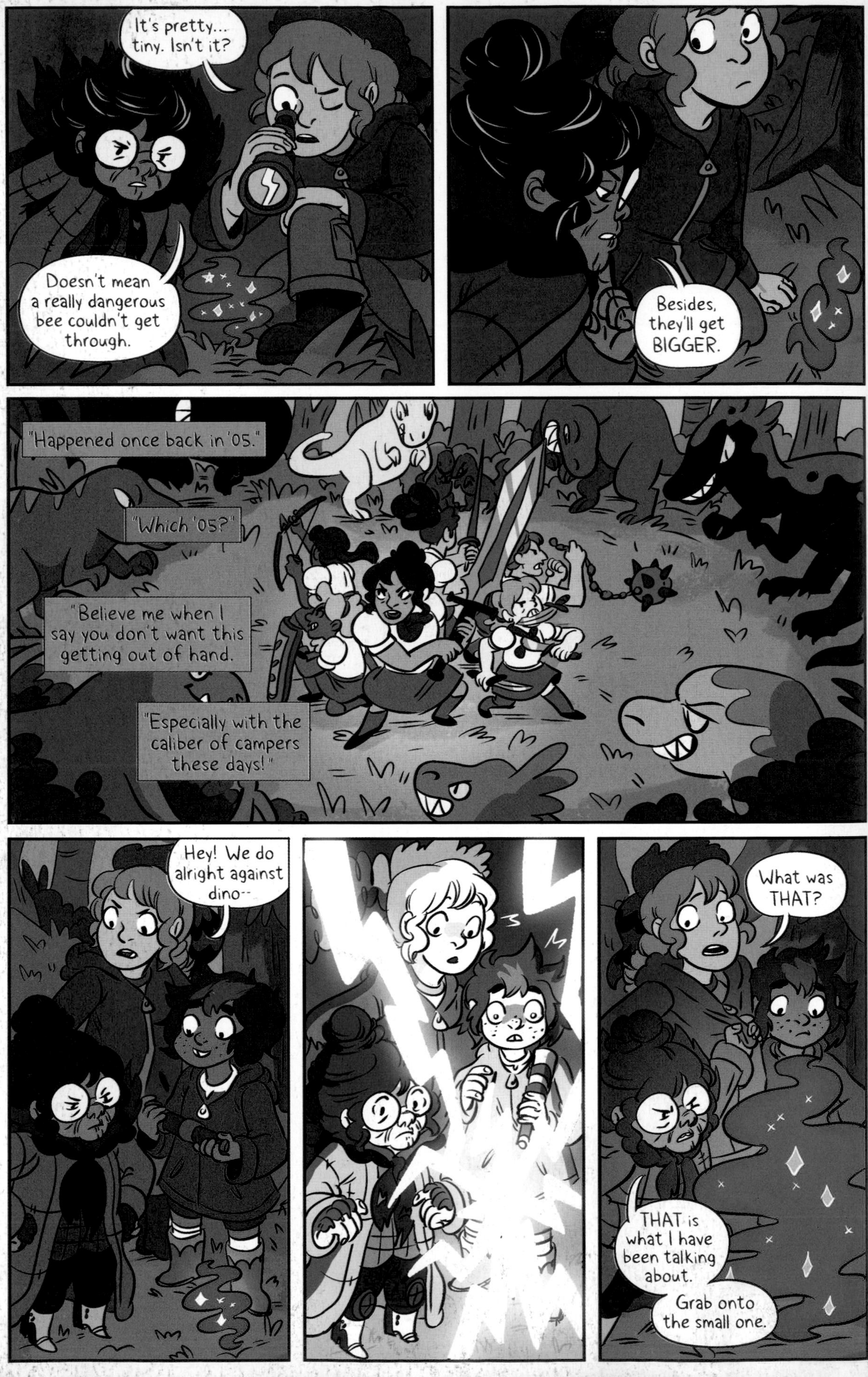
It's pretty... tiny. Isn't it?
Doesn't mean a really dangerous bee couldn't get through.
Besides, they'll get BIGGER.
"Happened once back in '05."
"Which '05?"
"Believe me when I say you don't want this getting out of hand.
"Especially with the caliber of campers these days!"
Hey! We do alright against dino--
What was THAT?
THAT is what I have been talking about.
Grab onto the small one.

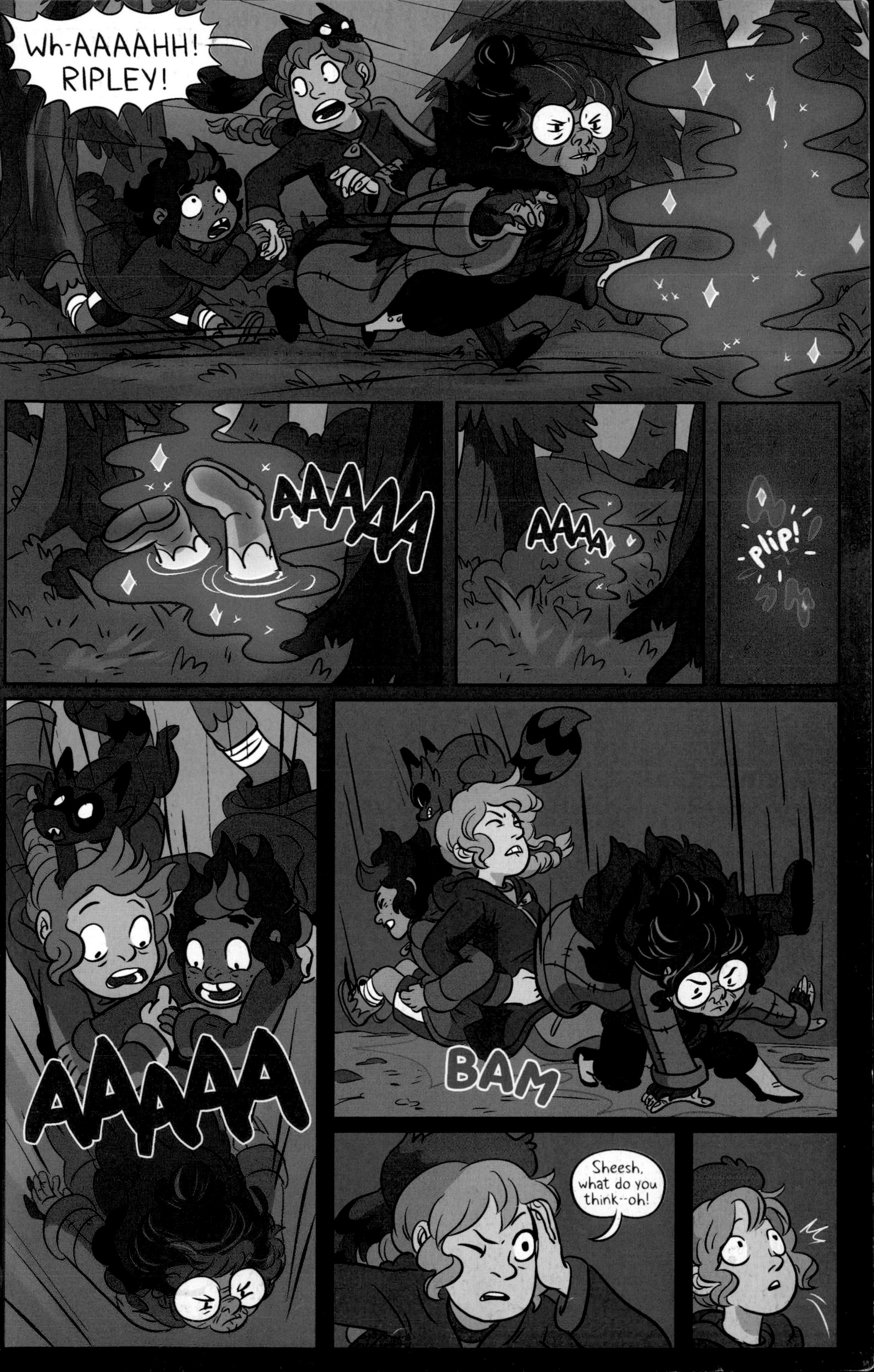
Wh-AAAAHH! RIPLEY!
AAAAAA
AAAA
plip!
AAAAA
BAM
Sheesh, what do you think--oh!

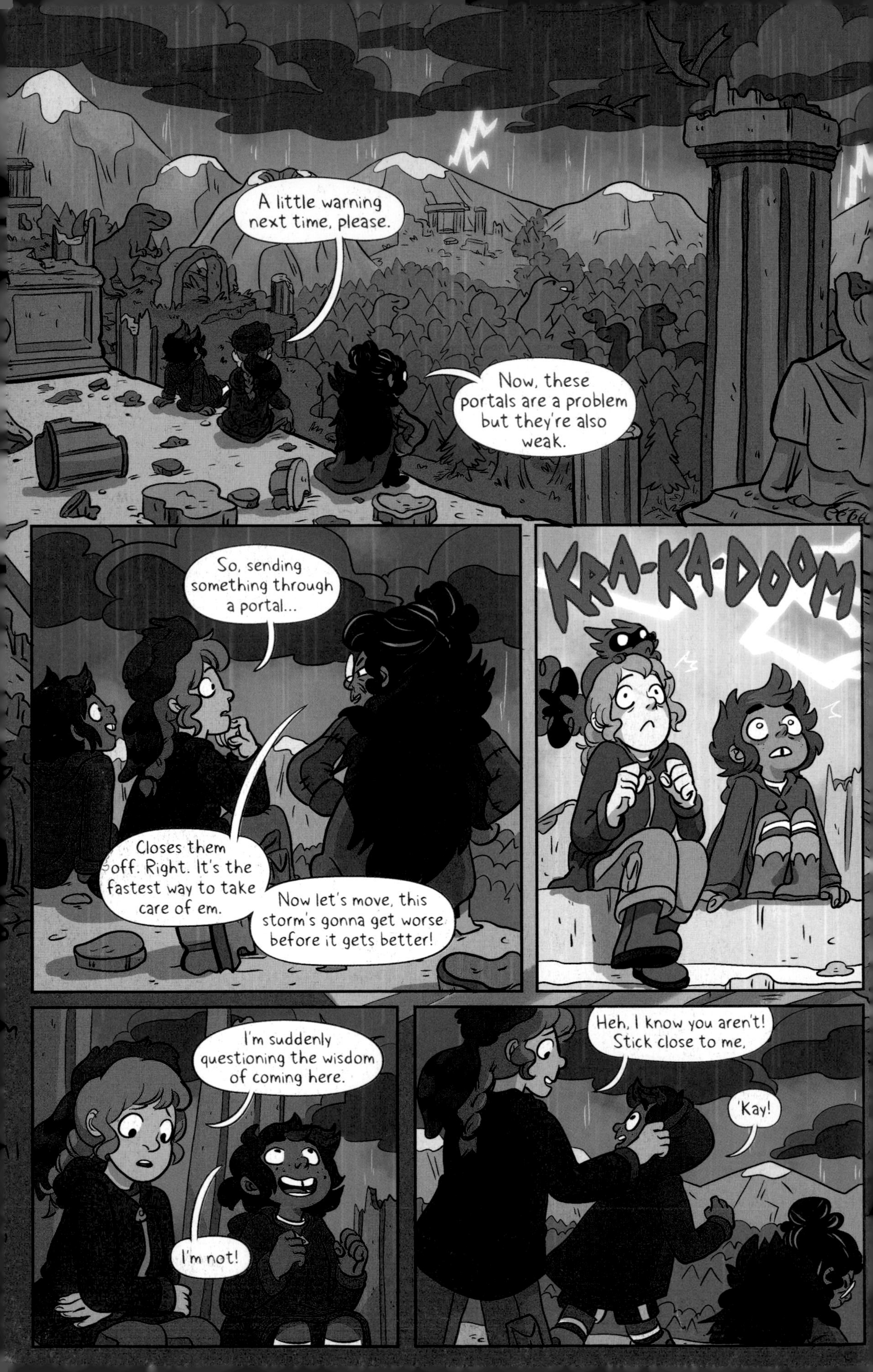
A little warning next time, please.
Now, these portals are a problem but they're also weak.
So, sending something through a portal...
Closes them off. Right. It's the fastest way to take care of em.
Now let's move, this storm's gonna get worse before it gets better!
KRA-KA-DOOM
I'm suddenly questioning the wisdom of coming here.
I'm not!
Heh, I know you aren't! Stick close to me.
'Kay!

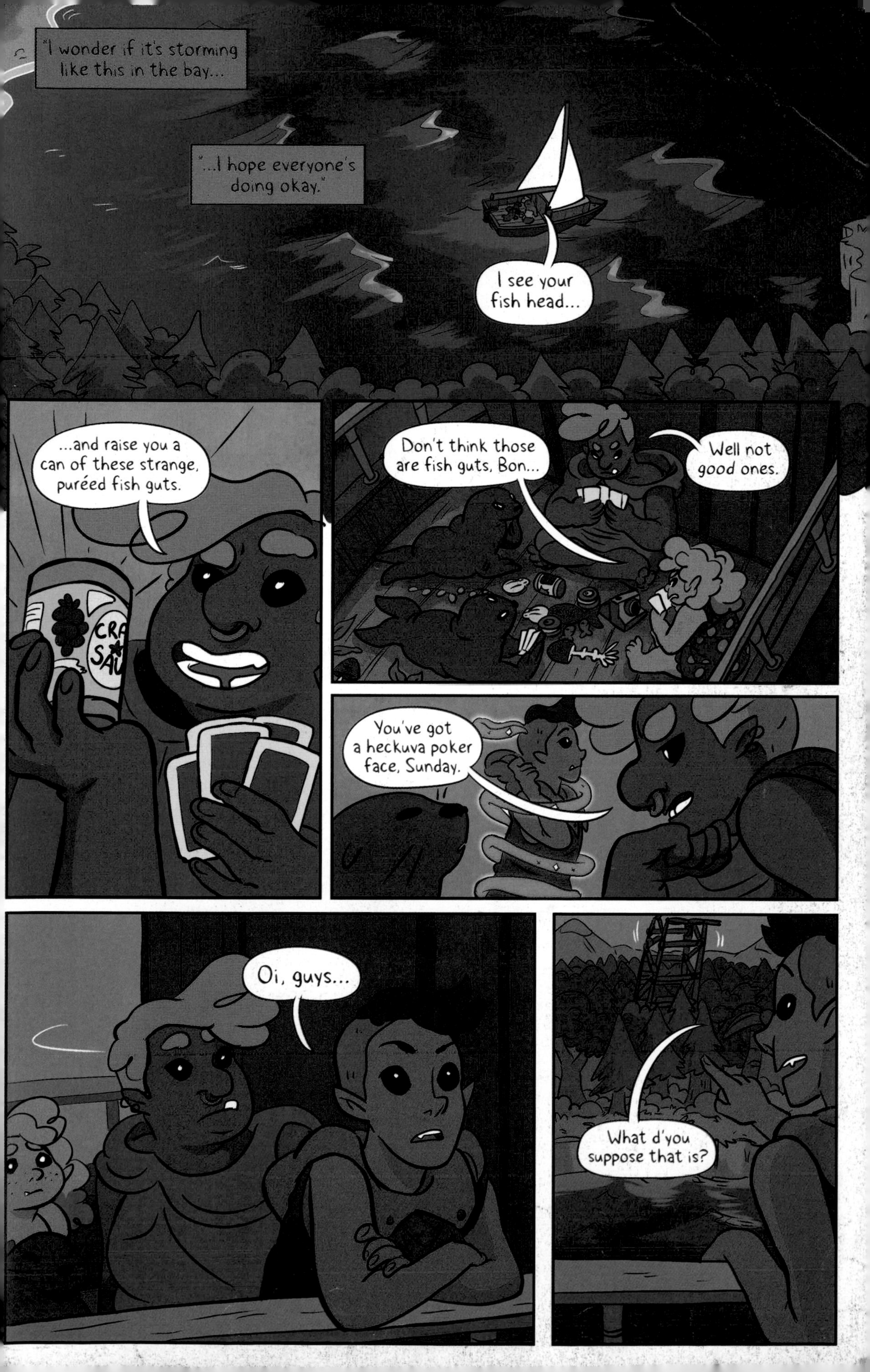
"I wonder if it's storming like this in the bay...
"...I hope everyone's doing okay."
I see your fish head...
...and raise you a can of these strange, puréed fish guts.
Don't think those are fish guts, Bon...
Well not good ones.
You've got a heckuva poker face, Sunday.
Oi, guys...
What d'you suppose that is?

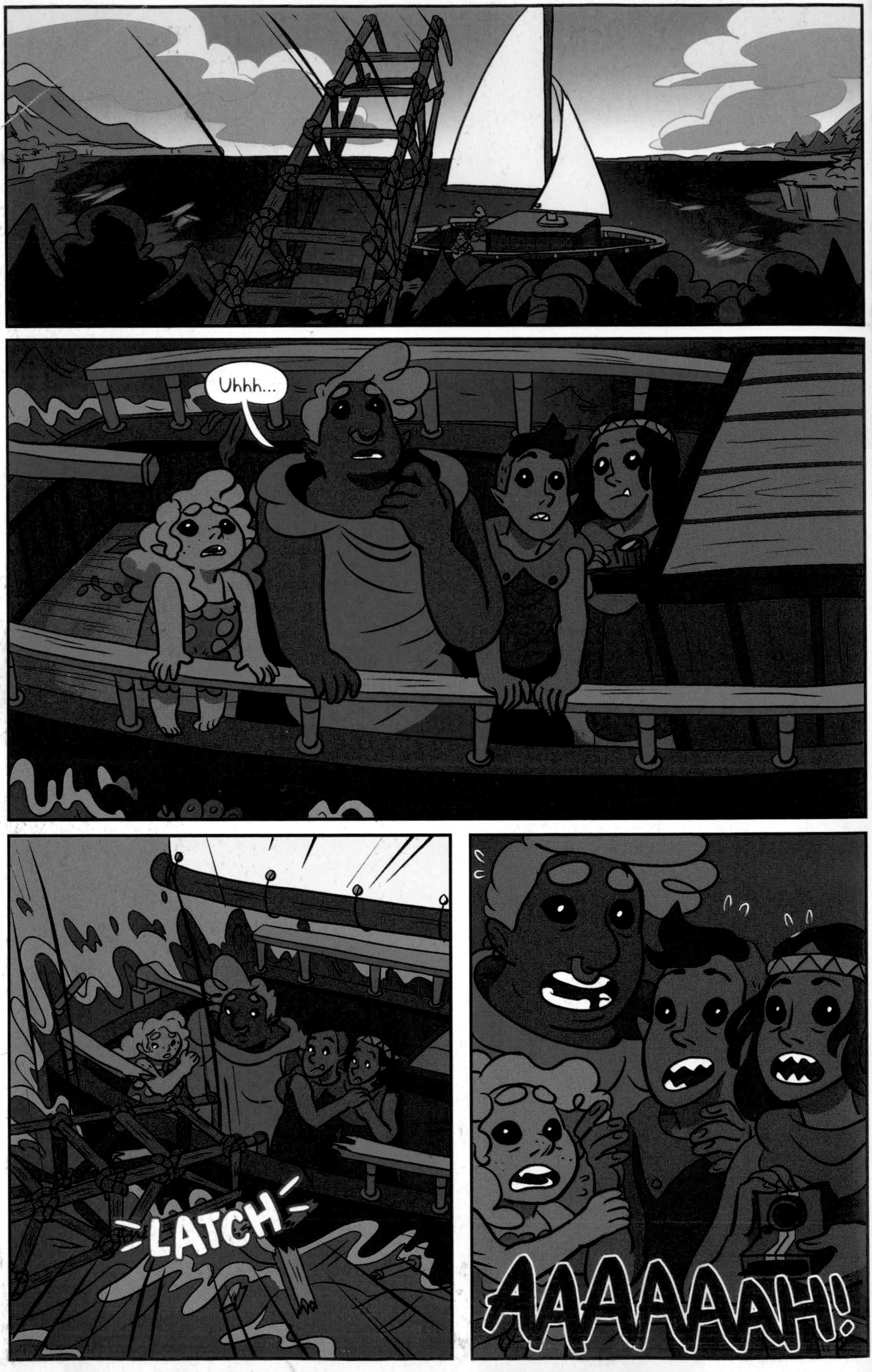
Uhhh...
LATCH
AAAAAAH!

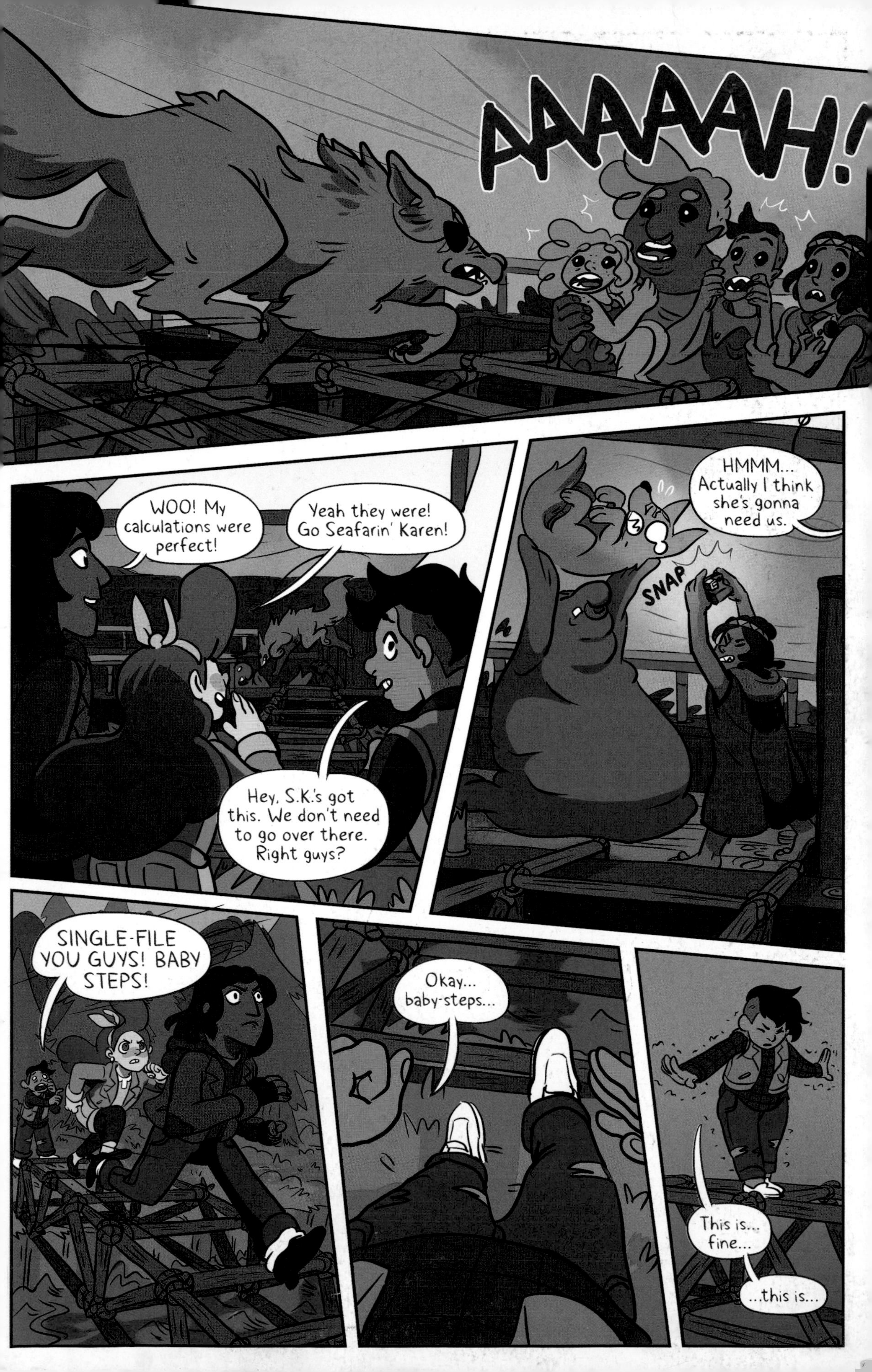
AAAAAH!
WOO! My calculations were perfect!
Yeah they were! Go Seafarin' Karen!
Hey, S.K.'s got this. We don't need to go over there. Right guys?
HMMM... Actually I think she's gonna need us.
SNAP
SINGLE-FILE YOU GUYS! BABY STEPS!
Okay... baby-steps...
This is... fine...
...this is...

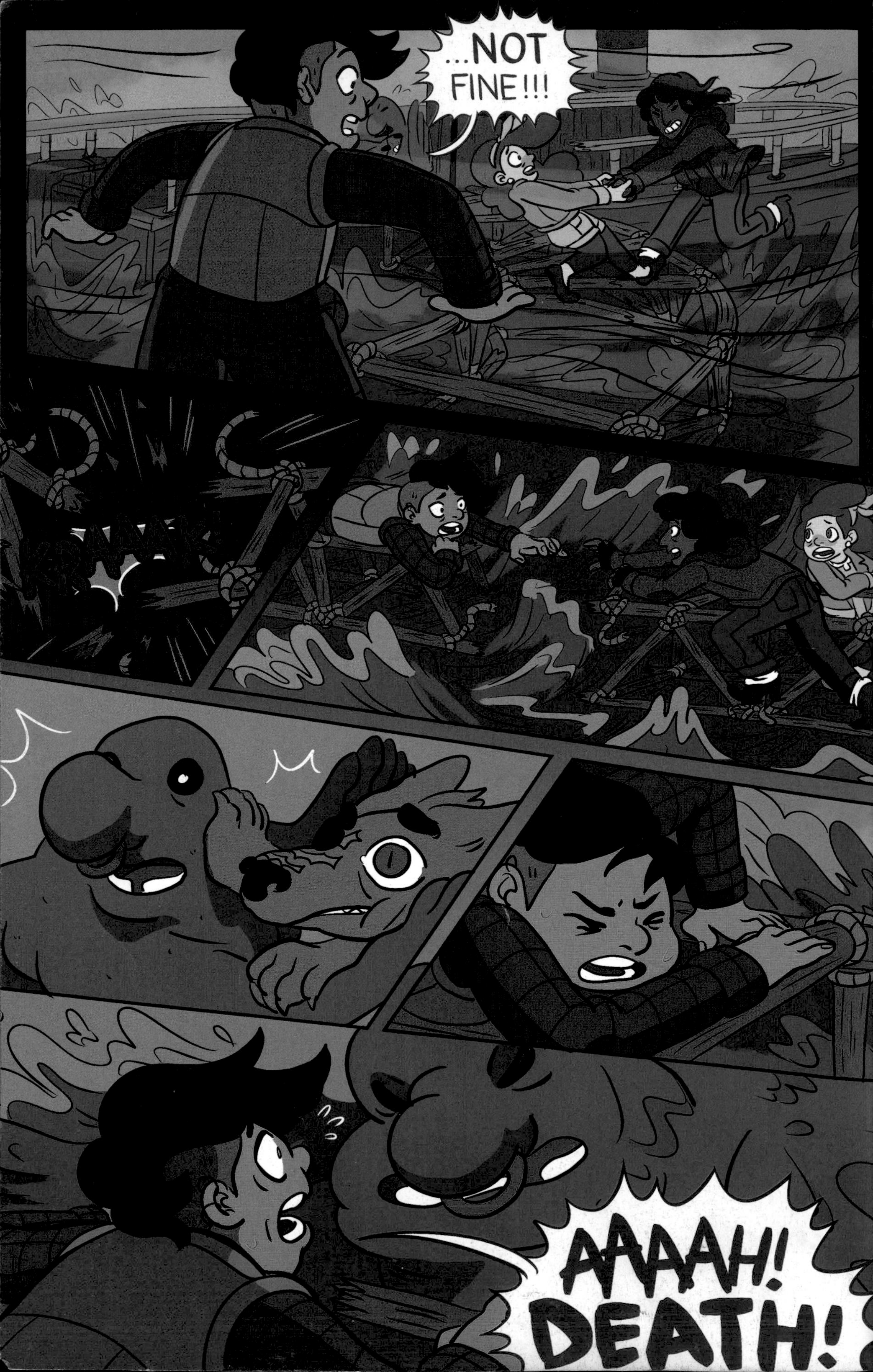
...NOT FINE!!!
AAAAH! DEATH!

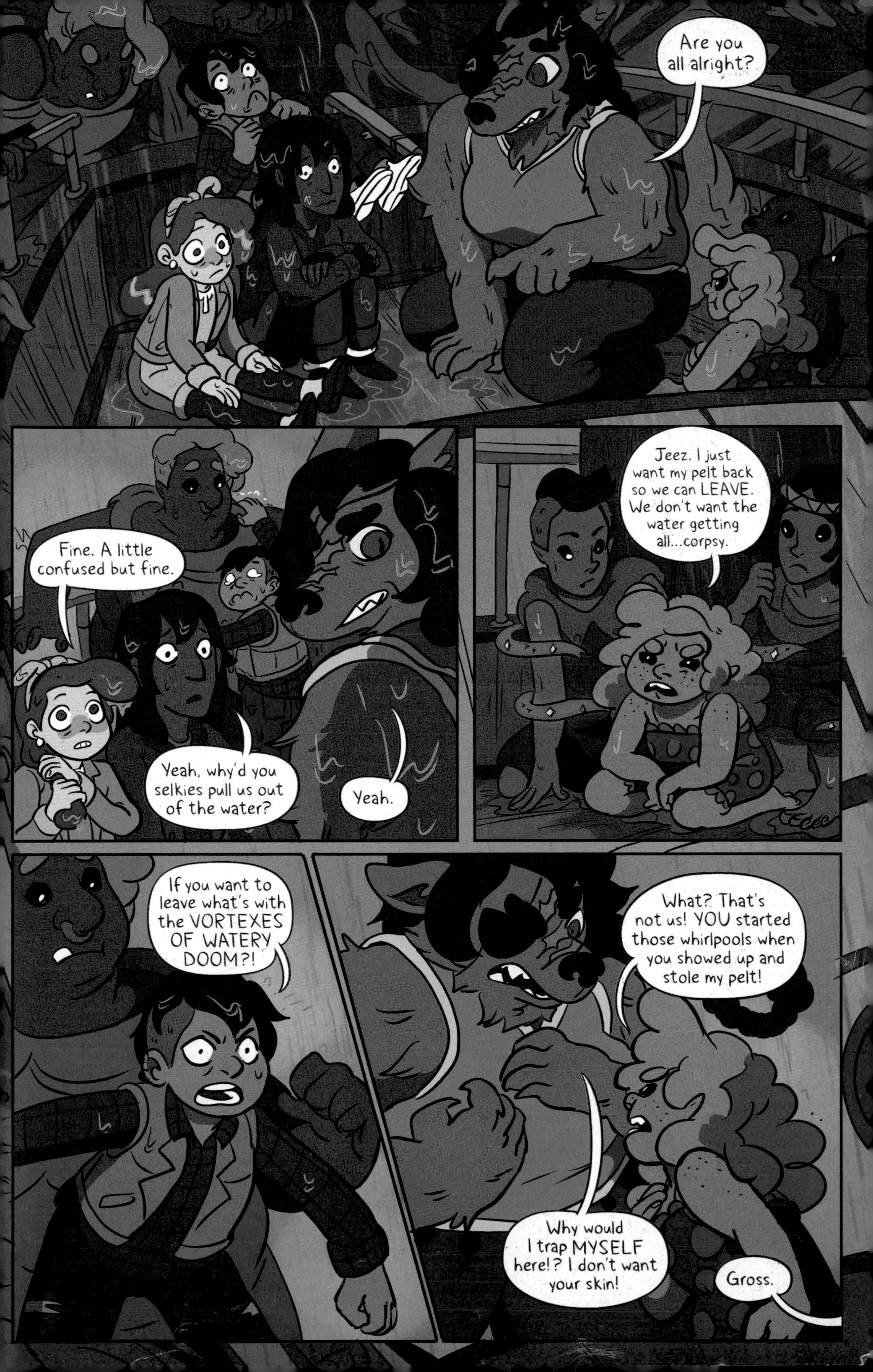
Are you all alright?
Fine. A little confused but fine.
Yeah, why'd you selkies pull us out of the water?
Yeah.
Jeez. I just want my pelt back so we can LEAVE. We don't want the water getting all...corpsy.
If you want to leave what's with the VORTEXES OF WATERY DOOM?!
What? That's not us! YOU started those whirlpools when you showed up and stole my pelt!
Why would I trap MYSELF here!? I don't want your skin!
Gross.

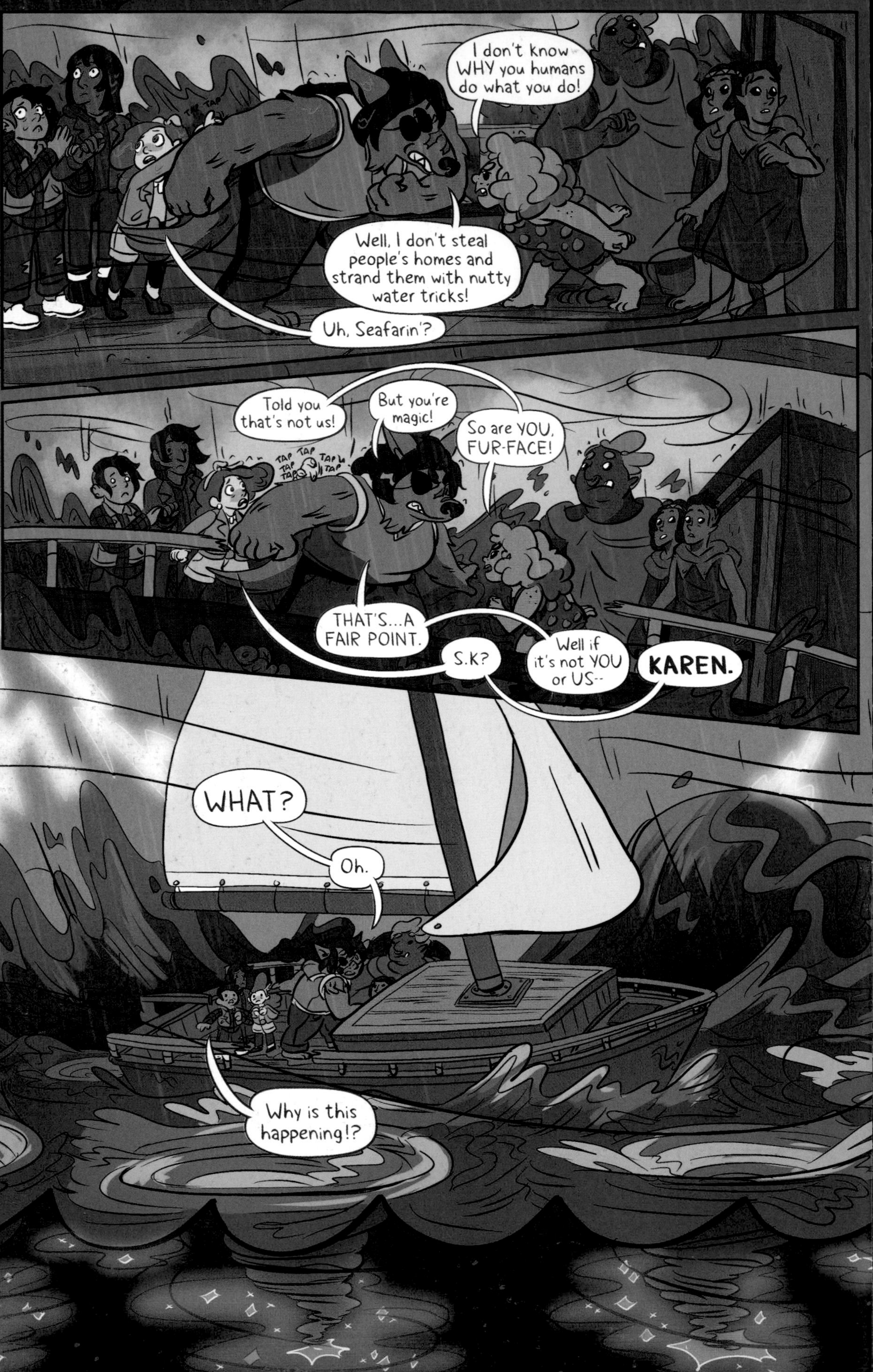

I don't know WHY you humans do what you do!
Well, I don't steal people's homes and strand them with nutty water tricks!
Uh, Seafarin'?
Told you that's not us!
But you're magic!
So are YOU, FUR-FACE!
TAP TAP TAP TAP TAP TAP
THAT'S...A FAIR POINT.
S.K?
Well if it's not YOU or US--
KAREN.
WHAT?
Oh.
Why is this happening!?

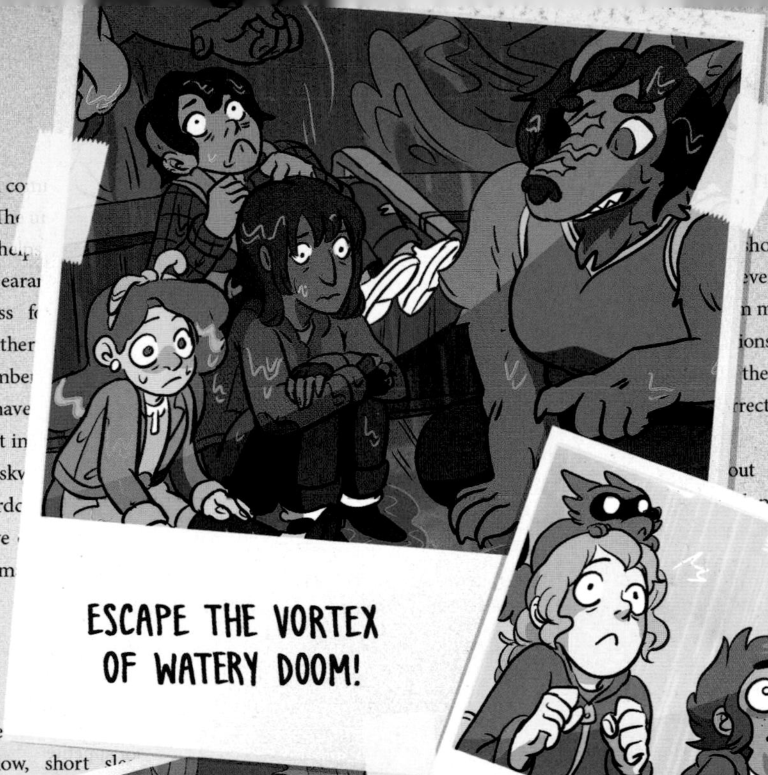
ESCAPE THE VORTEX
OF WATERY DOOM!

will co

The

It he

appearar

dress f

Further

Lumbe

to have

part in

Thiskv

Hardc

have

them

IE UNIFORM

should be worn at camp events when Lumberjanes n may also be worn at other ions. It should be worn as a the uniform dress with rrect shoes, and stocking or

out grows her uniform or ter Lumberjane. a she has her her

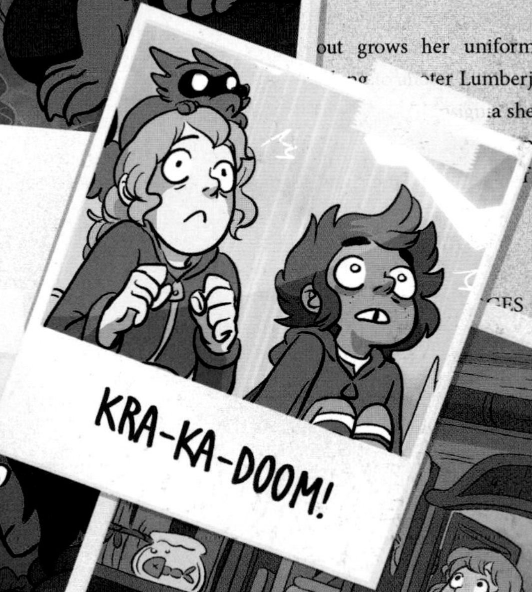
KRA-KA-DOOM!

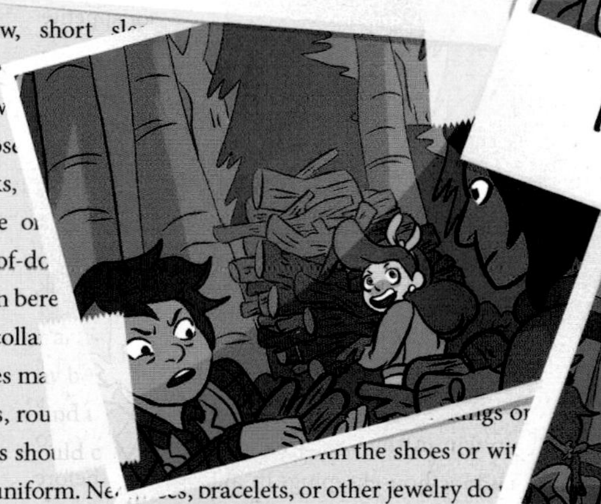

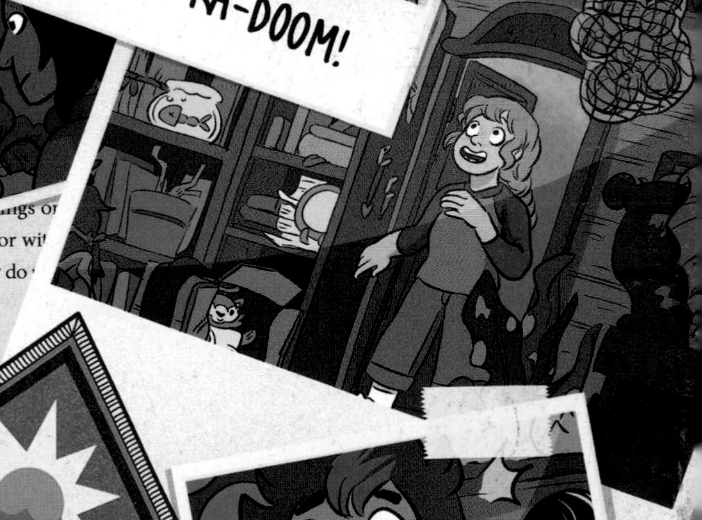

The

yellow, short sl

emb

the w

choose

slacks,

made o

out-of-do

green bere

the colla

Shoes ma

heels, rou kings or

socks shou with the shoes or wi

the uniform. Ne es, bracelets, or other jewelry do

belong with a Lumberjane uniform.

CES

HOW TO WEAR THE UNIFOR

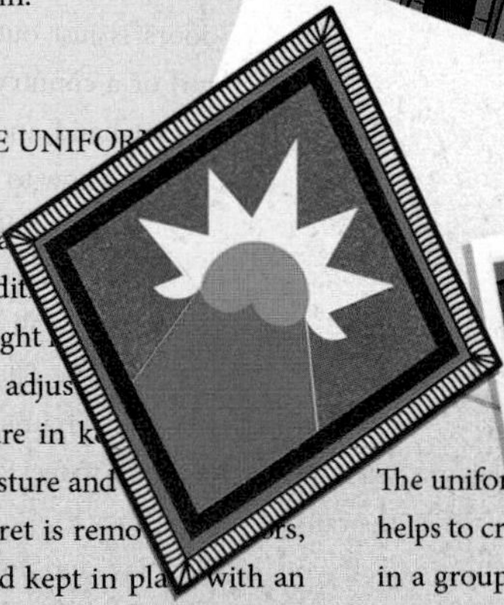

To look well in a uniform dema uniform be kept in good condit pressed. See that the skirt is the right height and build, that the belt is adjus that your shoes and stockings are in k uniform, that you watch your posture and with dignity and grace. If the beret is remo rs, be sure that your hair is neat and kept in pla with an insonspicuous clip or ribbon. When you wear a Lumberjane uniform you are identified as a member of this organization and you should be doubly careful to conduct yourself in a way that will show everyone that courtesy and thoughtfullness are part of being a Lumberjane. People are likely to judge a whole nation by the selfishness of a few individuals, to criticize a whole family because of the misconduct of one member, and to feel unkindly toward and organization because of the

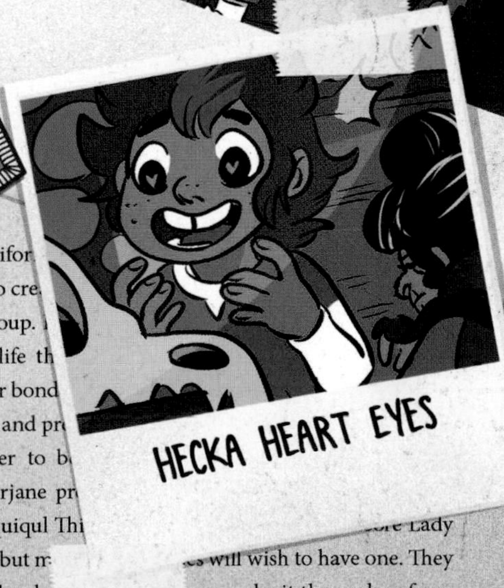
HECKA HEART EYES

The unifor helps to cre in a group. active life th another bond future, and pr in order to b Lumberjane pr Penniquiqul Thi ore Lady Types, but m es will wish to have one. They can either bu , or make it themselves from materials available at the trading post.

LUMBERJANES FIELD MANUAL
CHAPTER TWENTY-THREE

Lumberjanes "Out-of-Doors" Program Field

FOR THE HALIBUT BADGE

"Jumping in head first is always the best solution."

Life is a collection of choices. These choices help create who we become as individuals, and while everyone will have something that they might wish they could go back in time to change, we must learn to accept the events that have already happened and learn to embrace the future that we've made for ourselves. Not everything will be a choice that we're ready to make, and some of these decisions might be based on a reaction to someone else, but as a Lumberjane, we hope that every step that we take is the best one. It might not always be the case, but we have to learn to think on our feet and deal with the consequences regardless if they are positive or otherwise.

For The Halibut badge is about making decisions without any forethought. This badge is about jumping into a situation with no knowledge of what you might find on the other end and learning how to not only make

the best of the situation, but learn how to think on your feet. Life outside of camp, and even inside of camp, might not be as forgiving as we hope it is, but we want to make sure that everyone learns how to make those split-second decisions and how to hone your instincts in order to get more positive outcomes out of every situation.

There are a few ways to obtain the *For The Halibut* badge, and they all deal with water. It is important to have already earned the basic water safety badges before you will be able to earn the *For The Halibut* badge. The first task for this badge will be up to your counselor, as they will do their best to find a challenge for you that not only meets your level of difficulty but creates a problem that has several possible answers. It will be up to you to jump into the challenge with no forewarning and solve it with the best solution. Your counselor will evaluate your task and if they need to they will

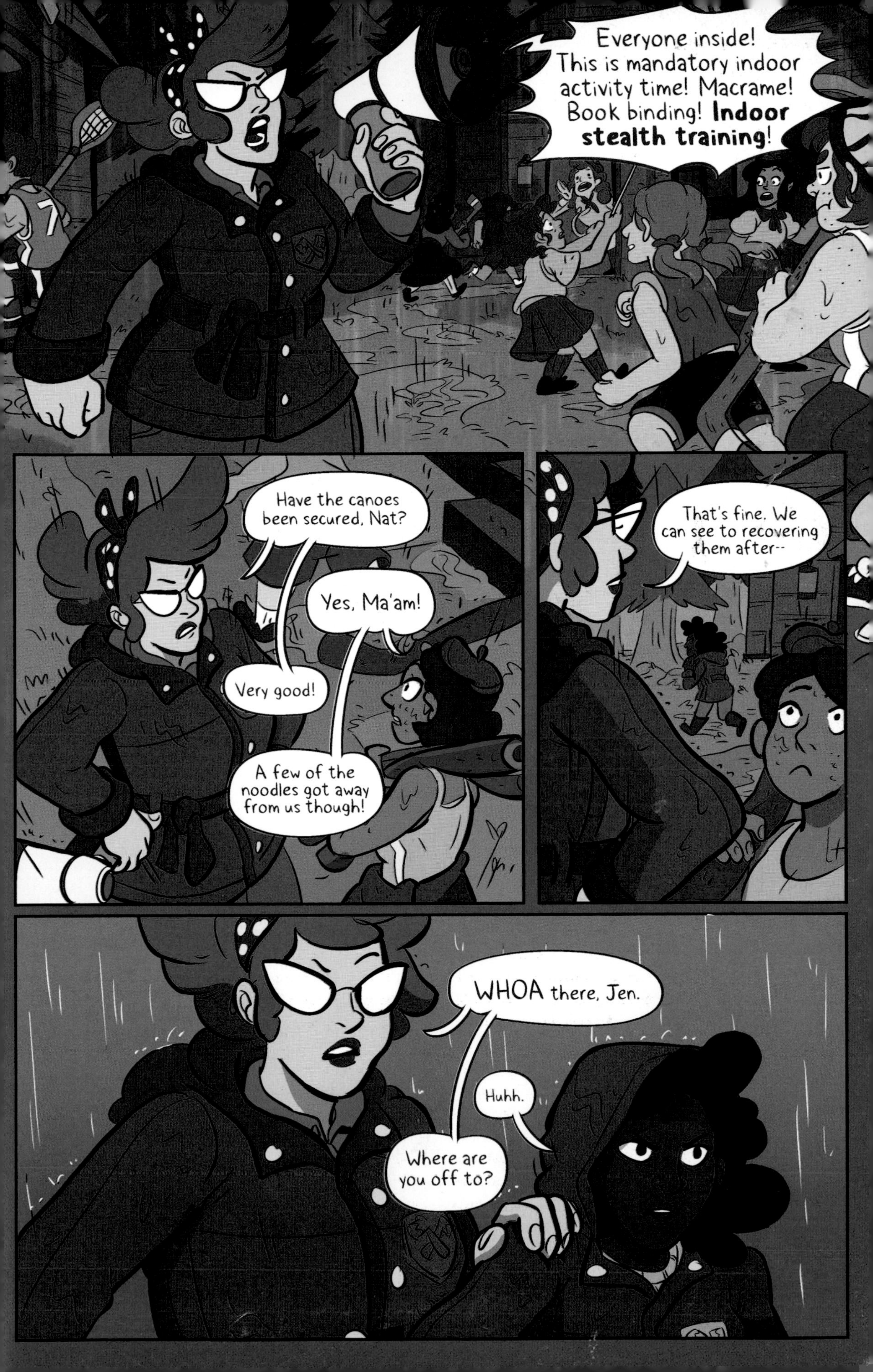
Everyone inside! This is mandatory indoor activity time! Macrame! Book binding! **Indoor stealth training**!
Have the canoes been secured, Nat?
Yes, Ma'am!
Very good!
A few of the noodles got away from us though!
That's fine. We can see to recovering them after--
WHOA there, Jen.
Huhh.
Where are you off to?

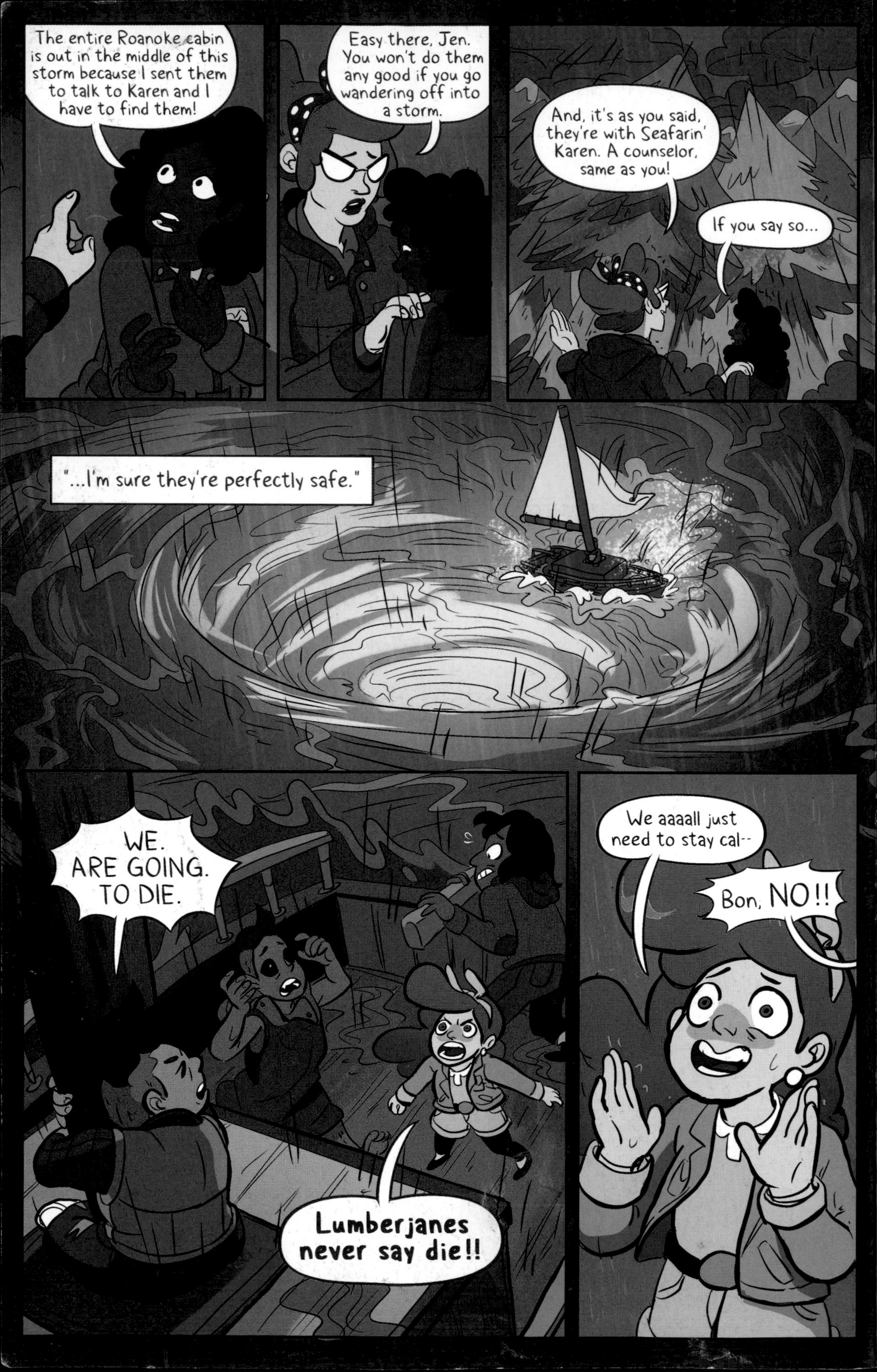

The entire Roanoke cabin is out in the middle of this storm because I sent them to talk to Karen and I have to find them!
Easy there, Jen. You won't do them any good if you go wandering off into a storm.
And, it's as you said, they're with Seafarin' Karen. A counselor, same as you!
If you say so...
"...I'm sure they're perfectly safe."
WE. ARE GOING. TO DIE.
Lumberjanes never say die!!
We aaaall just need to stay cal--
Bon, NO!!

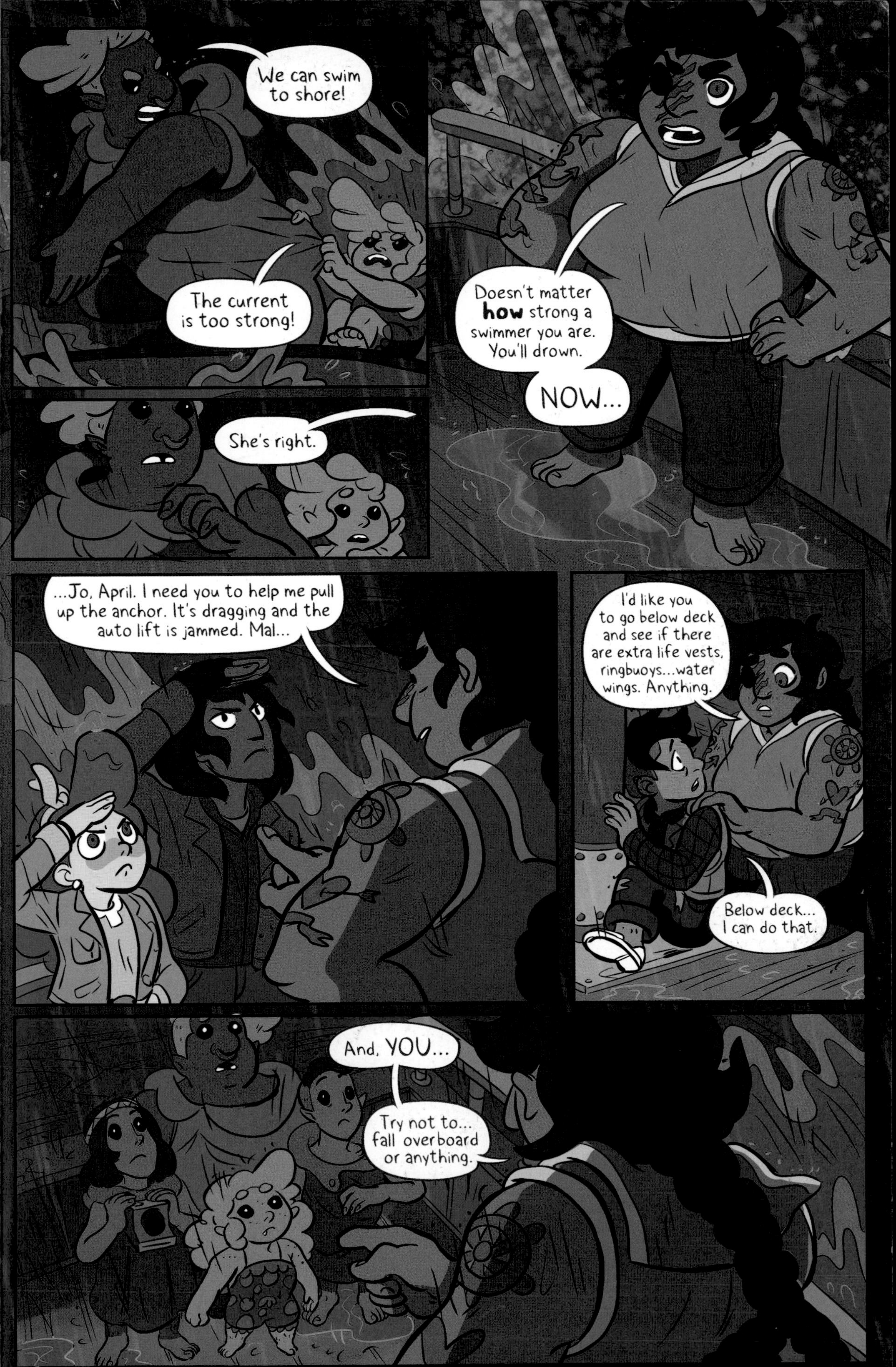
We can swim to shore!
The current is too strong!
Doesn't matter **how** strong a swimmer you are. You'll drown.
NOW...
She's right.
...Jo, April. I need you to help me pull up the anchor. It's dragging and the auto lift is jammed. Mal...
I'd like you to go below deck and see if there are extra life vests, ringbuoys...water wings. Anything.
Below deck... I can do that.
And, YOU...
Try not to... fall overboard or anything.

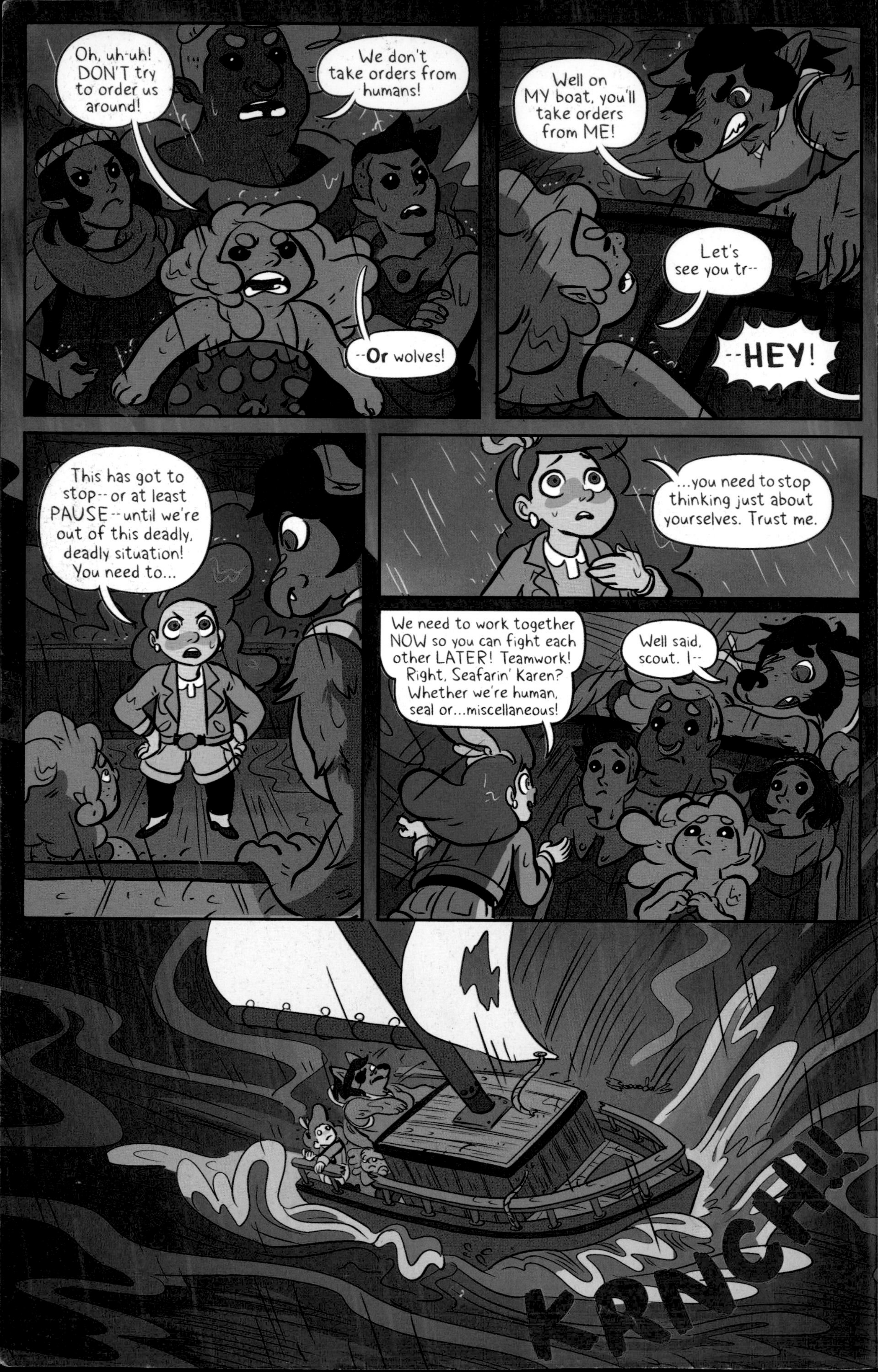
Oh, uh-uh! DON'T try to order us around!
We don't take orders from humans!
--Or wolves!
Well on MY boat, you'll take orders from ME!
Let's see you tr--
--HEY!
This has got to stop--or at least PAUSE--until we're out of this deadly, deadly situation! You need to...
...you need to stop thinking just about yourselves. Trust me.
We need to work together NOW so you can fight each other LATER! Teamwork! Right, Seafarin' Karen? Whether we're human, seal or...miscellaneous!
Well said, scout. I--
KRNCH!!

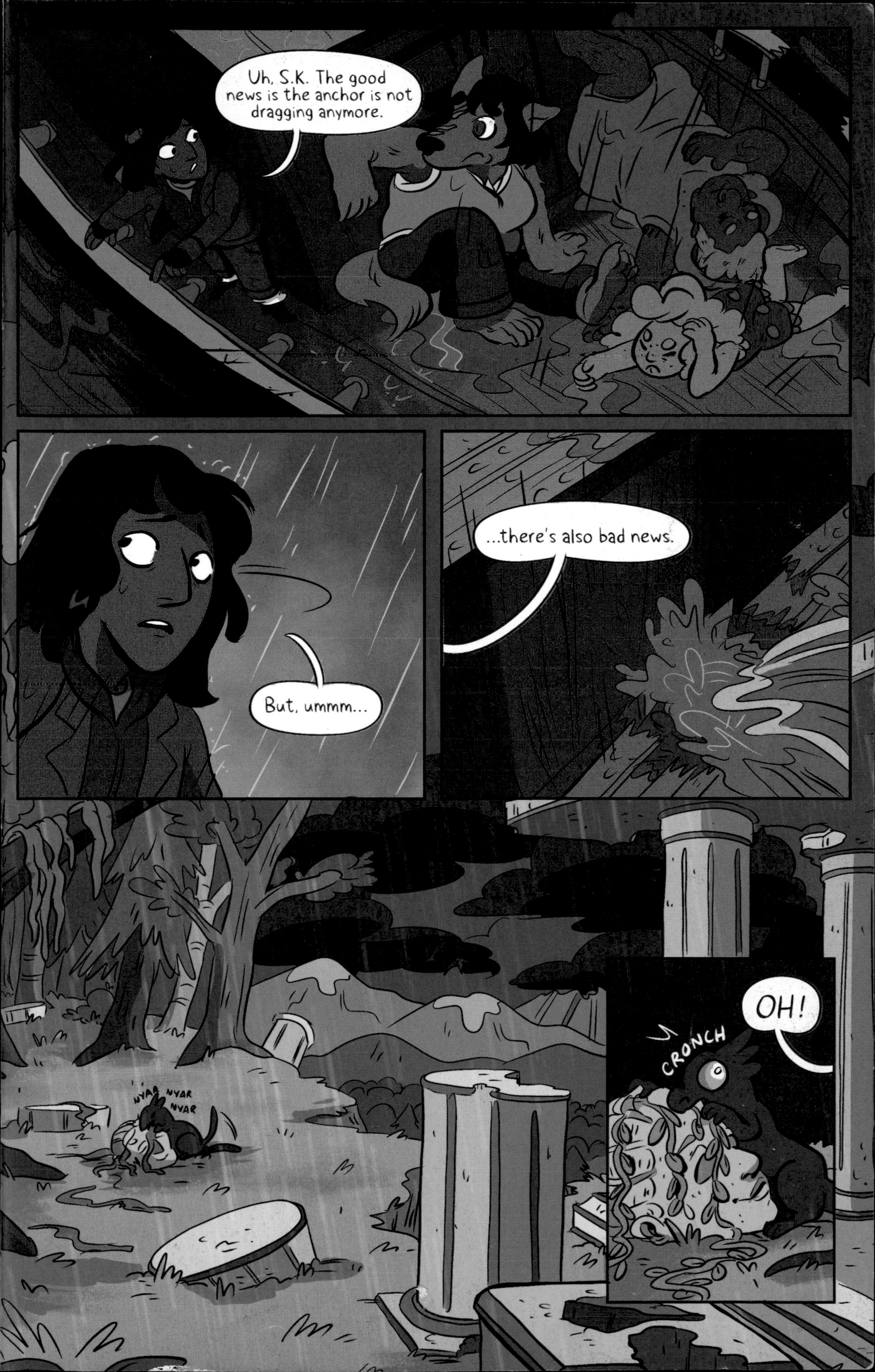
Uh, S.K. The good news is the anchor is not dragging anymore.
But, ummm...
...there's also bad news.
NYAR NYAR NYAR
CRONCH
OH!

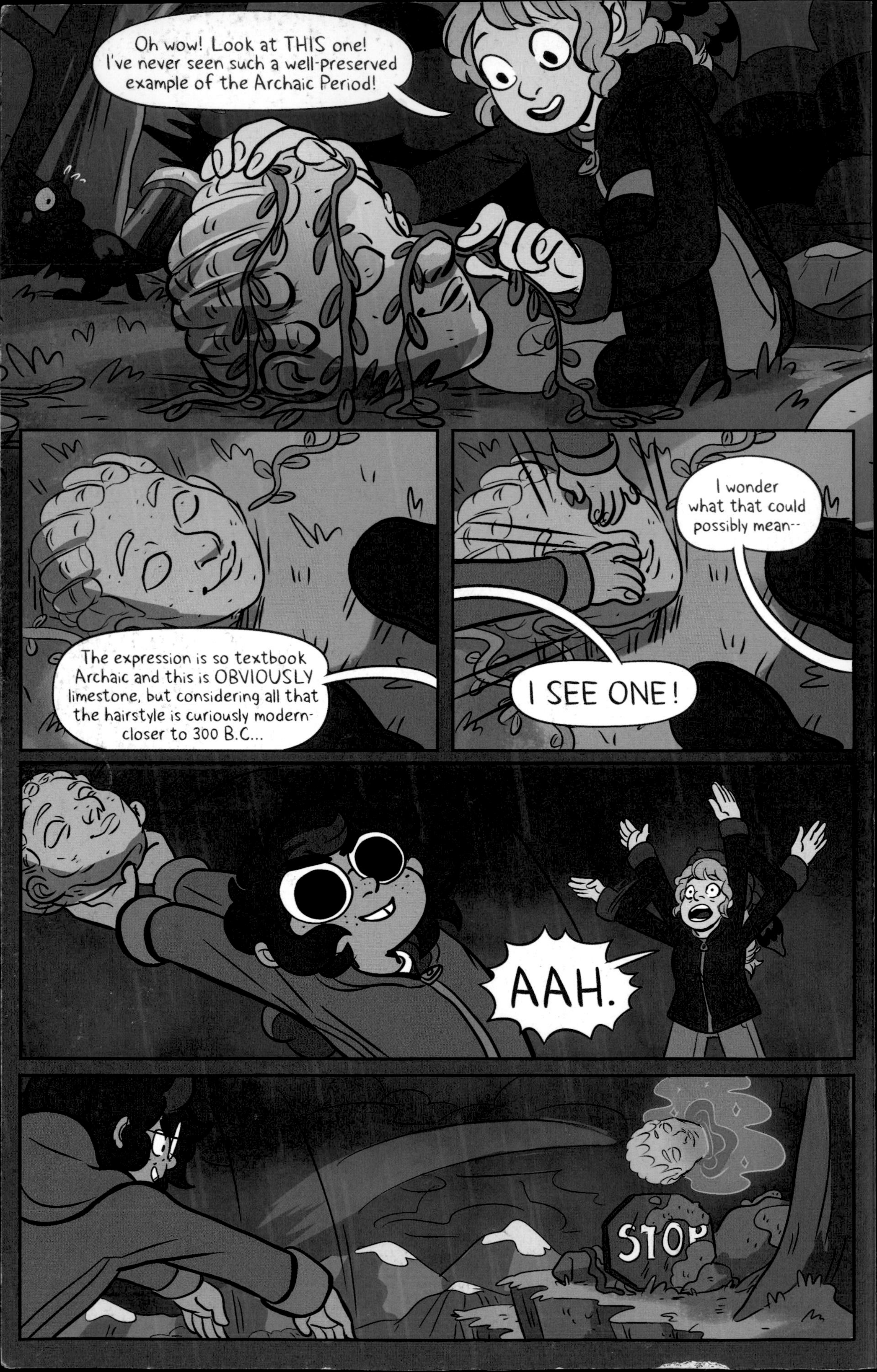
Oh wow! Look at THIS one! I've never seen such a well-preserved example of the Archaic Period!
The expression is so textbook Archaic and this is OBVIOUSLY limestone, but considering all that the hairstyle is curiously modern-closer to 300 B.C...
I wonder what that could possibly mean--
I SEE ONE!
AAH.
STOP

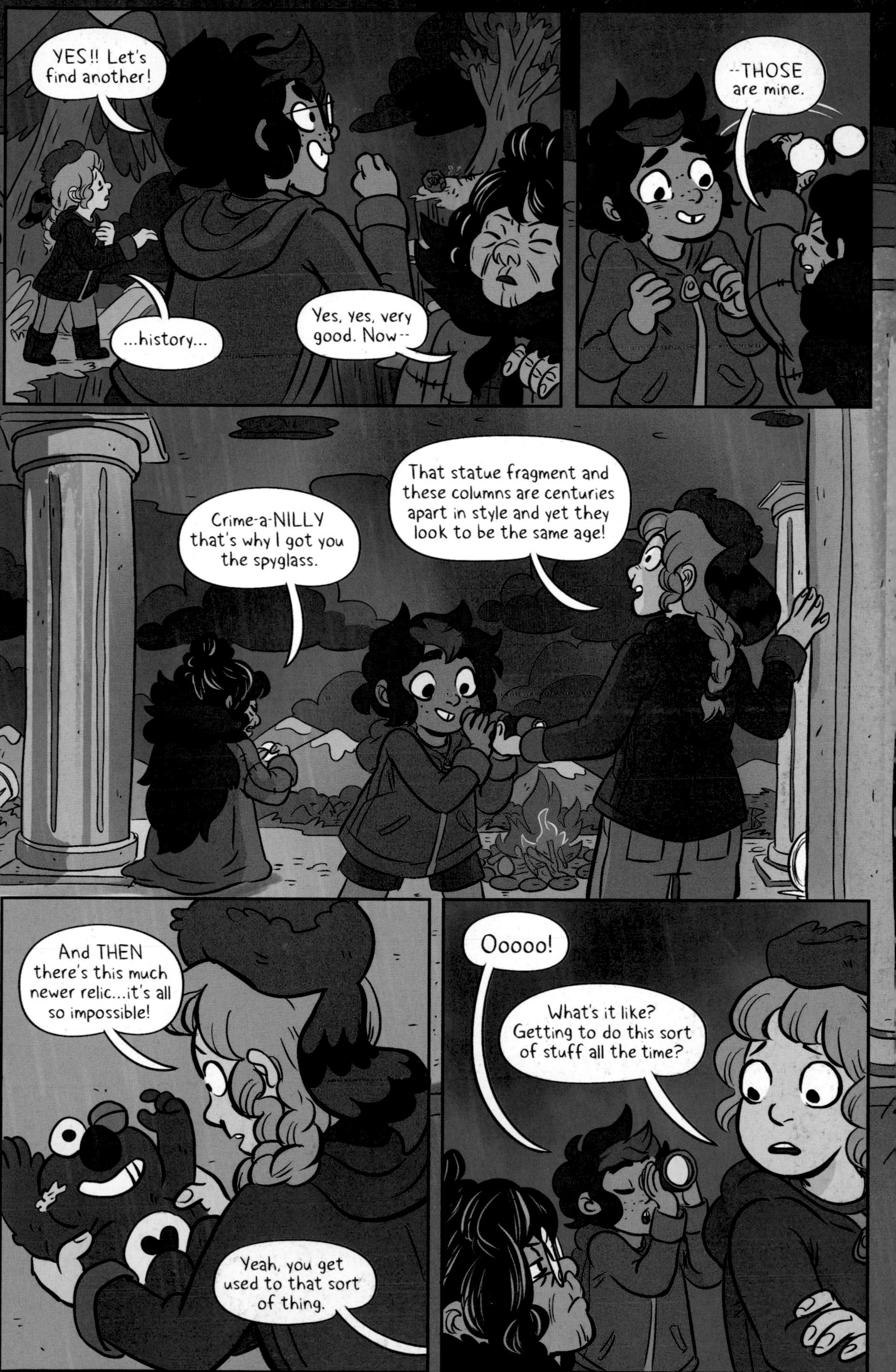
YES!! Let's find another!
...history...
Yes, yes, very good. Now--
--THOSE are mine.
Crime-a-NILLY that's why I got you the spyglass.
That statue fragment and these columns are centuries apart in style and yet they look to be the same age!
And THEN there's this much newer relic...it's all so impossible!
Yeah, you get used to that sort of thing.
Ooooo!
What's it like? Getting to do this sort of stuff all the time?

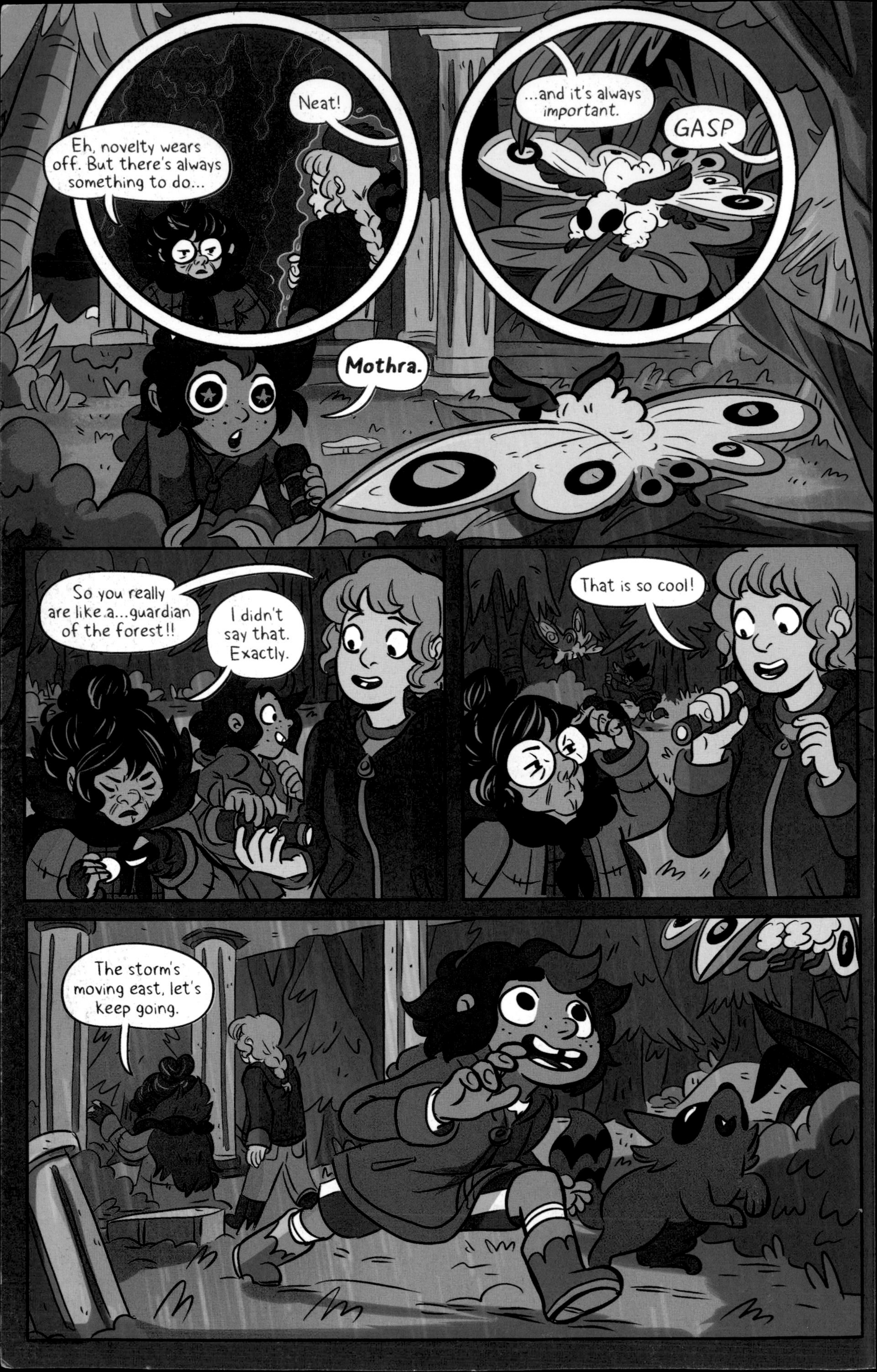
Eh, novelty wears off. But there's always something to do...
Neat!
...and it's always important.
GASP
Mothra.
So you really are like a...guardian of the forest!!
I didn't say that. Exactly.
That is so cool!
The storm's moving east, let's keep going.

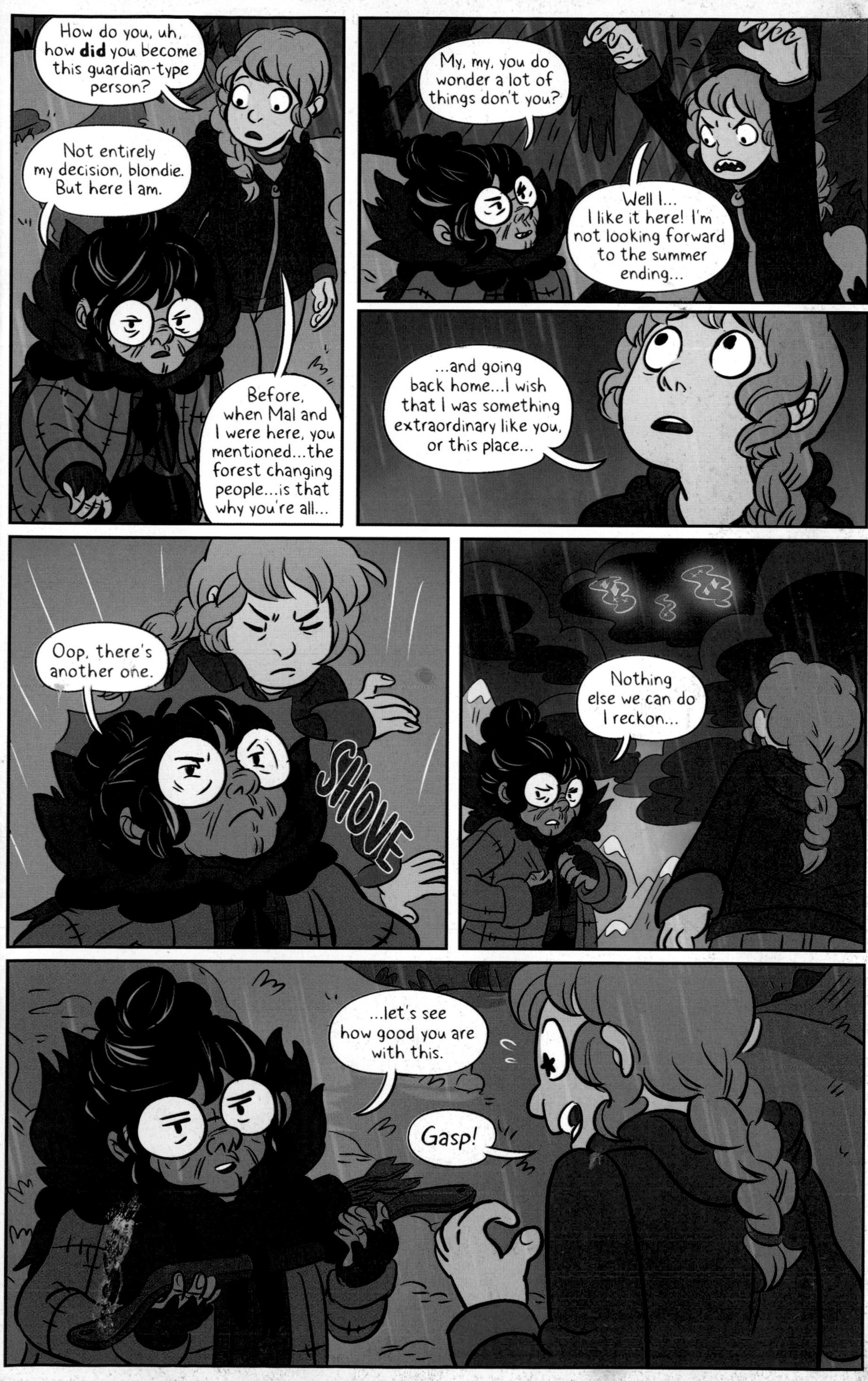
How do you, uh, how **did** you become this guardian-type person?
Not entirely my decision, blondie. But here I am.
Before, when Mal and I were here, you mentioned...the forest changing people...is that why you're all...
My, my, you do wonder a lot of things don't you?
Well I... I like it here! I'm not looking forward to the summer ending...
...and going back home...I wish that I was something extraordinary like you, or this place...
Oop, there's another one.
SHOVE
Nothing else we can do I reckon...
...let's see how good you are with this.
Gasp!

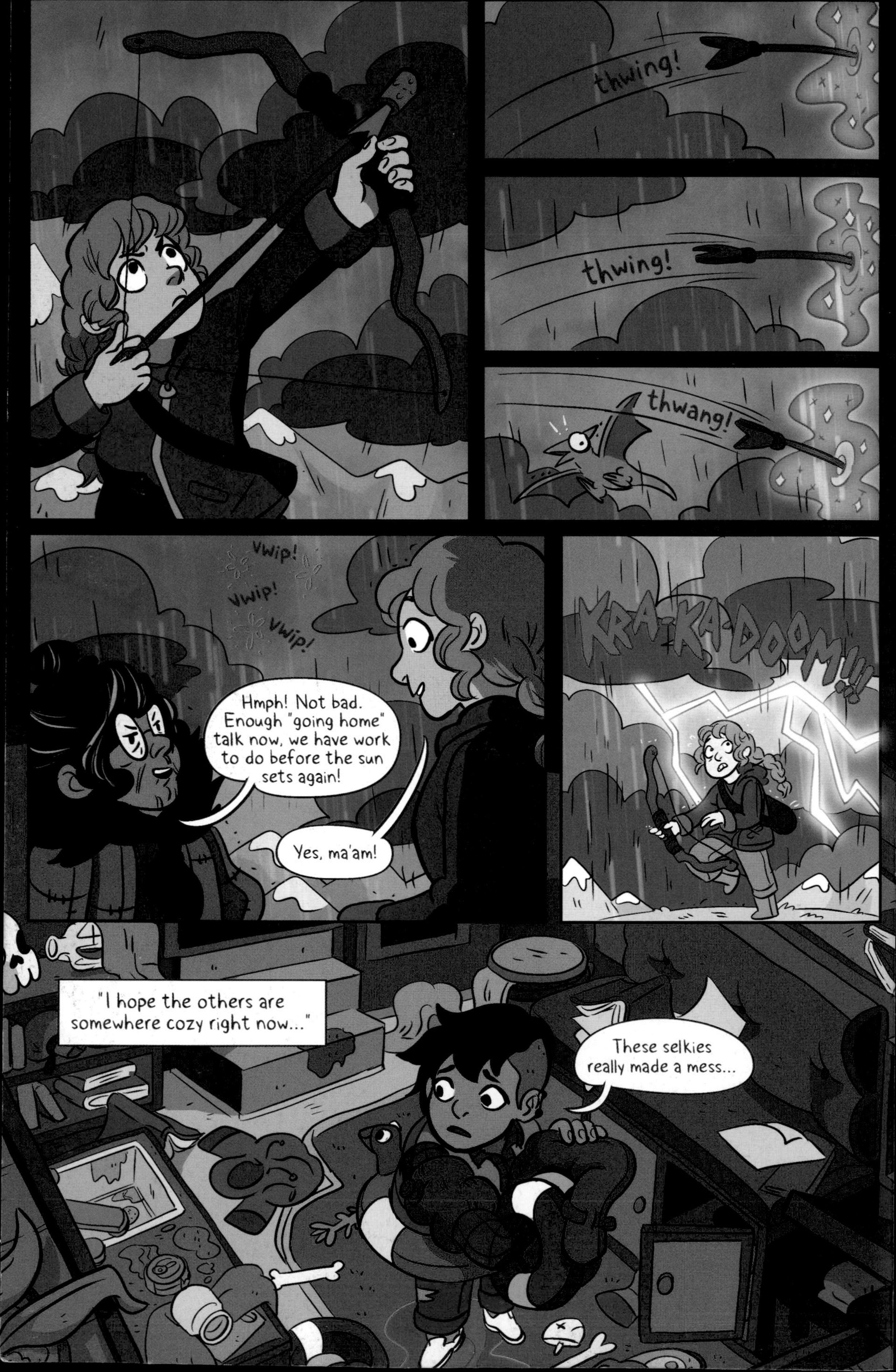
thwing!
thwing!
thwang!
vwip!
vwip!
vwip!
Hmph! Not bad. Enough "going home" talk now, we have work to do before the sun sets again!
Yes, ma'am!
KRA-KA-DOOM!!!
"I hope the others are somewhere cozy right now..."
These selkies really made a mess...

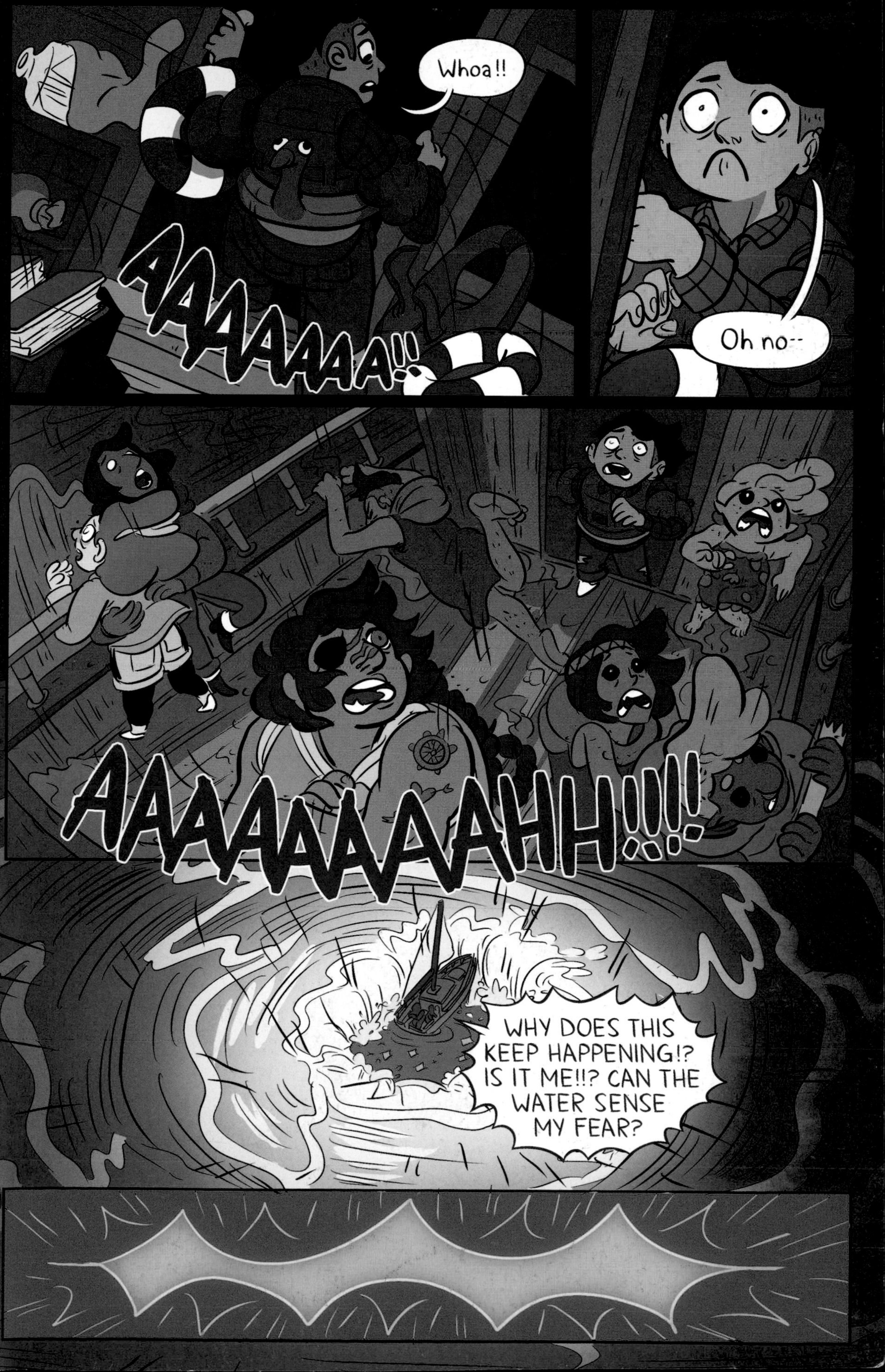
Whoa!!
AAAAAAAA!!
Oh no--
AAAAAAAAAHH!!!!
WHY DOES THIS KEEP HAPPENING!? IS IT ME!!? CAN THE WATER SENSE MY FEAR?

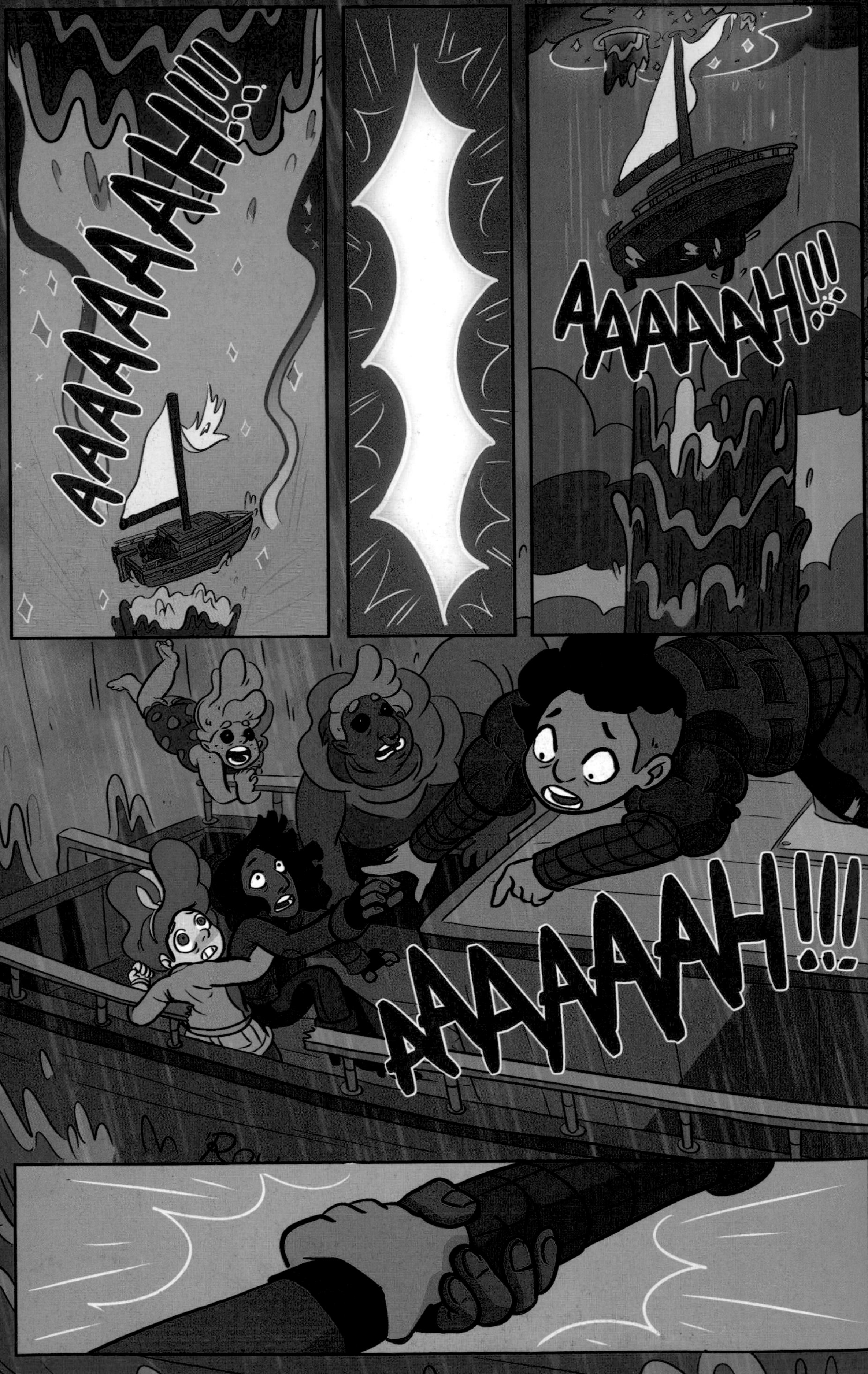
AAAAAAH!!!
AAAAAH!!!
AAAAAAH!!!

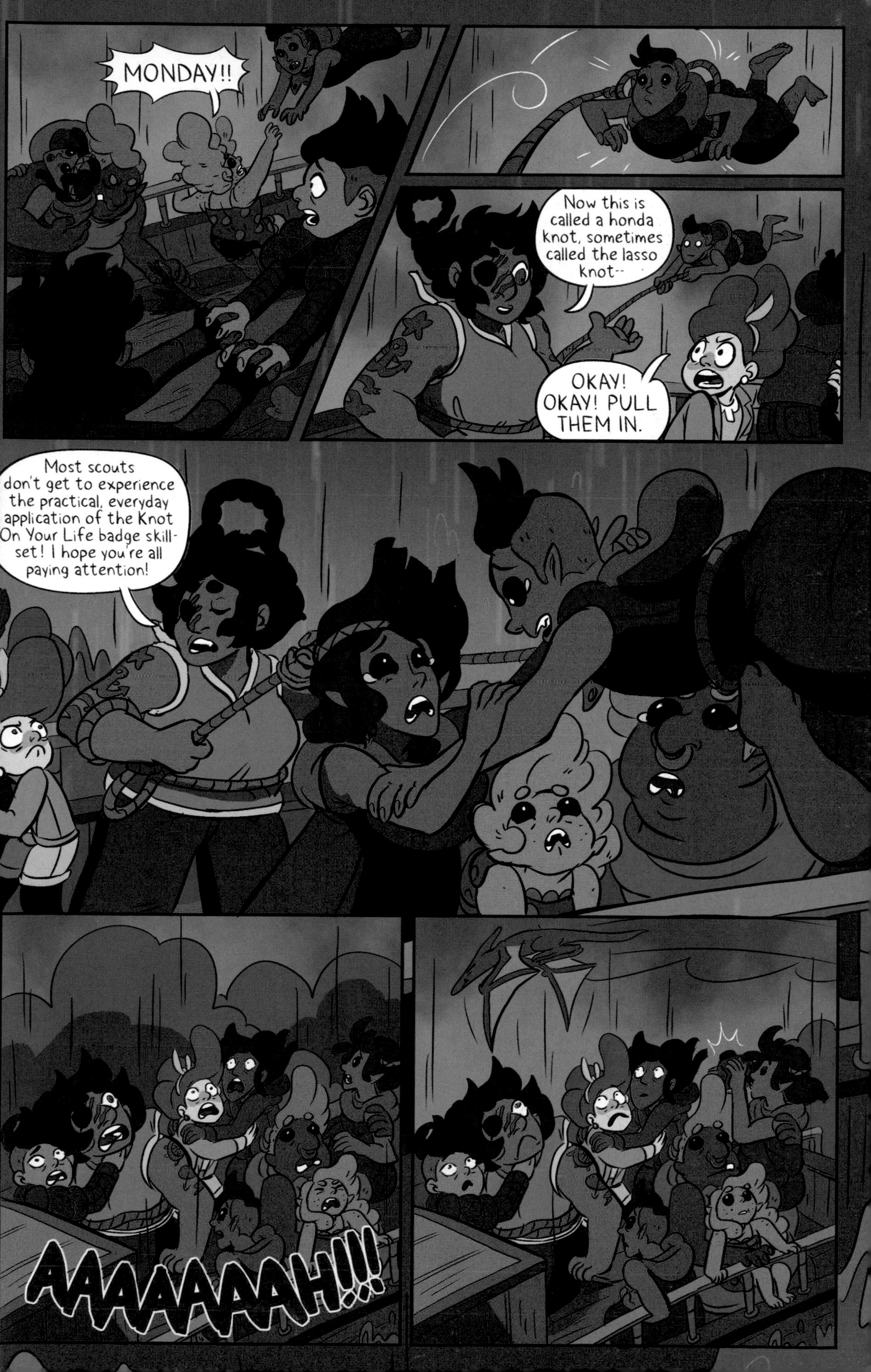
MONDAY!!
Now this is called a honda knot, sometimes called the lasso knot--
OKAY! OKAY! PULL THEM IN.
Most scouts don't get to experience the practical, everyday application of the Knot On Your Life badge skill-set! I hope you're all paying attention!
AAAAAAAH!!!

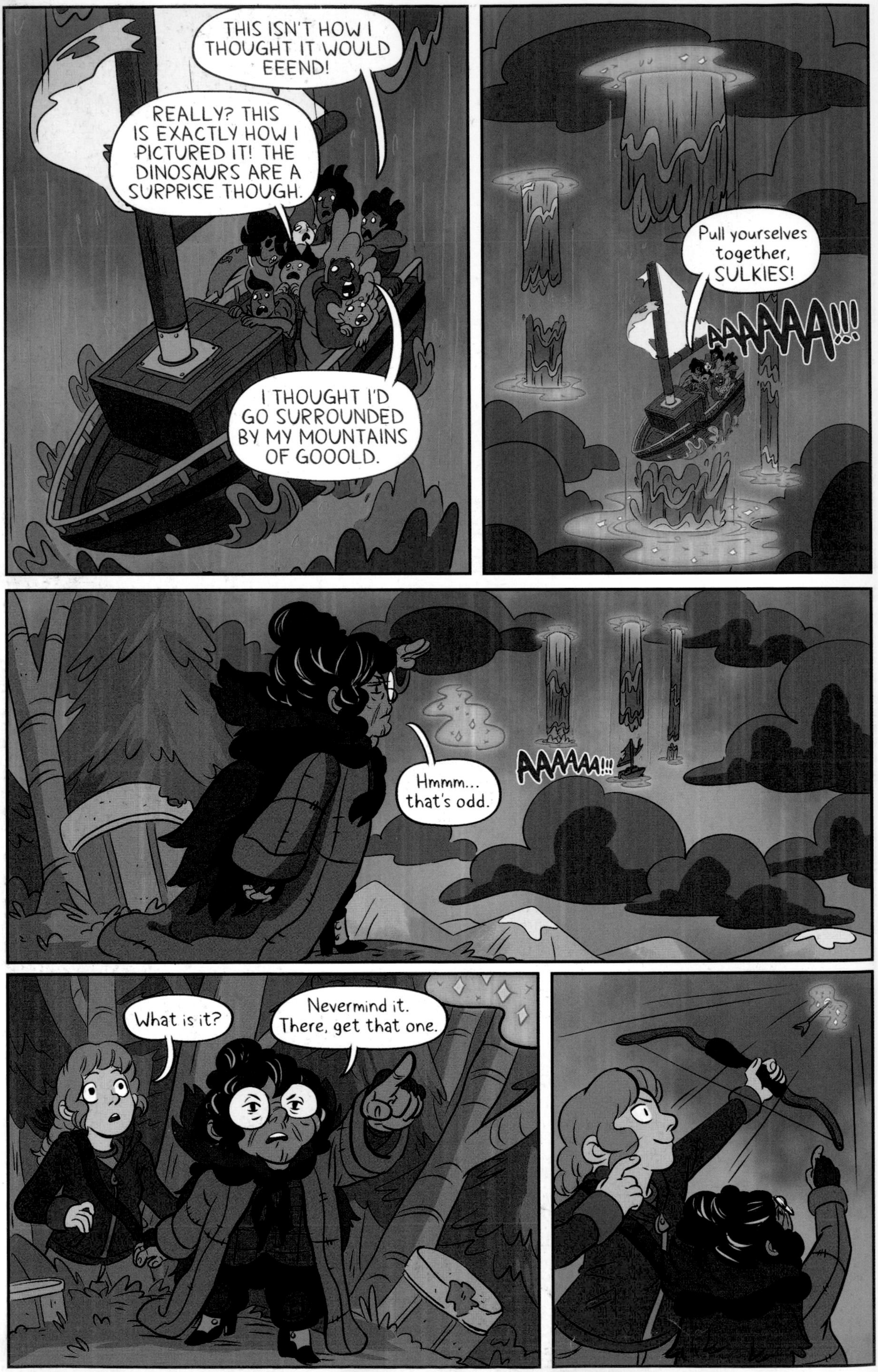
THIS ISN'T HOW I THOUGHT IT WOULD EEEND!
REALLY? THIS IS EXACTLY HOW I PICTURED IT! THE DINOSAURS ARE A SURPRISE THOUGH.
I THOUGHT I'D GO SURROUNDED BY MY MOUNTAINS OF GOOOLD.
Pull yourselves together, SULKIES!
AAAAAA!!!
AAAAAA!!!
Hmmm... that's odd.
What is it?
Nevermind it. There, get that one.

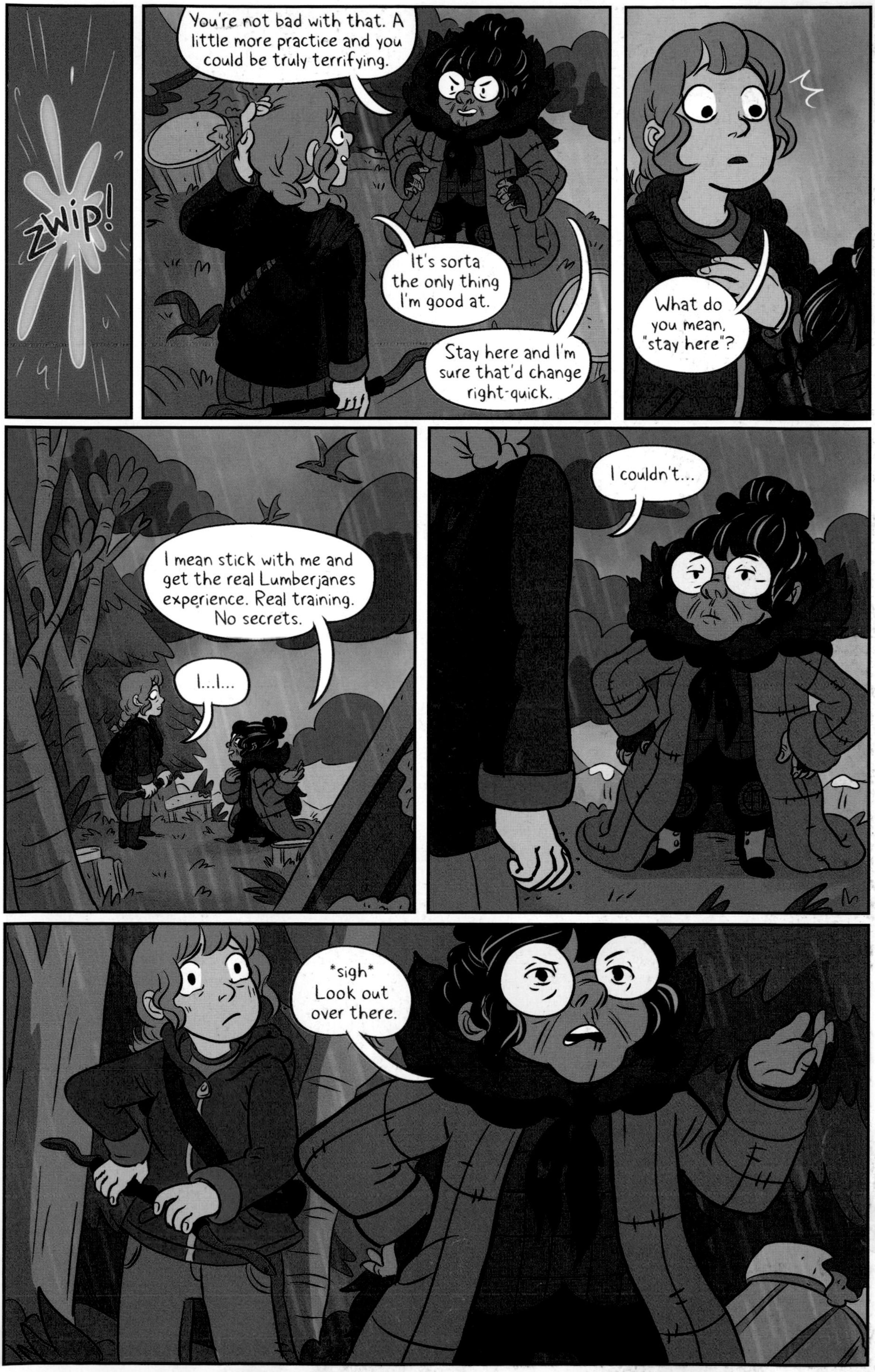
ZWIP!
You're not bad with that. A little more practice and you could be truly terrifying.
It's sorta the only thing I'm good at.
Stay here and I'm sure that'd change right-quick.
What do you mean, "stay here"?
I mean stick with me and get the real Lumberjanes experience. Real training. No secrets.
I...I...
I couldn't...
sigh Look out over there.

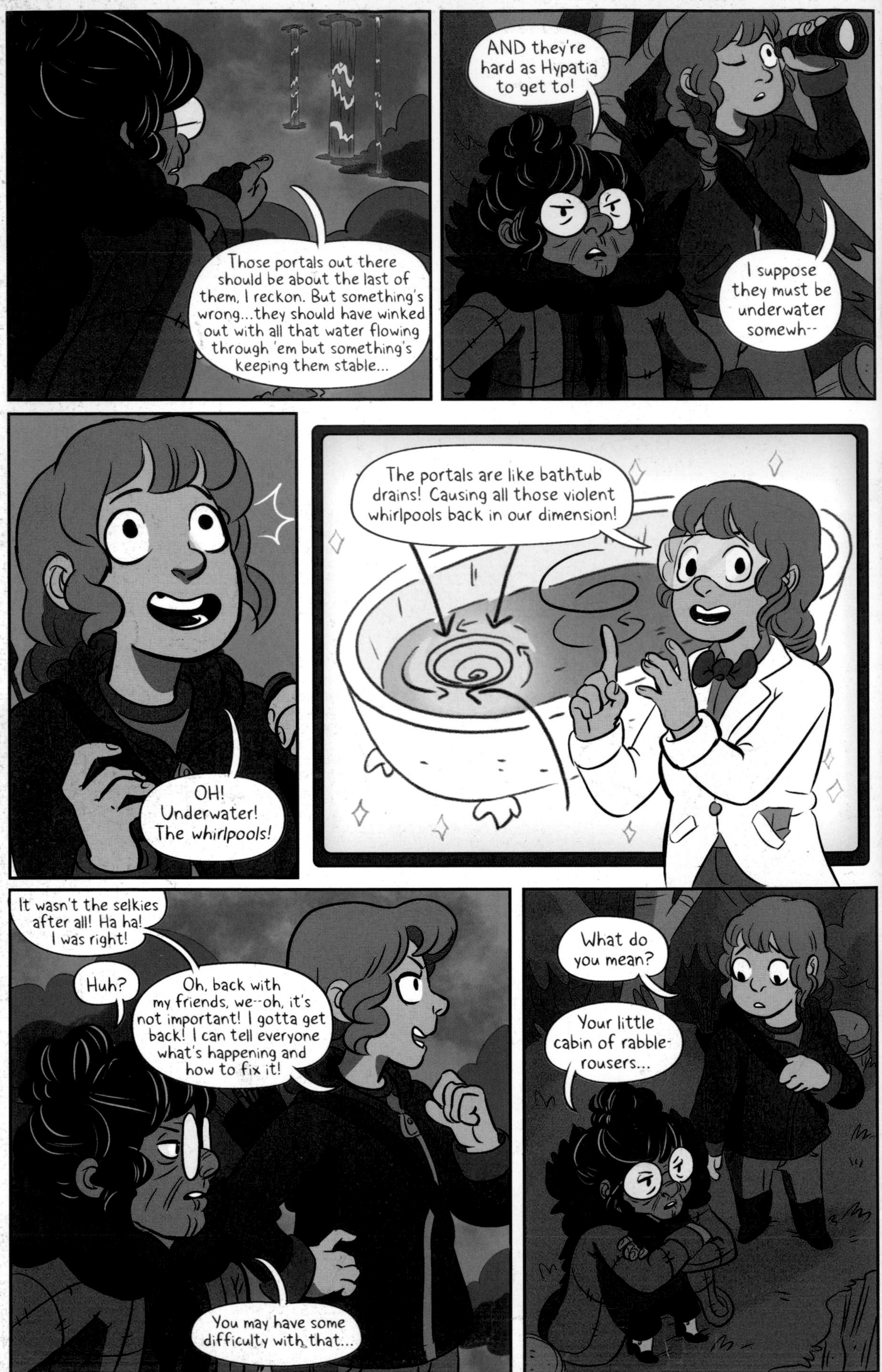
Those portals out there should be about the last of them, I reckon. But something's wrong...they should have winked out with all that water flowing through 'em but something's keeping them stable...
AND they're hard as Hypatia to get to!
I suppose they must be underwater somewh--
OH! Underwater! The whirlpools!
The portals are like bathtub drains! Causing all those violent whirlpools back in our dimension!
It wasn't the selkies after all! Ha ha! I was right!
Huh?
Oh, back with my friends, we--oh, it's not important! I gotta get back! I can tell everyone what's happening and how to fix it!
You may have some difficulty with that...
What do you mean?
Your little cabin of rabble-rousers...

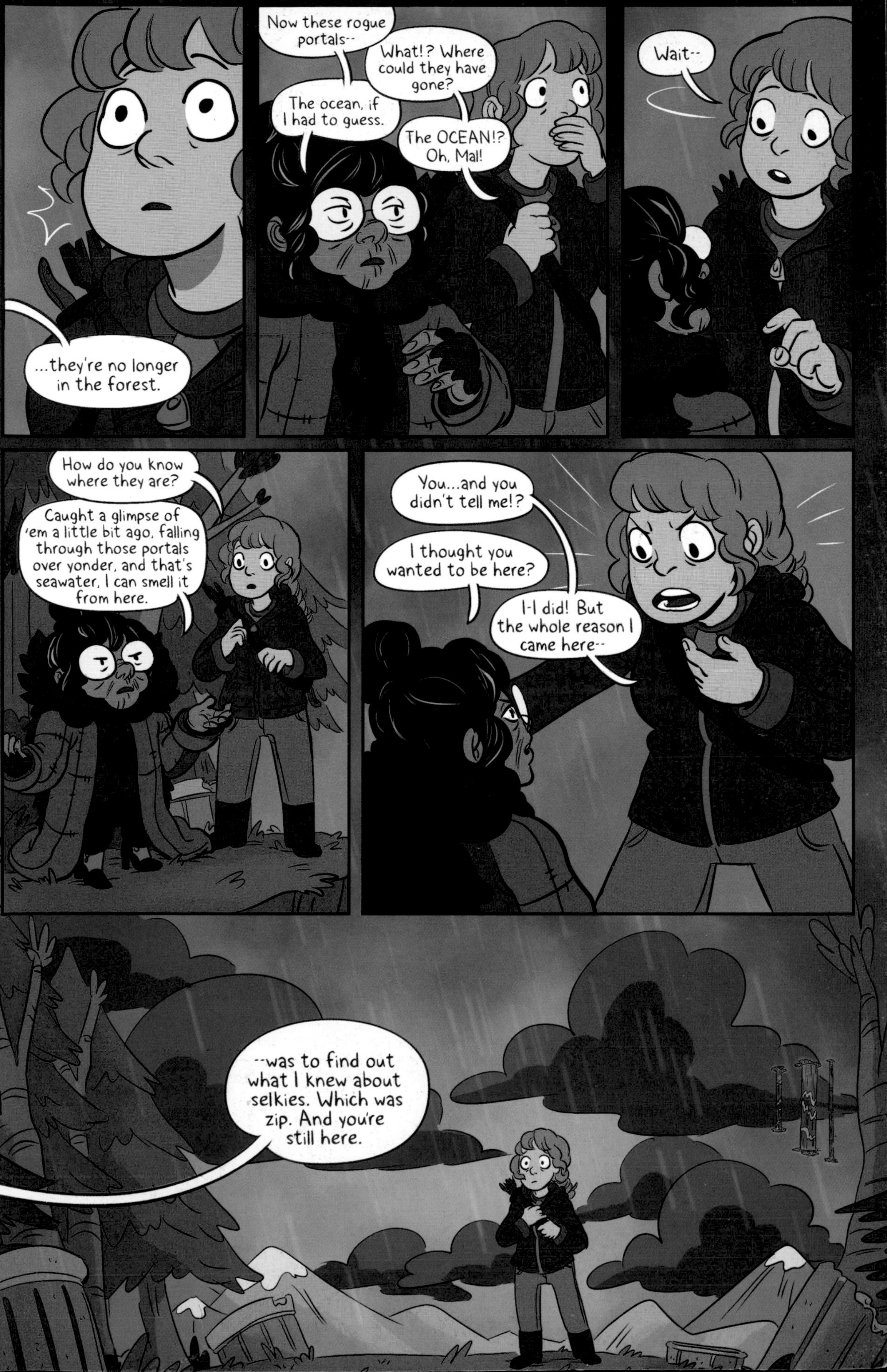
...they're no longer in the forest.
Now these rogue portals--
What!? Where could they have gone?
The ocean, if I had to guess.
The OCEAN!? Oh, Mal!
Wait--
How do you know where they are?
Caught a glimpse of 'em a little bit ago, falling through those portals over yonder, and that's seawater, I can smell it from here.
You...and you didn't tell me!?
I thought you wanted to be here?
I-I did! But the whole reason I came here--
--was to find out what I knew about selkies. Which was zip. And you're still here.

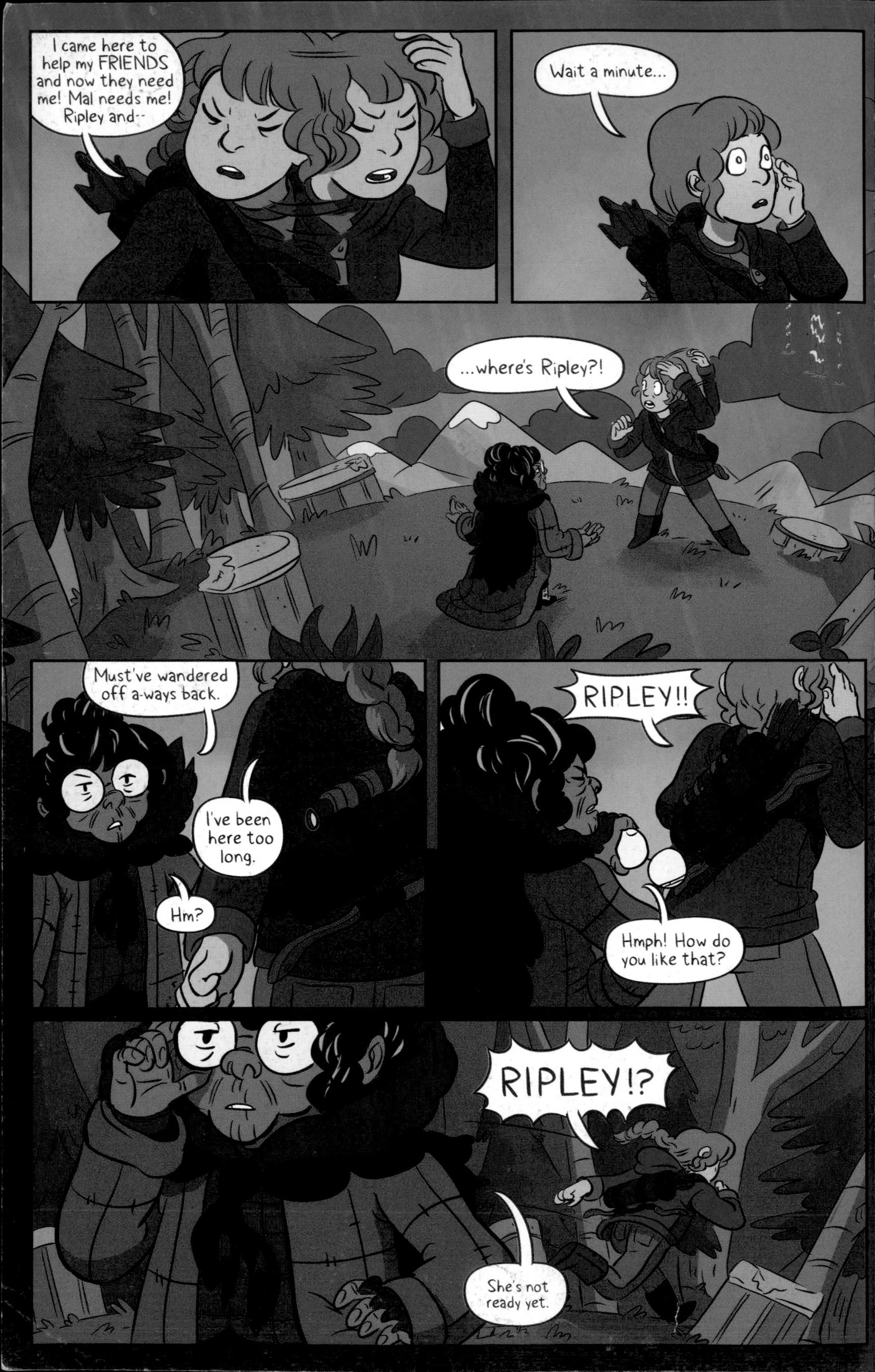
I came here to help my FRIENDS and now they need me! Mal needs me! Ripley and--
Wait a minute...
...where's Ripley?!
Must've wandered off a-ways back.
I've been here too long.
Hm?
RIPLEY!!
Hmph! How do you like that?
RIPLEY!?
She's not ready yet.

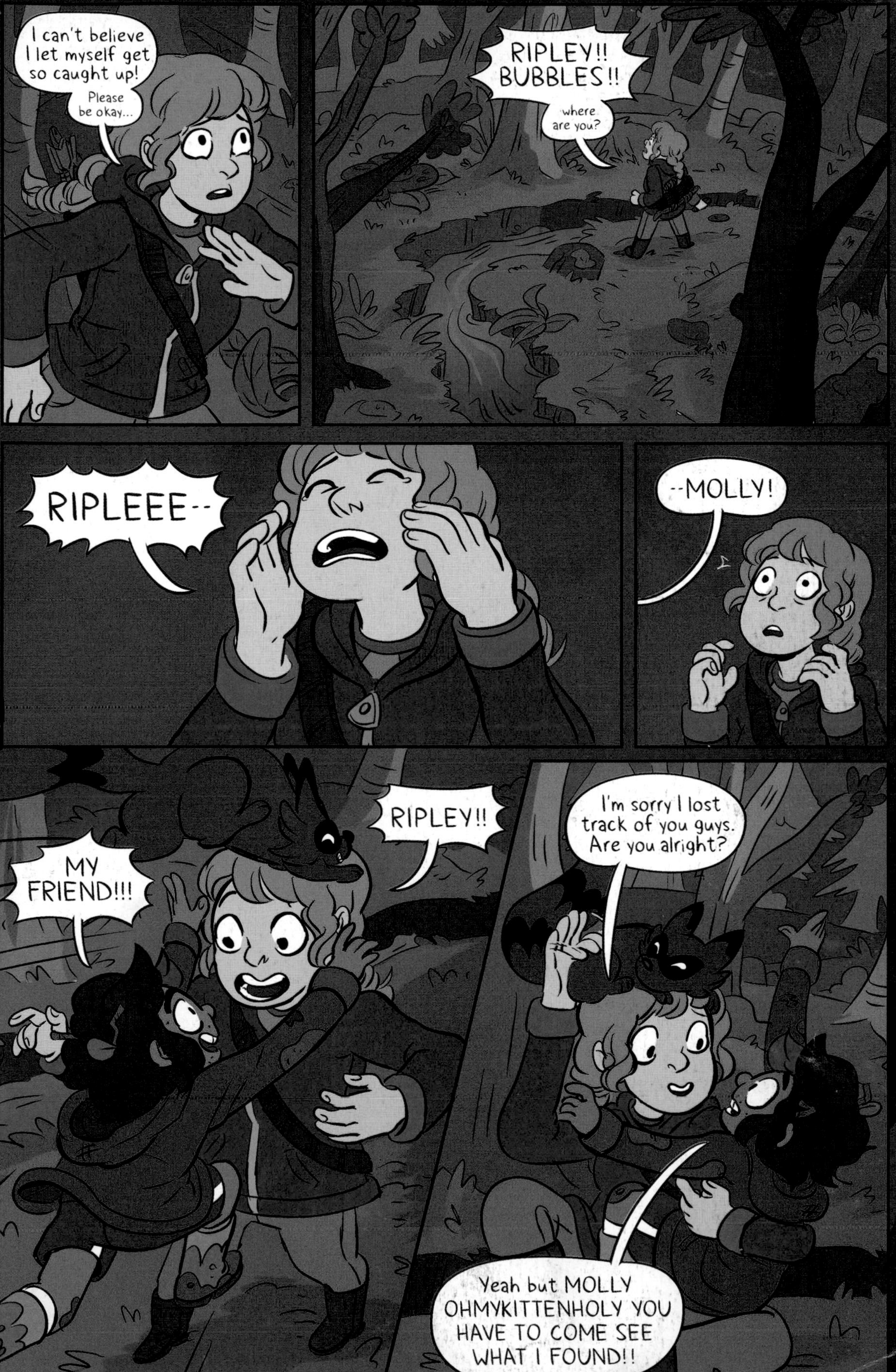
I can't believe I let myself get so caught up!
Please be okay...
RIPLEY!! BUBBLES!!
where are you?
RIPLEEE--
--MOLLY!
MY FRIEND!!!
RIPLEY!!
I'm sorry I lost track of you guys. Are you alright?
Yeah but MOLLY OHMYKITTENHOLY YOU HAVE TO COME SEE WHAT I FOUND!!

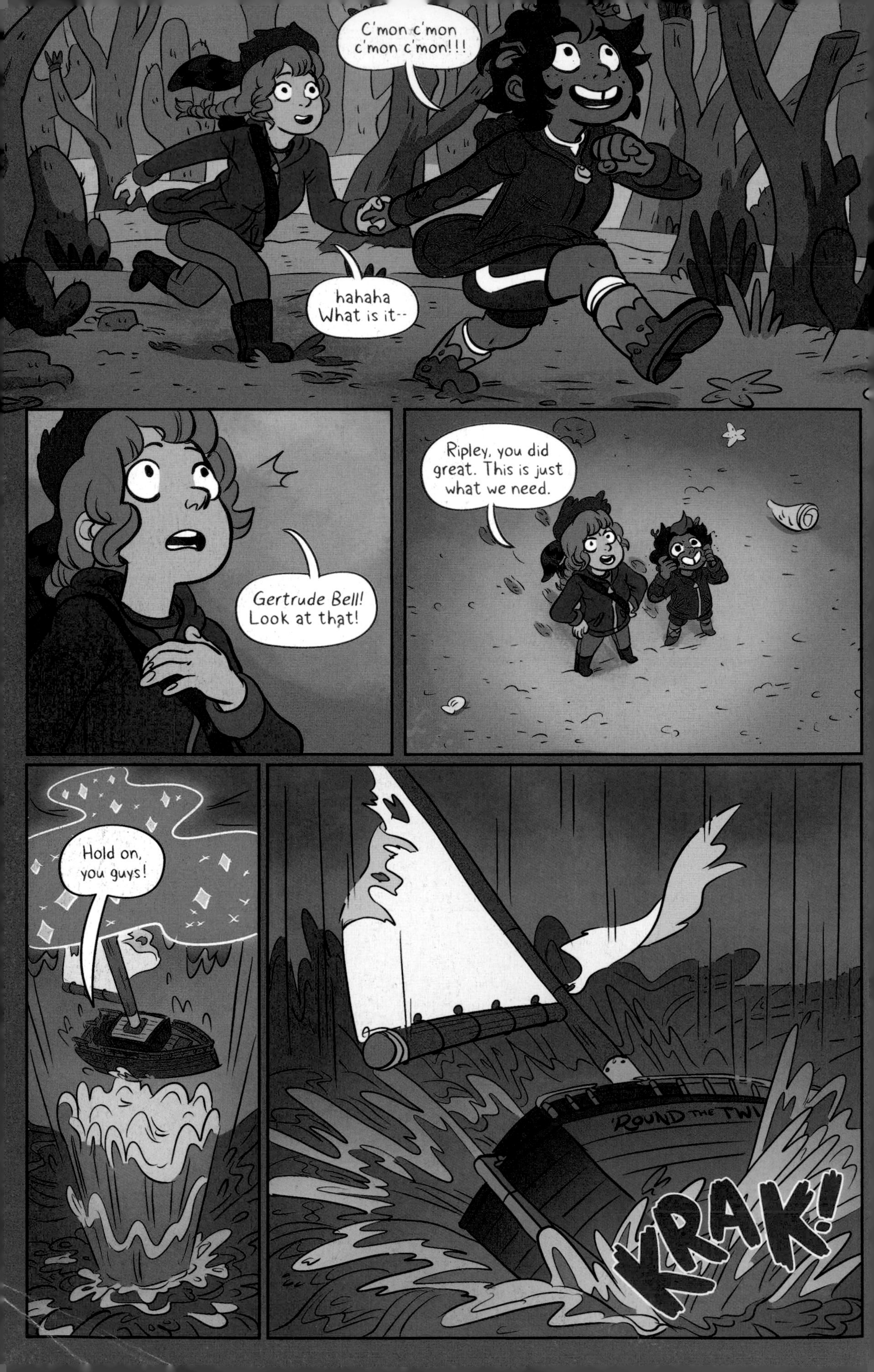

C'mon c'mon c'mon c'mon!!!
hahaha What is it--
Gertrude Bell! Look at that!
Ripley, you did great. This is just what we need.
Hold on, you guys!
'ROUND THE TWI
KRAK!

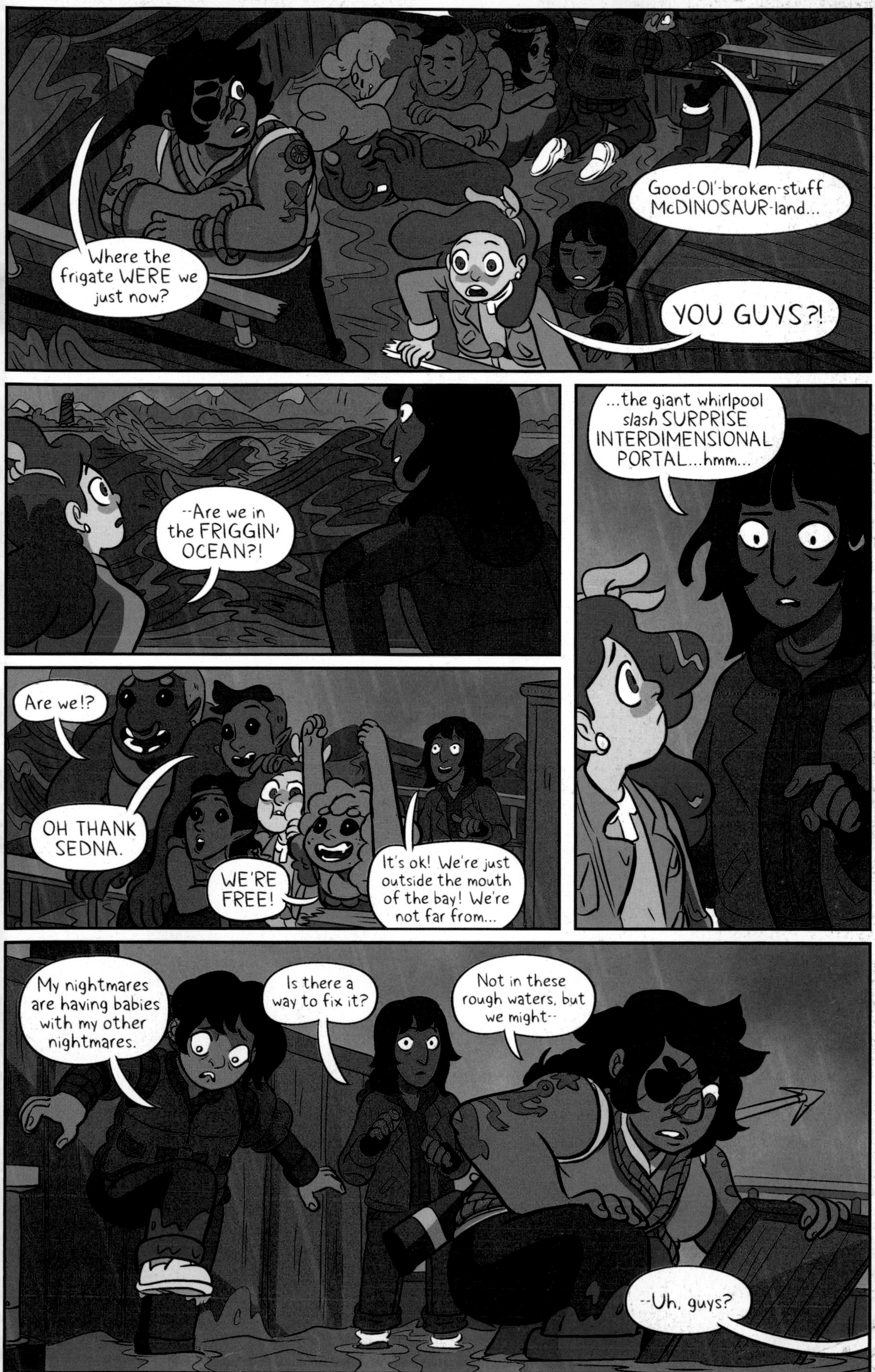
Where the frigate WERE we just now?
Good-Ol'-broken-stuff McDINOSAUR-land...
YOU GUYS?!
--Are we in the FRIGGIN' OCEAN?!
...the giant whirlpool slash SURPRISE INTERDIMENSIONAL PORTAL...hmm...
Are we!?
OH THANK SEDNA.
WE'RE FREE!
It's ok! We're just outside the mouth of the bay! We're not far from...
My nightmares are having babies with my other nightmares.
Is there a way to fix it?
Not in these rough waters, but we might--
--Uh, guys?

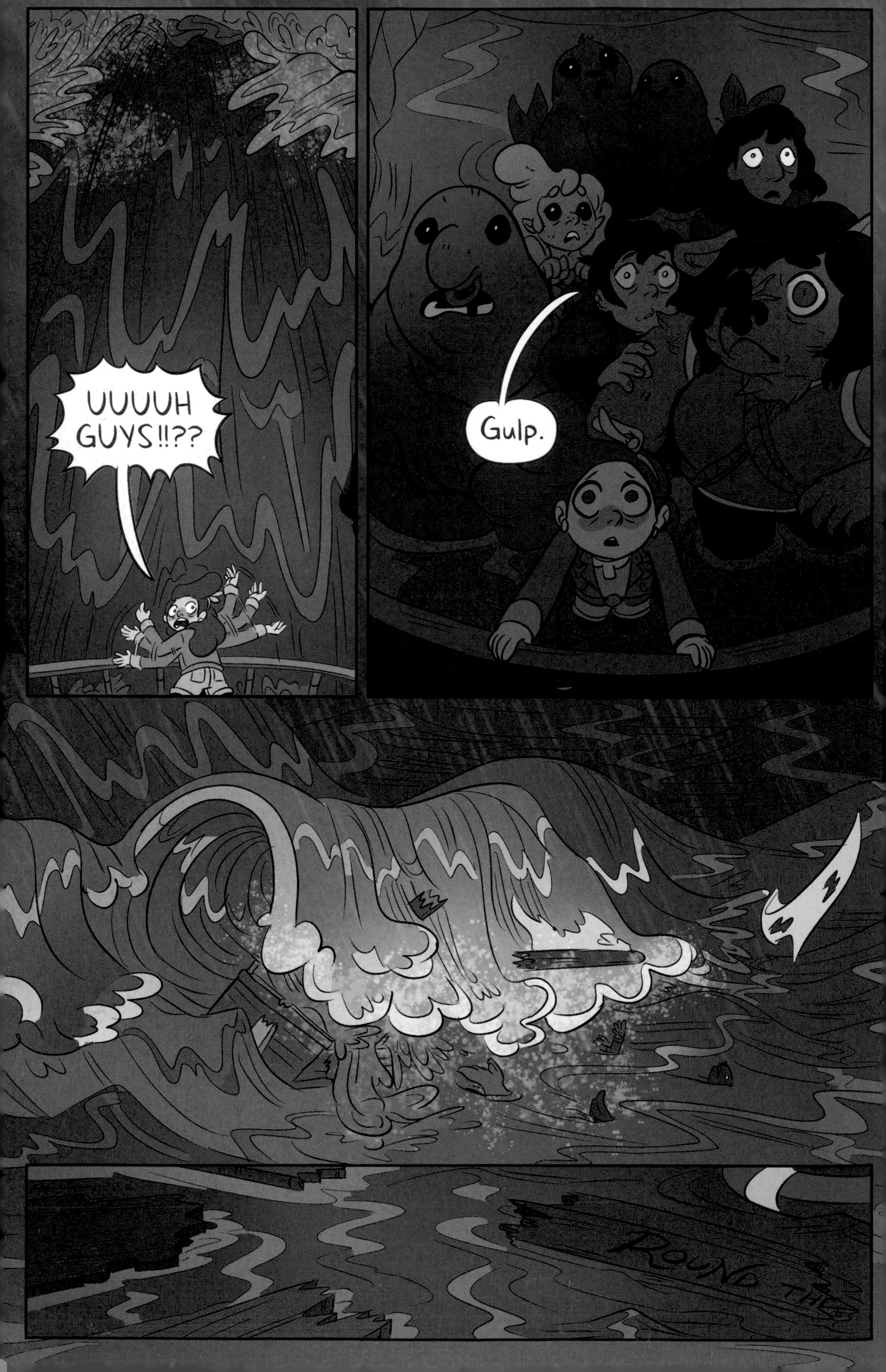
UUUUH GUYS!!??
Gulp.
ROUND

will co   E UNIFORM

The

It he   hould be worn at camp
appearan   vents when Lumberjanes
dress f   n may also be worn at other
Further   ons. It should be worn as a
Lumber   the uniform dress with
to have   rect shoes, and stocking or
part in

Thiskw   out grows her uniform or
Hardc   ter Lumberjane
have   a she has
them   her
                                                                  her

The
yellow, short sl
emb
the w
choose
slacks,
made o
out-of-do
green bere
the colla
Shoes ma
heels, rou   ngs or
socks shou   th the shoes or wi
the uniform. Ne   ces, bracelets, or other jewelry do
belong with a Lumberjane uniform.

HOW TO WEAR THE U

To look well in a uniform demar
uniform be kept in good condi
pressed. See that the skirt is the rig
height and build, that the belt is adj
that your shoes and stockings are in
uniform, that you watch your posture and   nifor
with dignity and grace. If the beret is removed   helps to cre
be sure that your hair is neat and kept in place with an   in a group.
insconspicuous clip or ribbon. When you wear a   active life th
Lumberjane uniform you are identified as a member of   another bond
this organization and you should be doubly careful to   future, and pr
conduct yourself in a way that will show everyone that   in order to b
courtesy and thoughtfullness are part of being a   Lumberjane pr
Lumberjane. People are likely to judge a whole nation by   Penniquiqul Thi   re Lady
the selfishness of a few individuals, to criticize a whole   Types, but m   es will wish to have one. They
family because of the misconduct of one member, and to   can either b   or make it themselves from
feel unkindly toward and organization because of the   materials available at the trading post.

LUMBERJANES FIELD MANUAL

CHAPTER TWENTY-FOUR

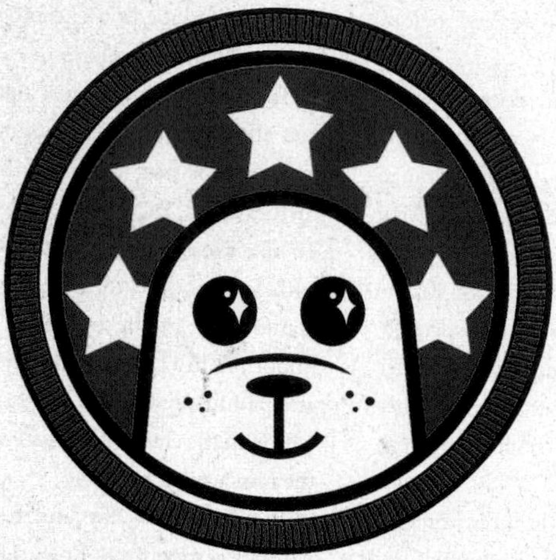

Lumberjanes "Out-of-Doors" Program Field

SEAL OF APPROVAL BADGE

"Criticism and approval often come hand in hand."

There are many things in life that we are grateful for, even if we don't realize it at the time. There is one thing in life that we are constantly searching for, and even if it can come from a variety of sources, most often the harder we work for it, the more satisfying it is to finally receive it. Approval drives all of us, and on some level, it is something we need just as much as security. Lumberjanes will find approval at this camp. They will find acceptance for who they are and they will find a community that has been built on love and was created as a home for anyone who feels that they are a hardcore lady-type.

This badge, the *Seal Of Approval* badge, is about learning to accept criticism and approval together. Learning that some words, while not the words that we might want to hear, are a different form of approval. The *Seal Of Approval* badge is different from other Lumberjane badges as it is not actions that are needed to complete this badge but more the understanding of words, and the power behind every language, spoken or written. This badge is considered one of the more obscure badges at camp, and while some find it easy to earn, some find it hard. But at the end of the day, every Lumberjane will earn this badge regardless if they have realized it or not.

Obtaining the *Seal Of Approval* badge is a closely guarded secret among the High Council. Every head counselor will know the needed steps that must be taken to earn this badge and will relay them to the counselors at the beginning of camp so that every counselor will know what to look for. Lumberjanes will earn this badge when they have completed the steps necessary, on their own and without any guidance. The advice that we offer to all of the campers is that when they start their tenure at camp this summer, they enter with an open mind and a love for their fellow campers. That they are kind, and honest, in any advice or recognition that they pass along.

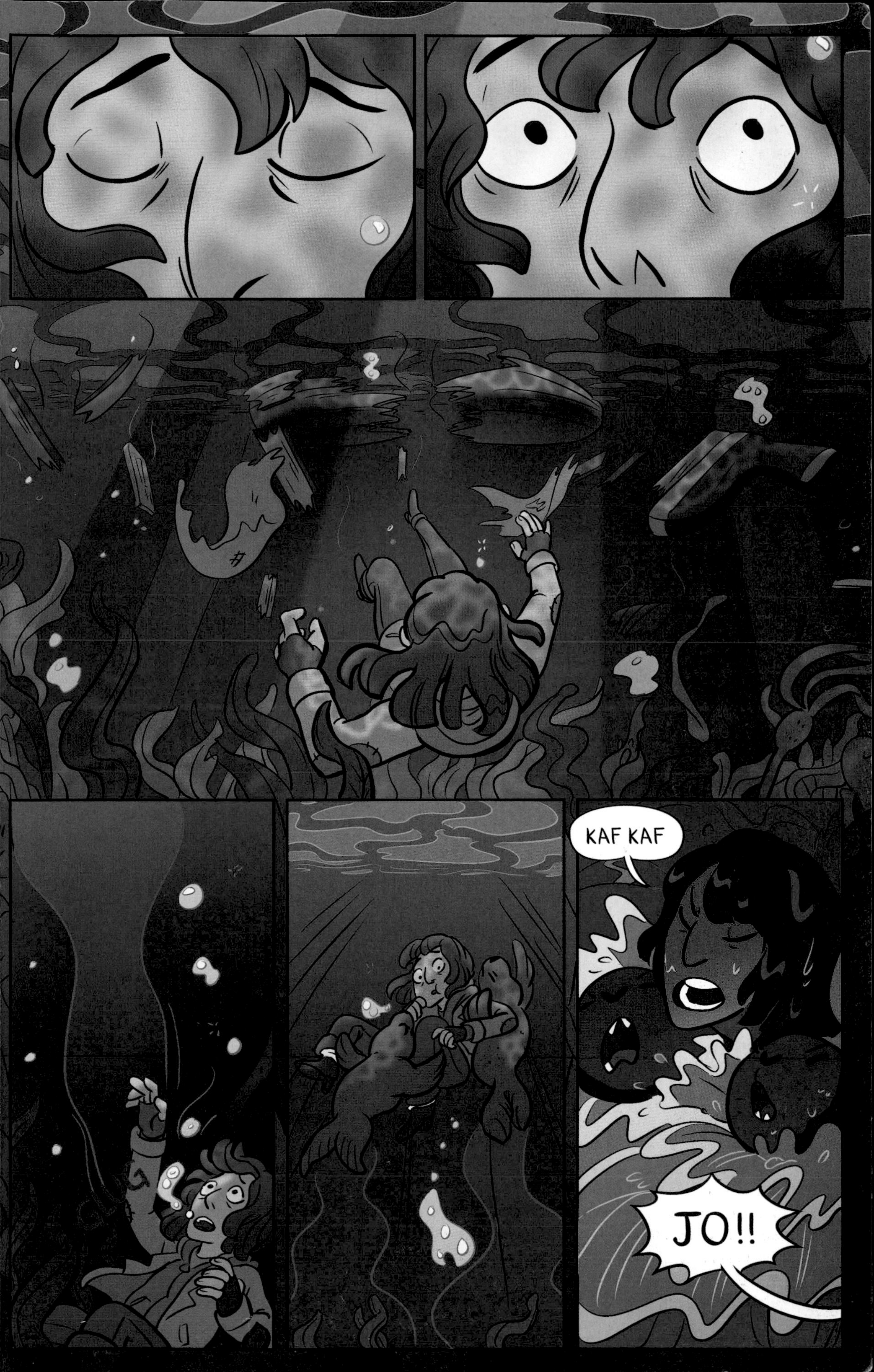
KAF KAF
JO!!

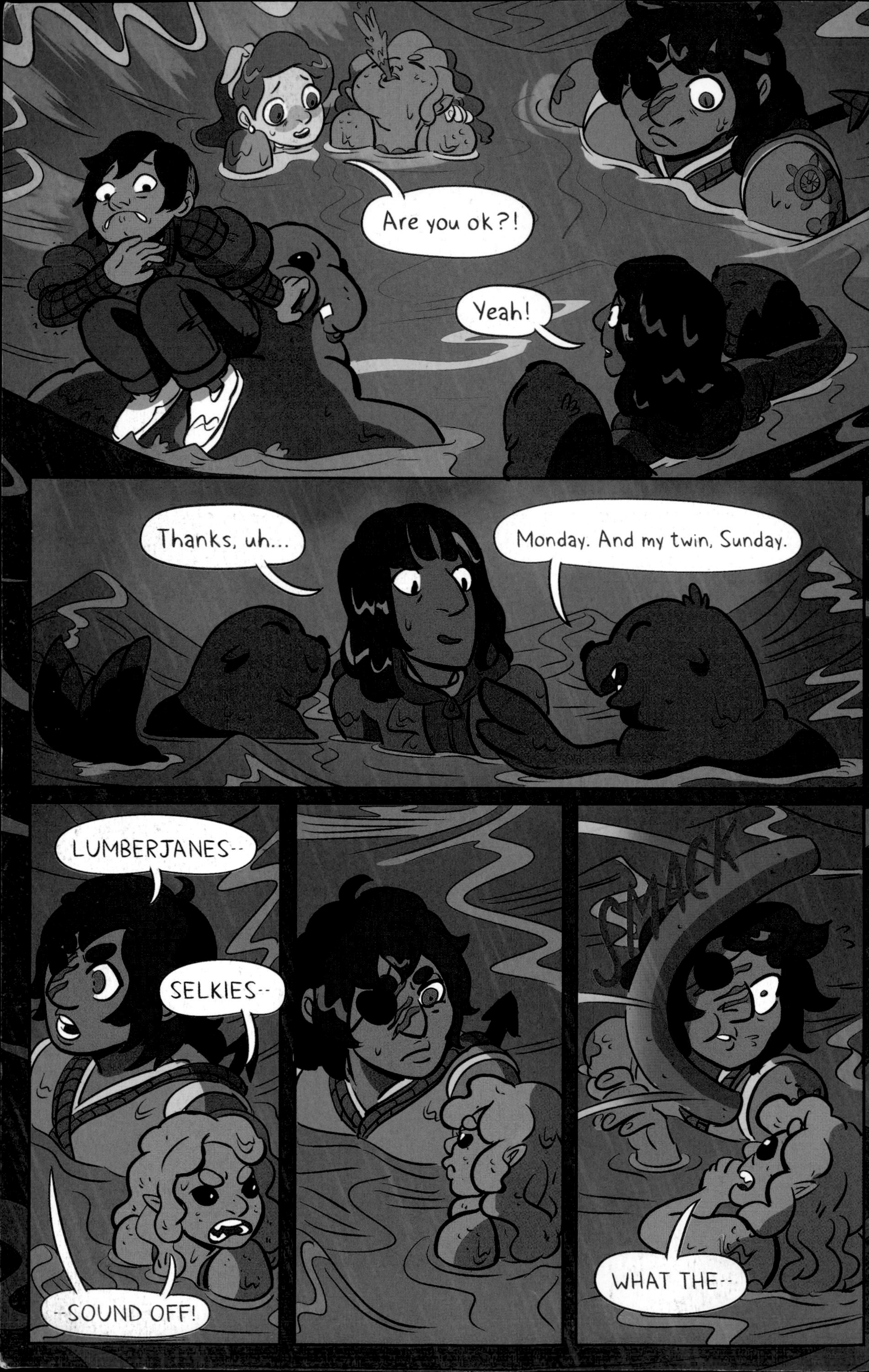
Are you ok?!
Yeah!
Thanks, uh...
Monday. And my twin, Sunday.
LUMBERJANES--
SELKIES--
--SOUND OFF!
SMACK
WHAT THE--

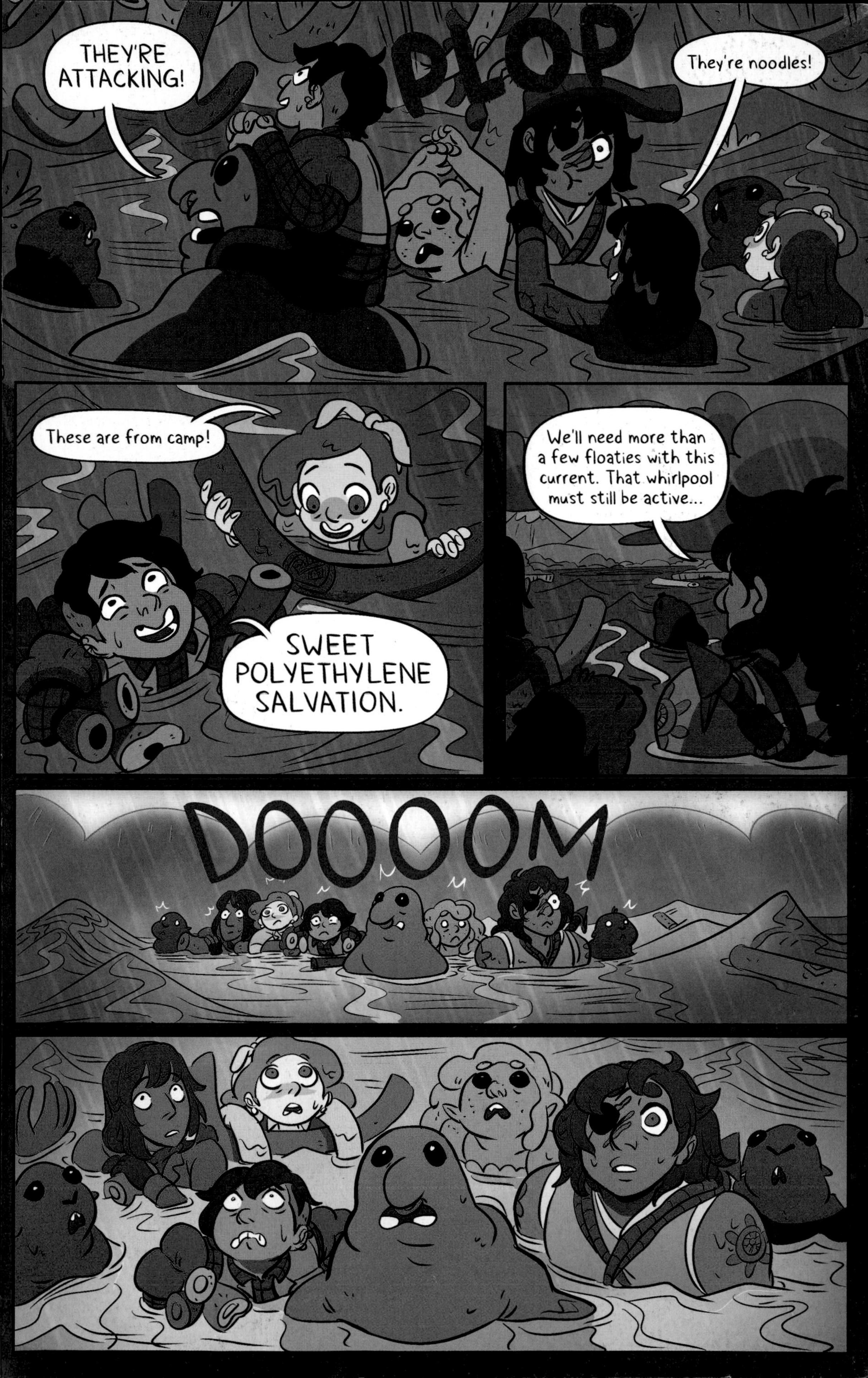
THEY'RE ATTACKING!
PLOP
They're noodles!
These are from camp!
SWEET POLYETHYLENE SALVATION.
We'll need more than a few floaties with this current. That whirlpool must still be active...
DOOOOM

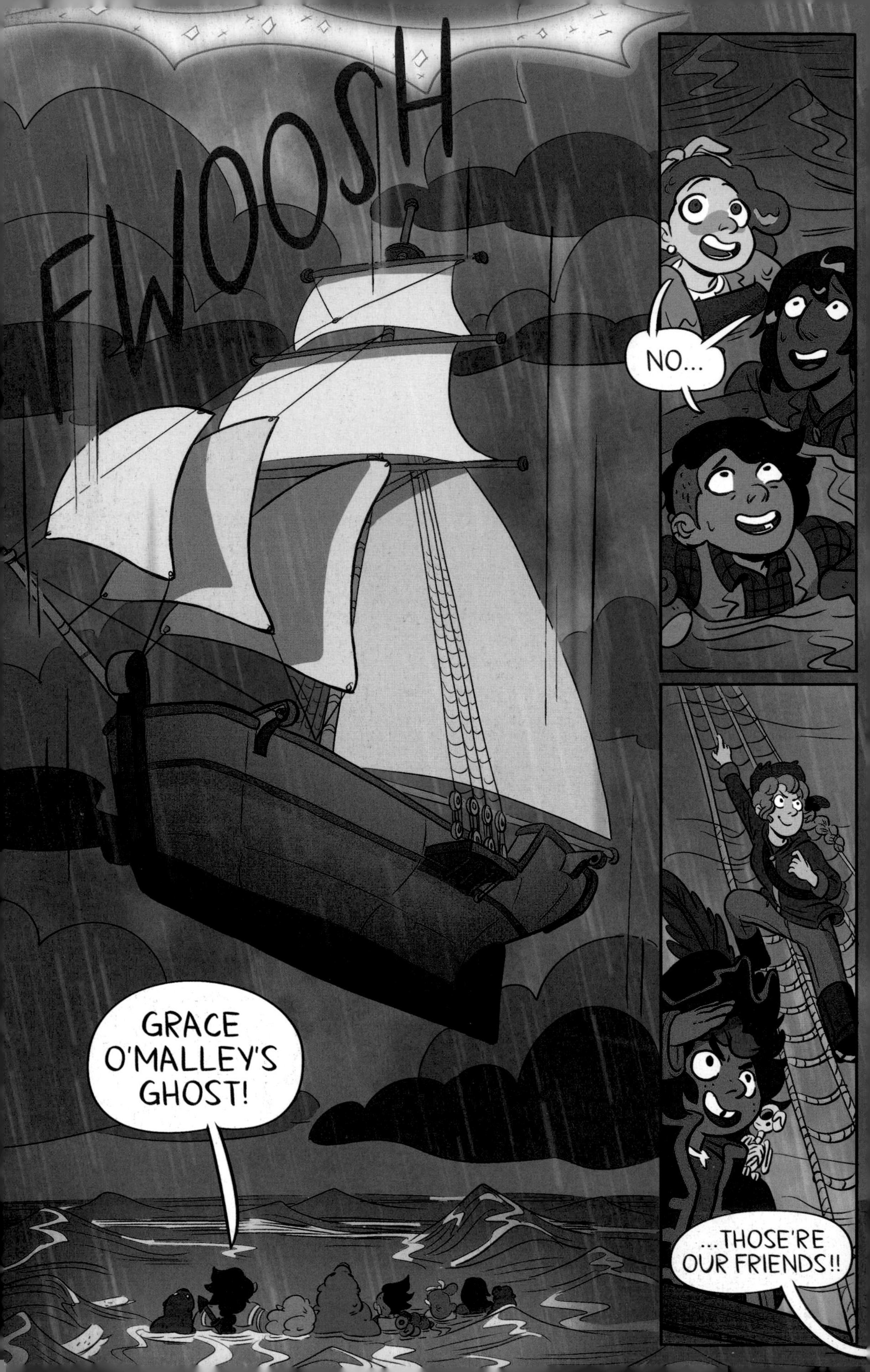
FWOOSH
GRACE O'MALLEY'S GHOST!
NO...
...THOSE'RE OUR FRIENDS!!

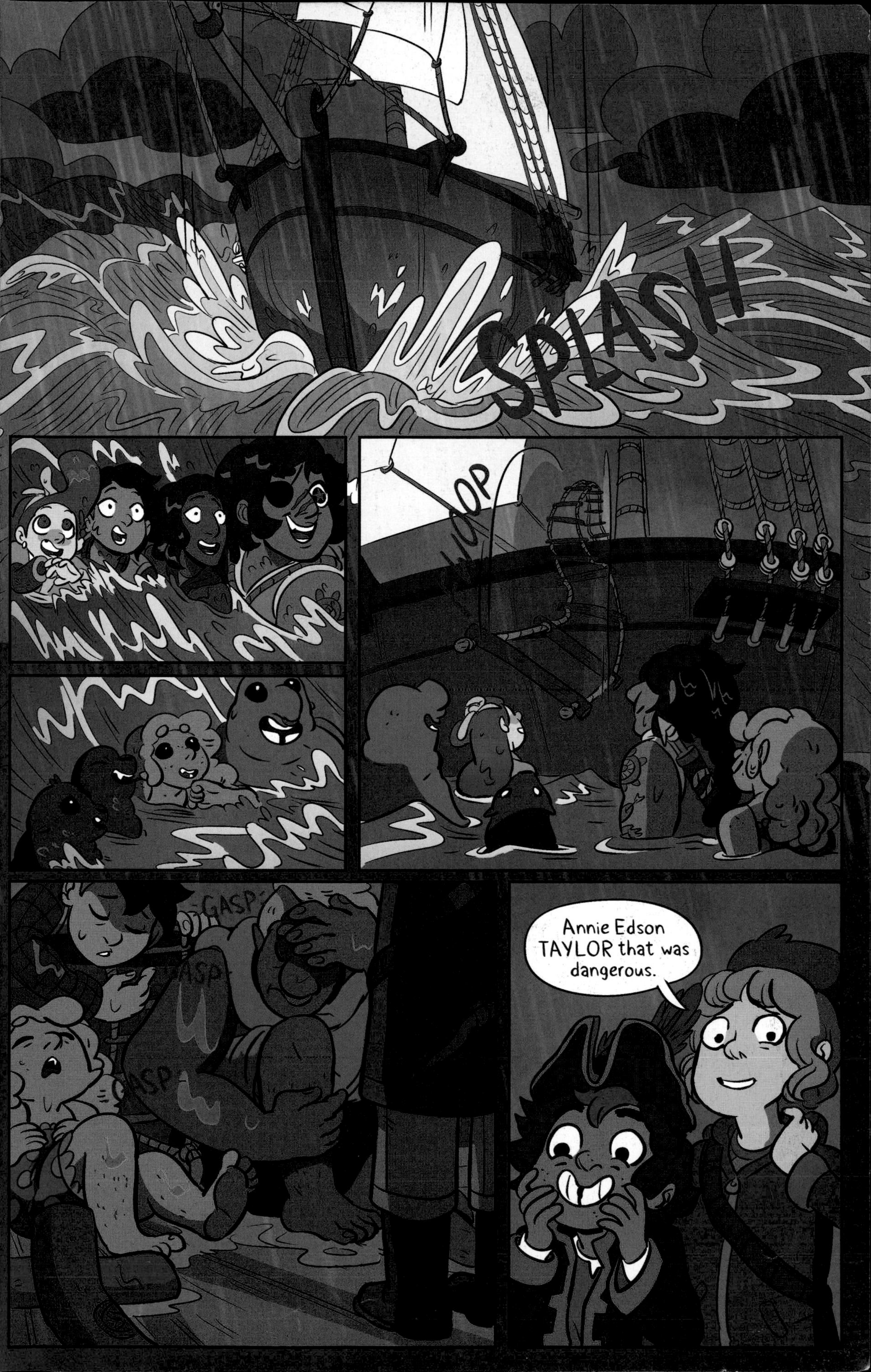
SPLASH
WHOOP
GASP
GASP
GASP
Annie Edson TAYLOR that was dangerous.

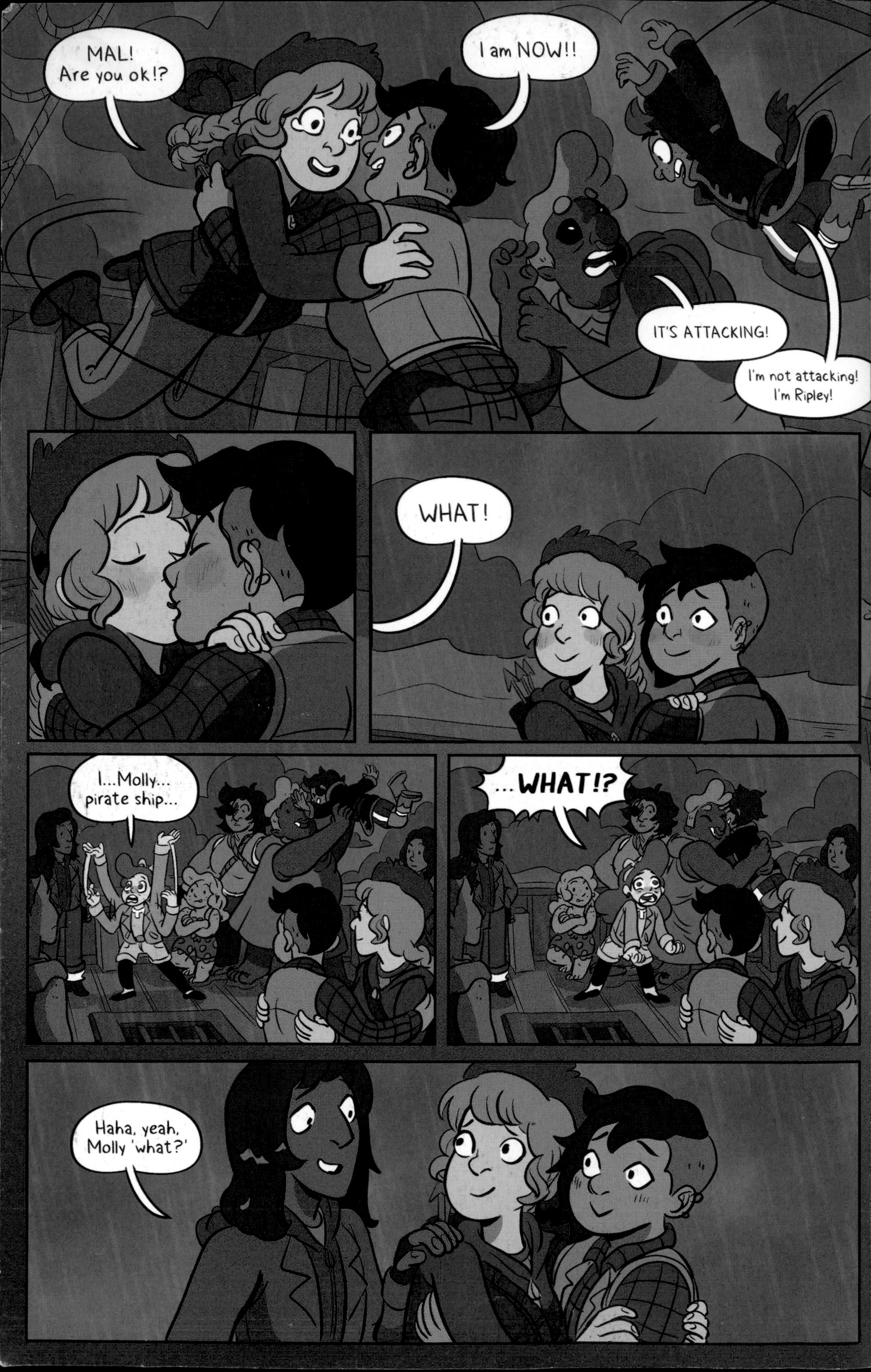
MAL! Are you ok!?
I am NOW!!
IT'S ATTACKING!
I'm not attacking! I'm Ripley!
WHAT!
I...Molly... pirate ship...
...WHAT!?
Haha, yeah, Molly 'what?'

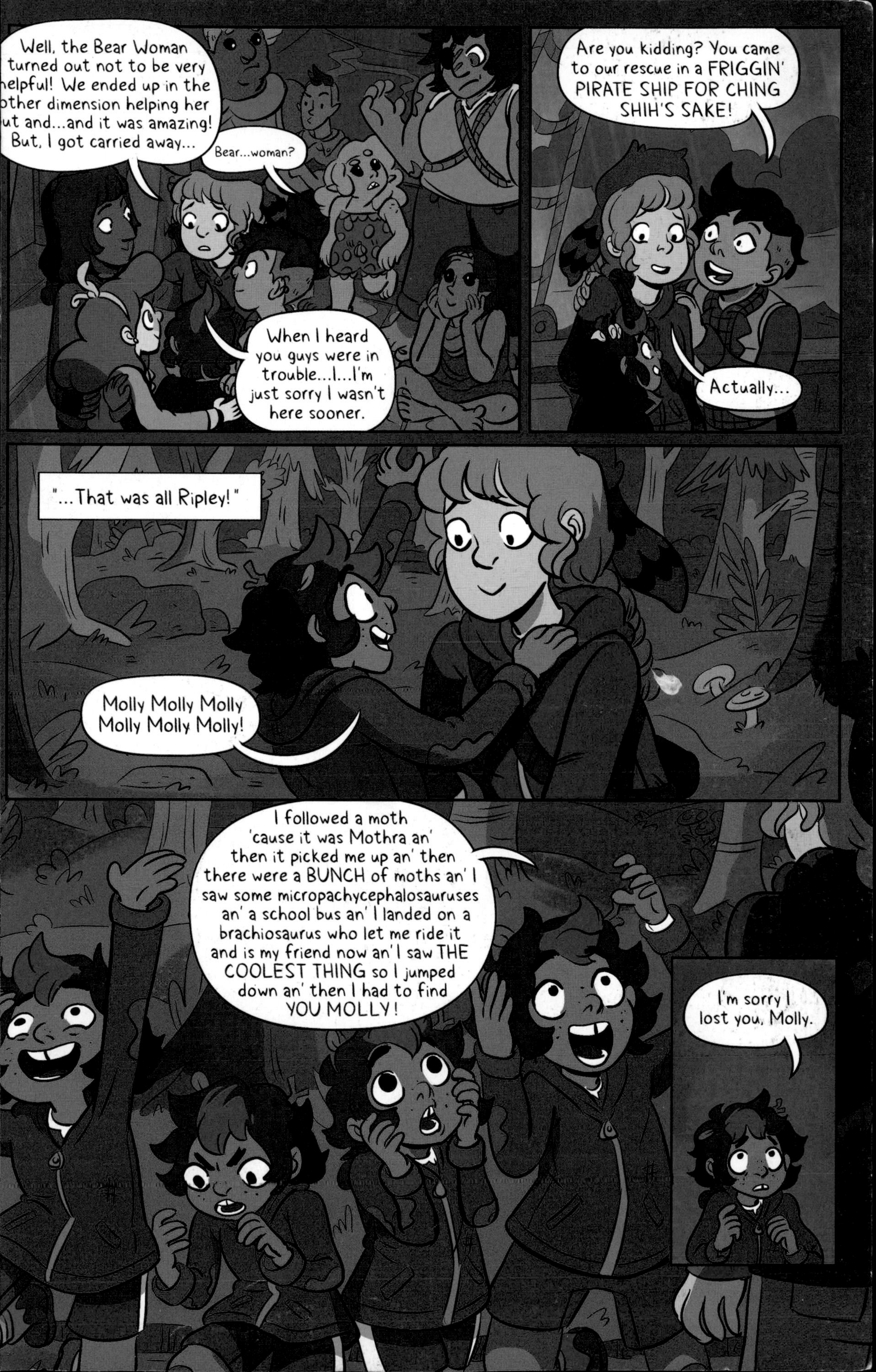
Well, the Bear Woman turned out not to be very helpful! We ended up in the other dimension helping her out and...and it was amazing! But, I got carried away...
Bear...woman?
When I heard you guys were in trouble...I...I'm just sorry I wasn't here sooner.
Are you kidding? You came to our rescue in a FRIGGIN' PIRATE SHIP FOR CHING SHIH'S SAKE!
Actually...
"...That was all Ripley!"
Molly Molly Molly Molly Molly Molly!
I followed a moth 'cause it was Mothra an' then it picked me up an' then there were a BUNCH of moths an' I saw some micropachycephalosauruses an' a school bus an' I landed on a brachiosaurus who let me ride it and is my friend now an' I saw THE COOLEST THING so I jumped down an' then I had to find YOU MOLLY!
I'm sorry I lost you, Molly.

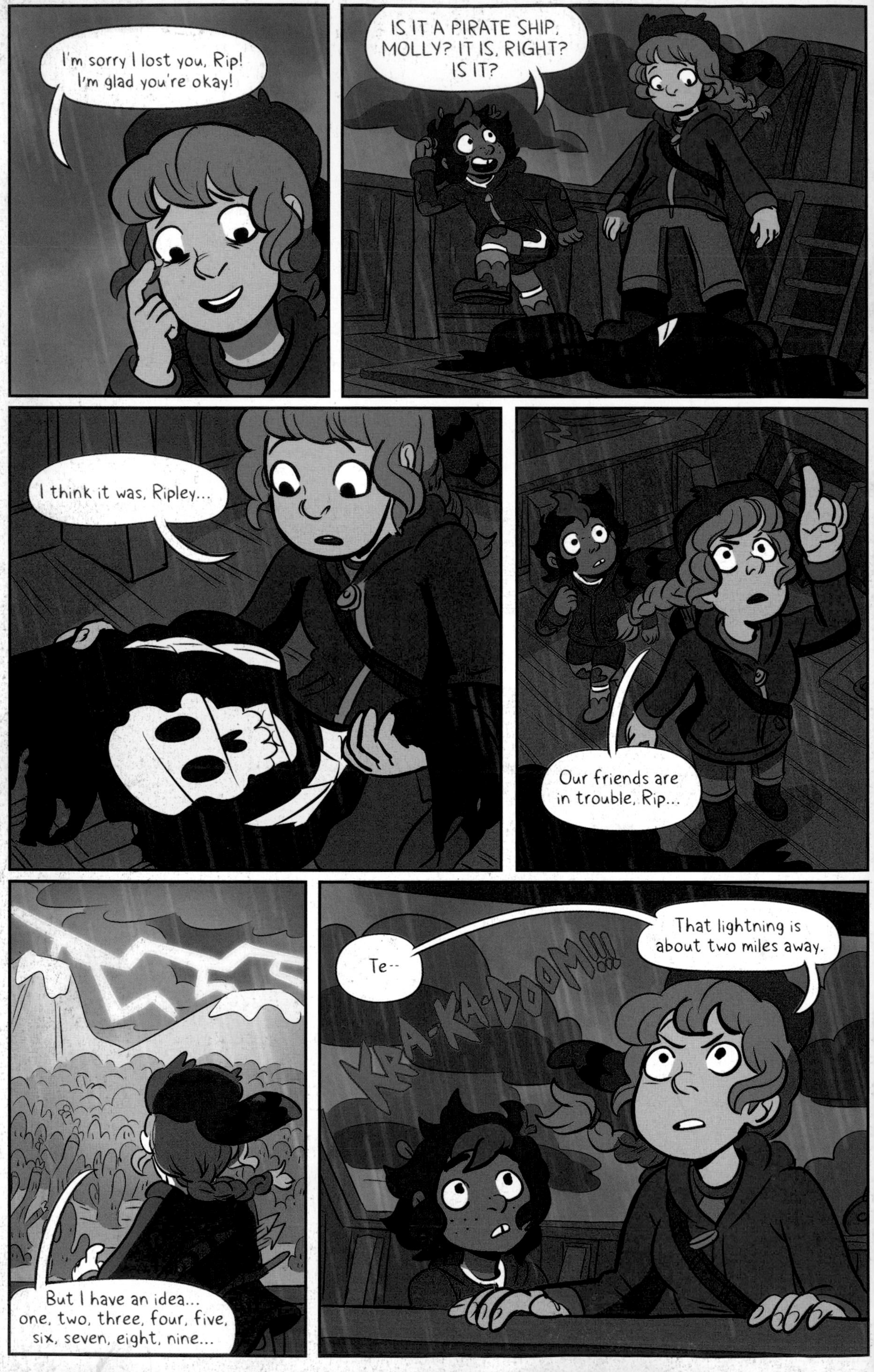
I'm sorry I lost you, Rip! I'm glad you're okay!
IS IT A PIRATE SHIP, MOLLY? IT IS, RIGHT? IS IT?
I think it was, Ripley...
Our friends are in trouble, Rip...
But I have an idea... one, two, three, four, five, six, seven, eight, nine...
Te--
That lightning is about two miles away.
KRA-KA-DOOM!!!

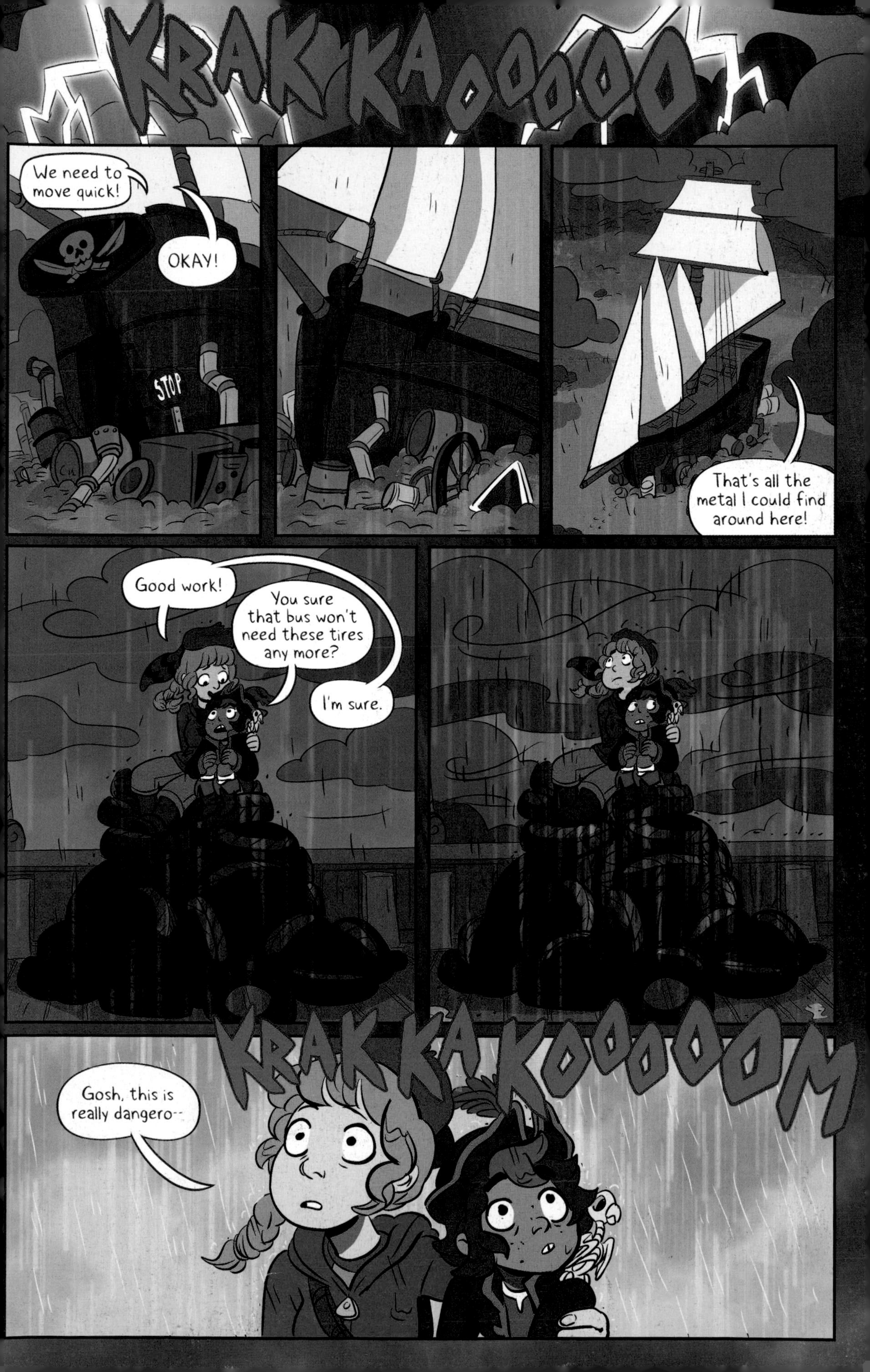
KRAKKAOOOOO
We need to move quick!
OKAY!
STOP
That's all the metal I could find around here!
Good work!
You sure that bus won't need these tires any more?
I'm sure.
KRAKKAKOOOOOM
Gosh, this is really dangero--

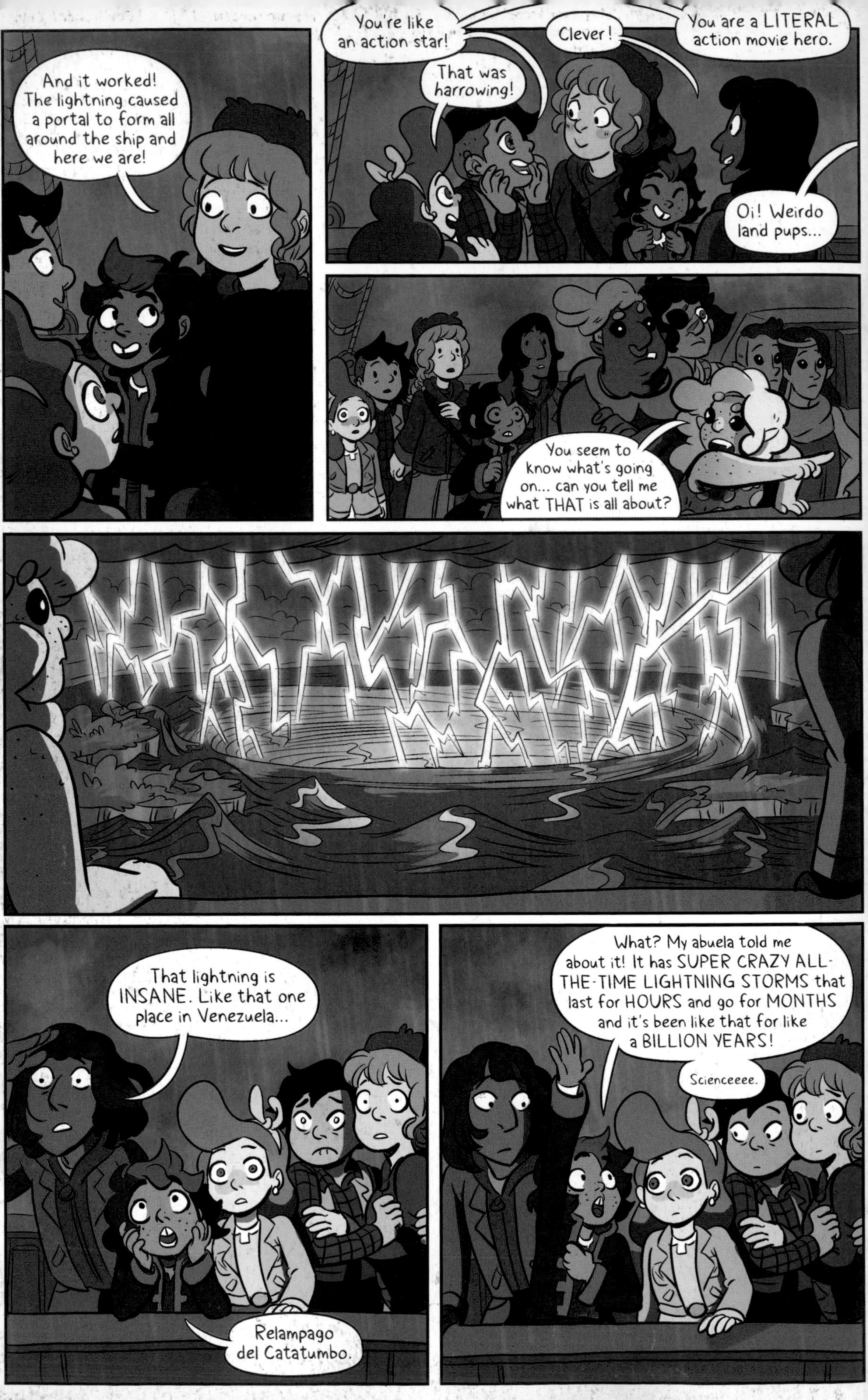
And it worked! The lightning caused a portal to form all around the ship and here we are!
You're like an action star!
Clever!
You are a LITERAL action movie hero.
That was harrowing!
Oi! Weirdo land pups...
You seem to know what's going on... can you tell me what THAT is all about?
That lightning is INSANE. Like that one place in Venezuela...
Relampago del Catatumbo.
What? My abuela told me about it! It has SUPER CRAZY ALL-THE-TIME LIGHTNING STORMS that last for HOURS and go for MONTHS and it's been like that for like a BILLION YEARS!
Scienceeee.

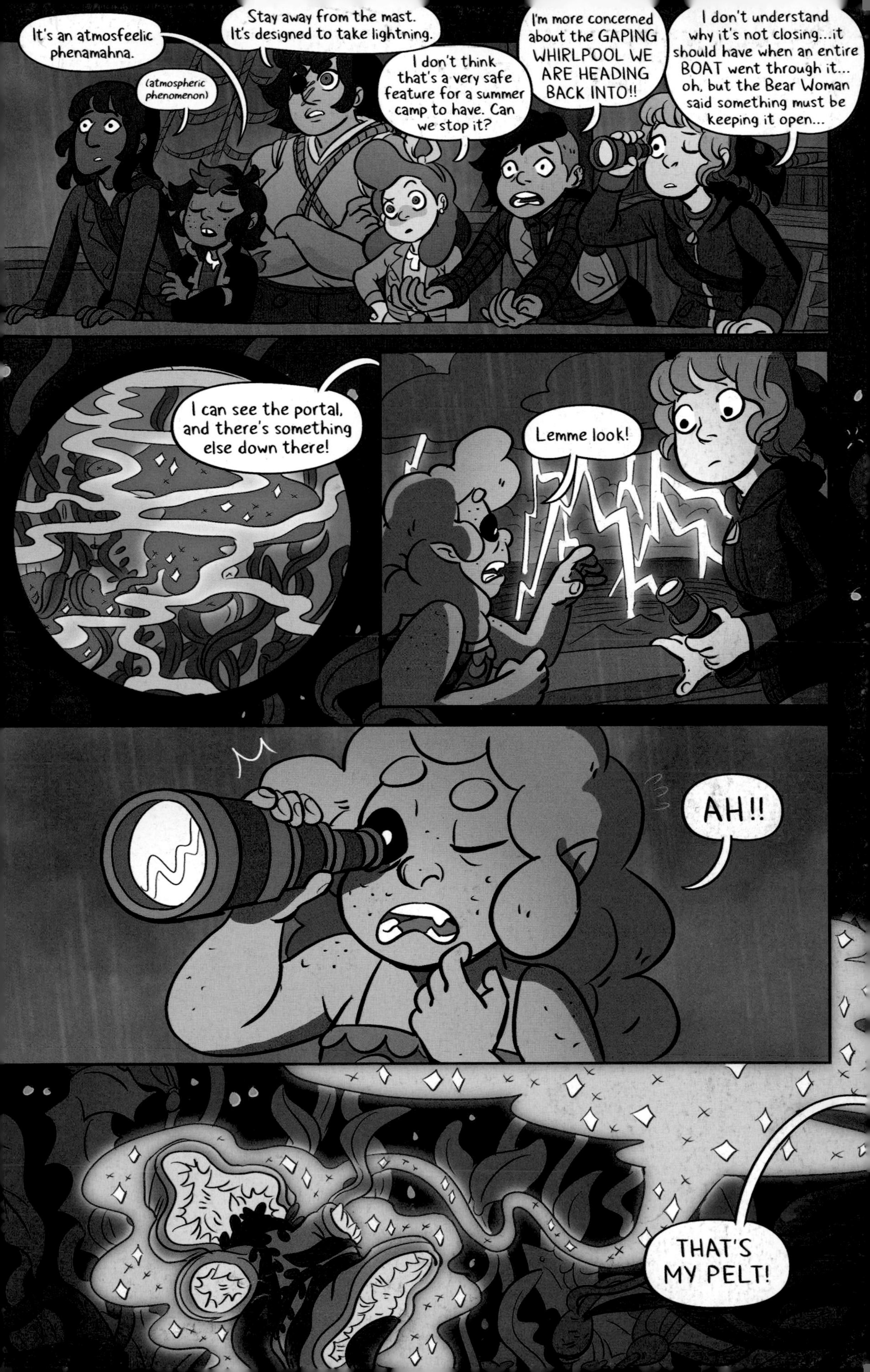
It's an atmosfeelic phenamahna.
(atmospheric phenomenon)
Stay away from the mast. It's designed to take lightning.
I don't think that's a very safe feature for a summer camp to have. Can we stop it?
I'm more concerned about the GAPING WHIRLPOOL WE ARE HEADING BACK INTO!!
I don't understand why it's not closing...it should have when an entire BOAT went through it... oh, but the Bear Woman said something must be keeping it open...
I can see the portal, and there's something else down there!
Lemme look!
AH!!
THAT'S MY PELT!

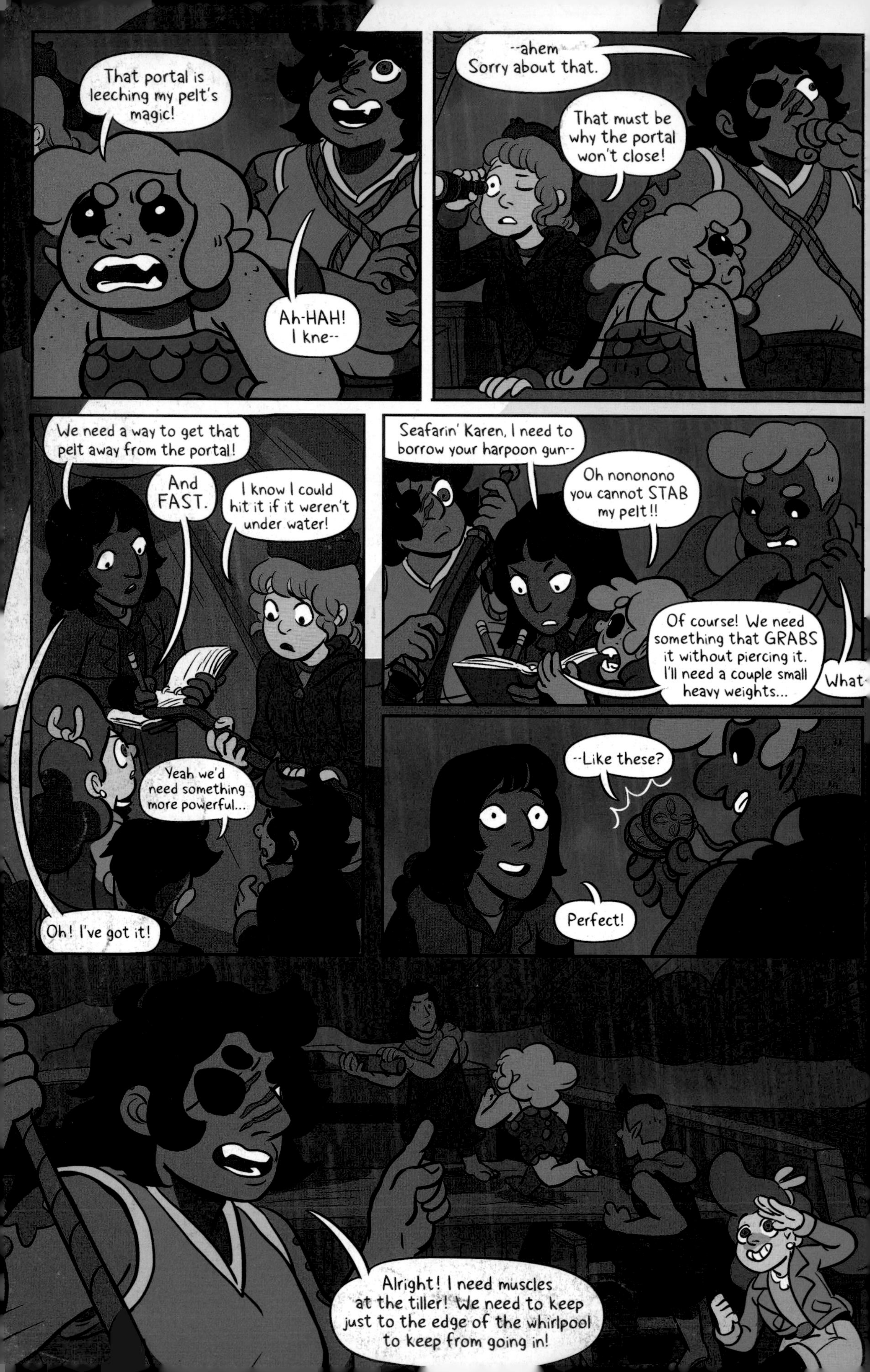
That portal is leeching my pelt's magic!
Ah-HAH! I kne--
--ahem Sorry about that.
That must be why the portal won't close!
We need a way to get that pelt away from the portal!
And FAST.
I know I could hit it if it weren't under water!
Yeah we'd need something more powerful...
Oh! I've got it!
Seafarin' Karen, I need to borrow your harpoon gun--
Oh nononono you cannot STAB my pelt!!
Of course! We need something that GRABS it without piercing it. I'll need a couple small heavy weights...
What-
--Like these?
Perfect!
Alright! I need muscles at the tiller! We need to keep just to the edge of the whirlpool to keep from going in!

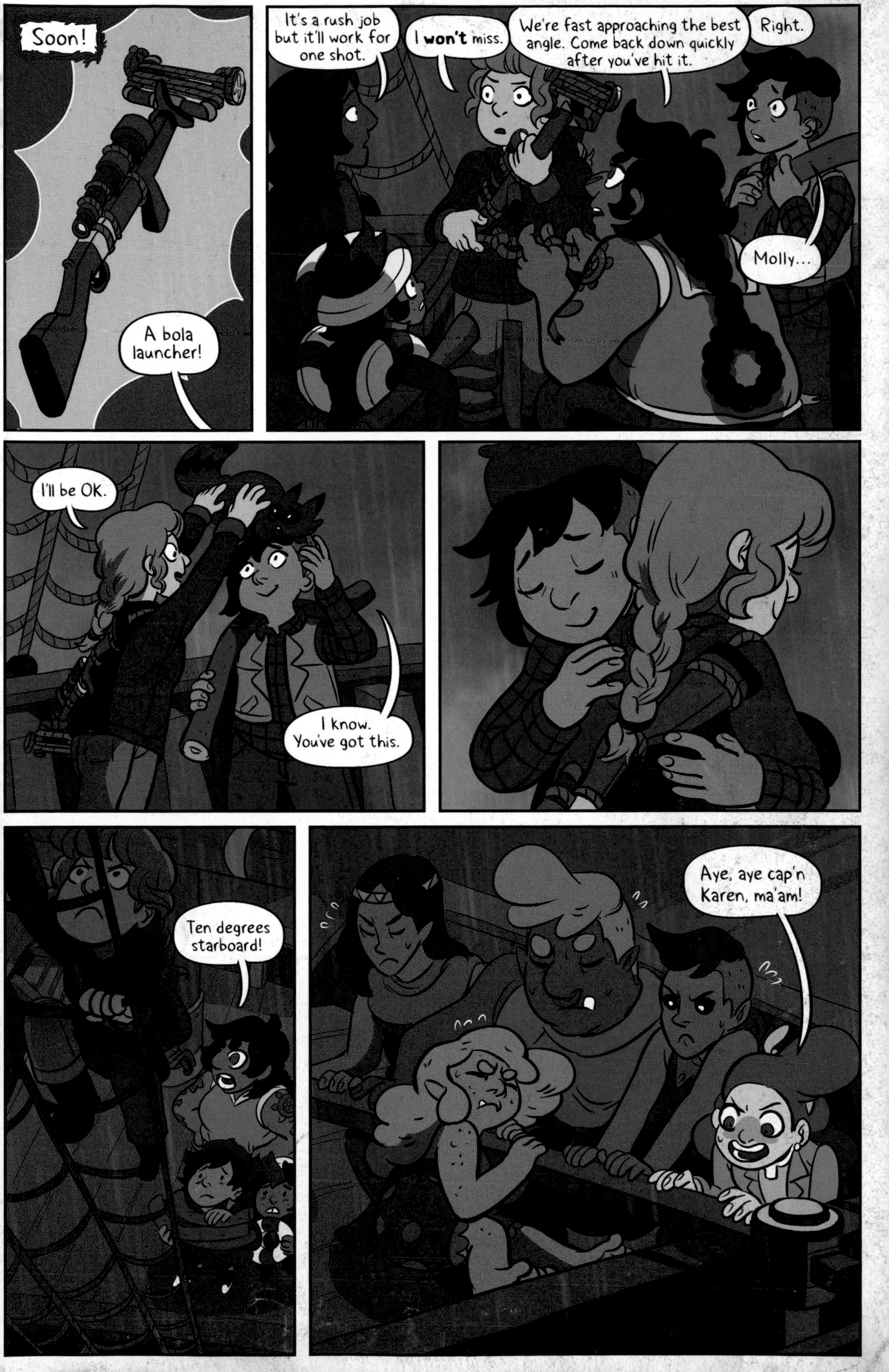
Soon!
A bola launcher!
It's a rush job but it'll work for one shot.
I won't miss.
We're fast approaching the best angle. Come back down quickly after you've hit it.
Right.
Molly...
I'll be OK.
I know. You've got this.
Ten degrees starboard!
Aye, aye cap'n Karen, ma'am!

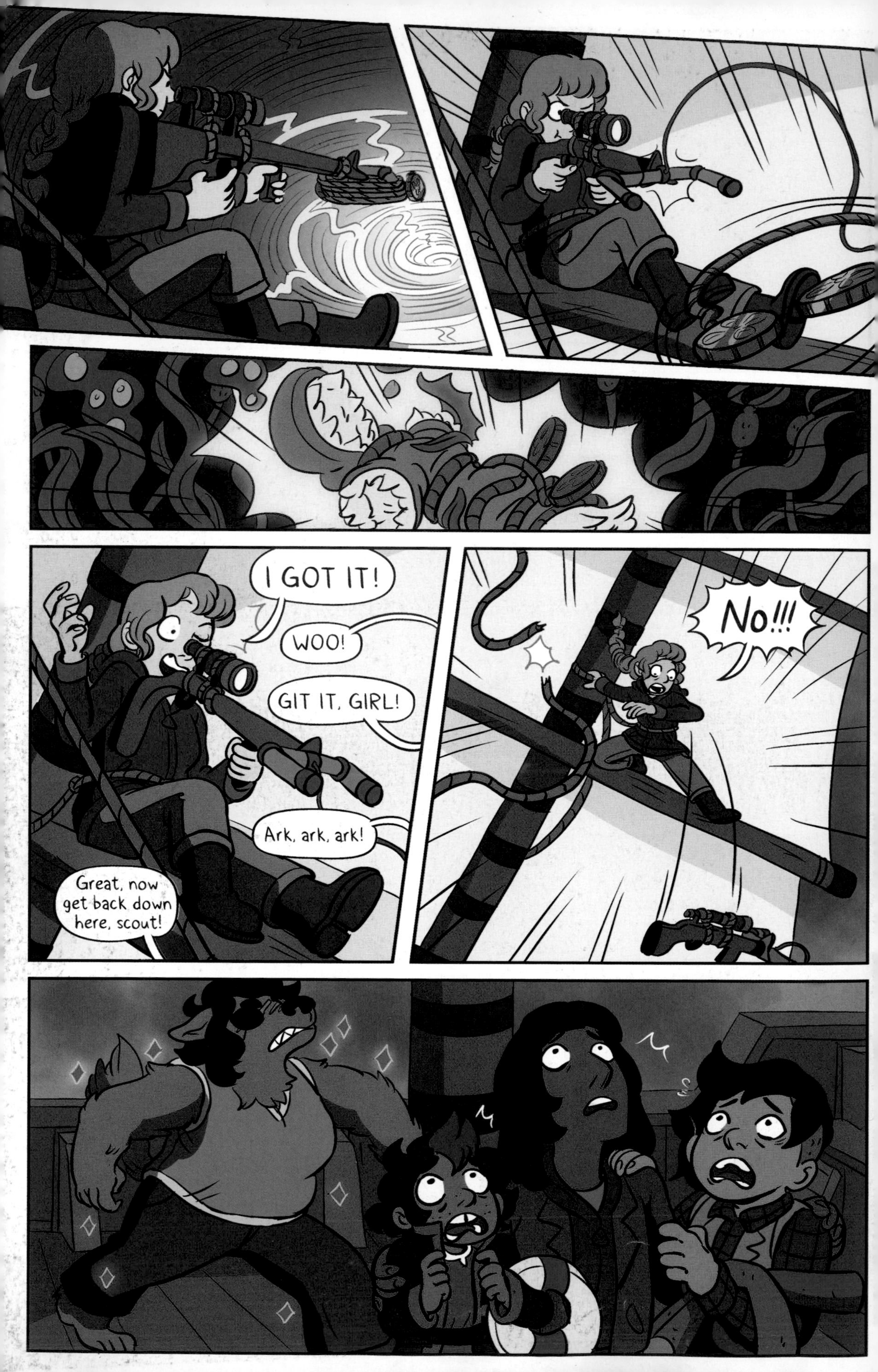
I GOT IT!
WOO!
GIT IT, GIRL!
Ark, ark, ark!
Great, now get back down here, scout!
No!!!

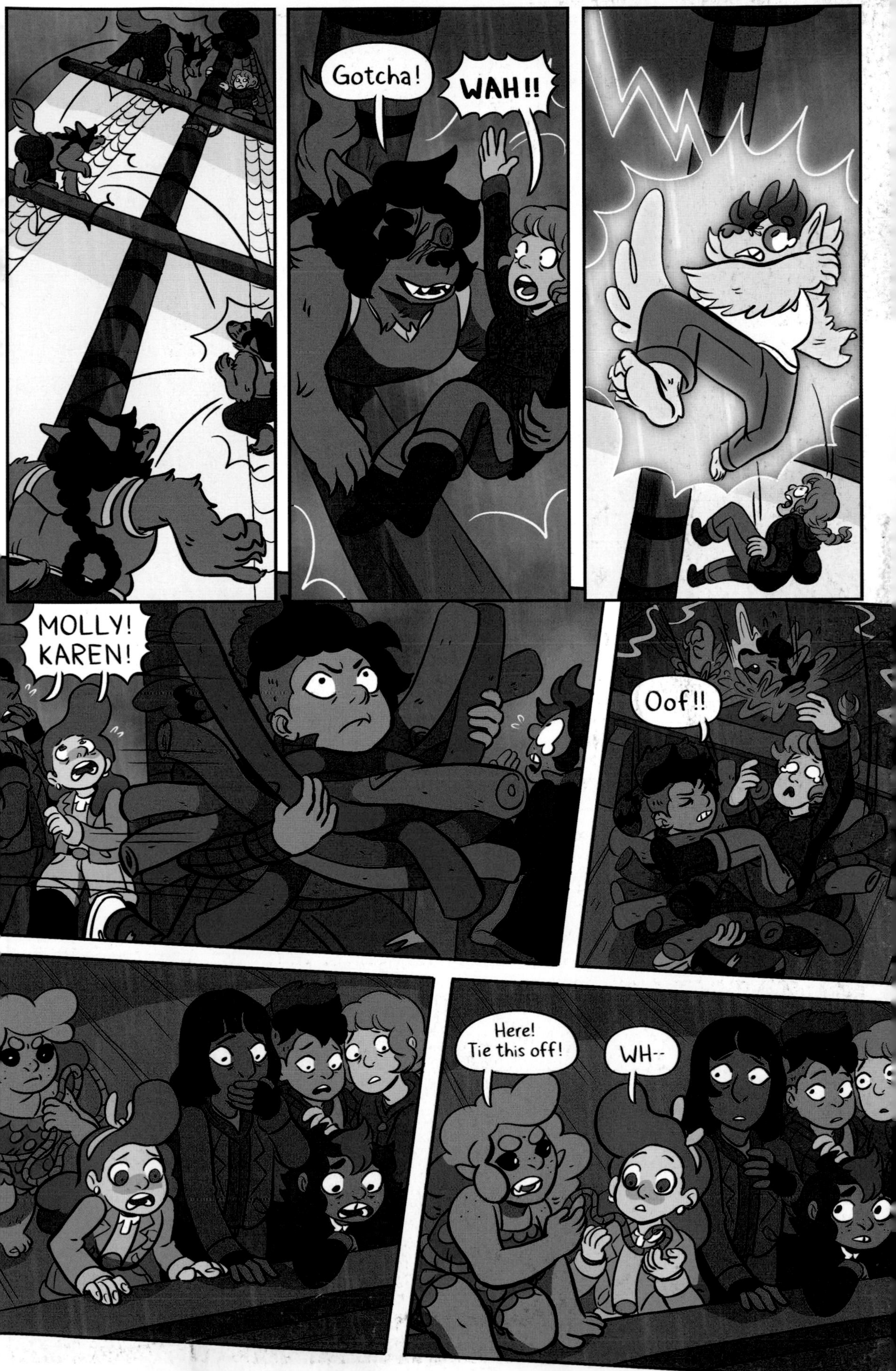
Gotcha!
WAH!!
MOLLY! KAREN!
Oof!!
Here! Tie this off!
WH--

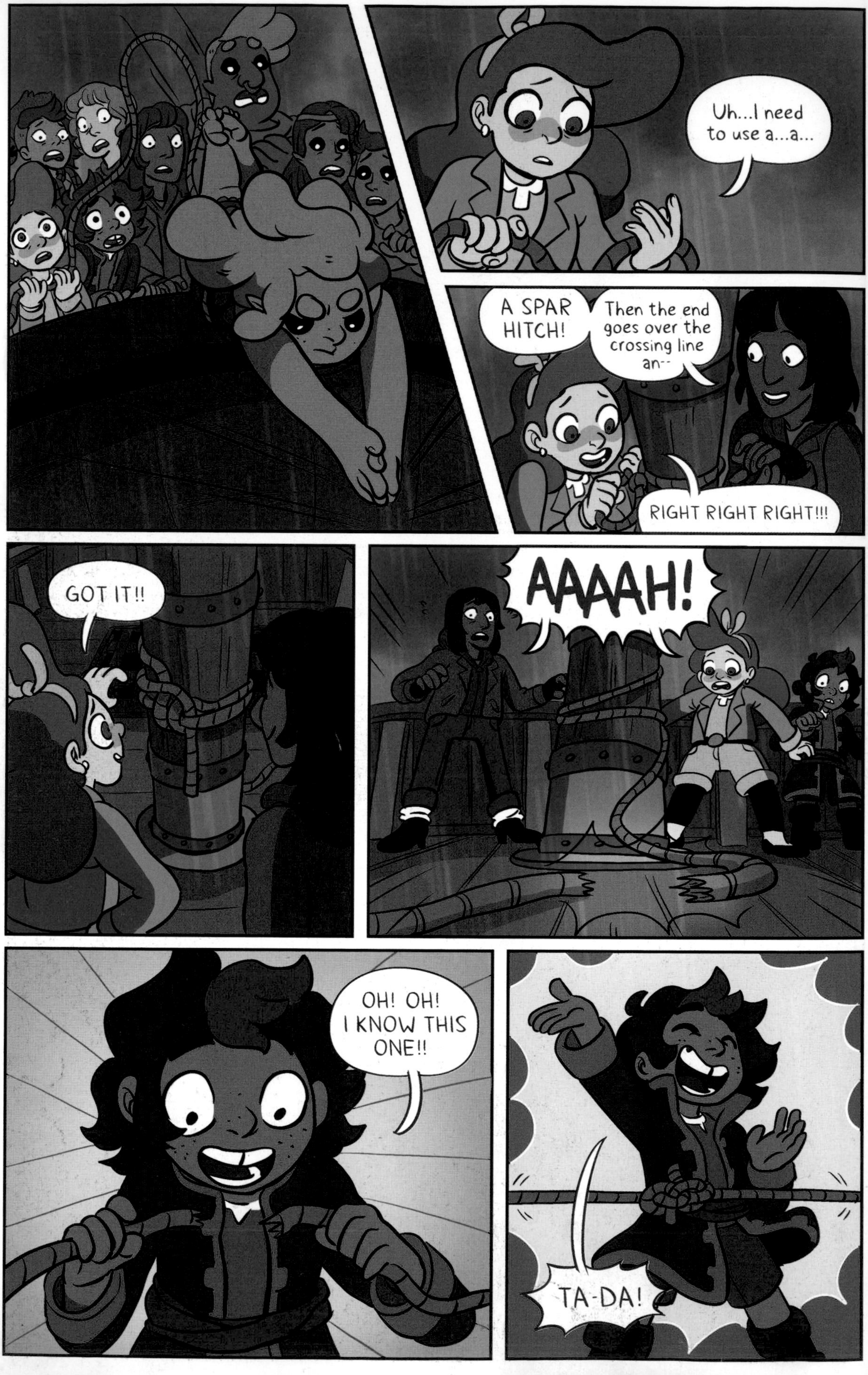
Uh...I need to use a...a...
A SPAR HITCH!
Then the end goes over the crossing line an--
RIGHT RIGHT RIGHT!!!
GOT IT!!
AAAAH!
OH! OH! I KNOW THIS ONE!!
TA-DA!

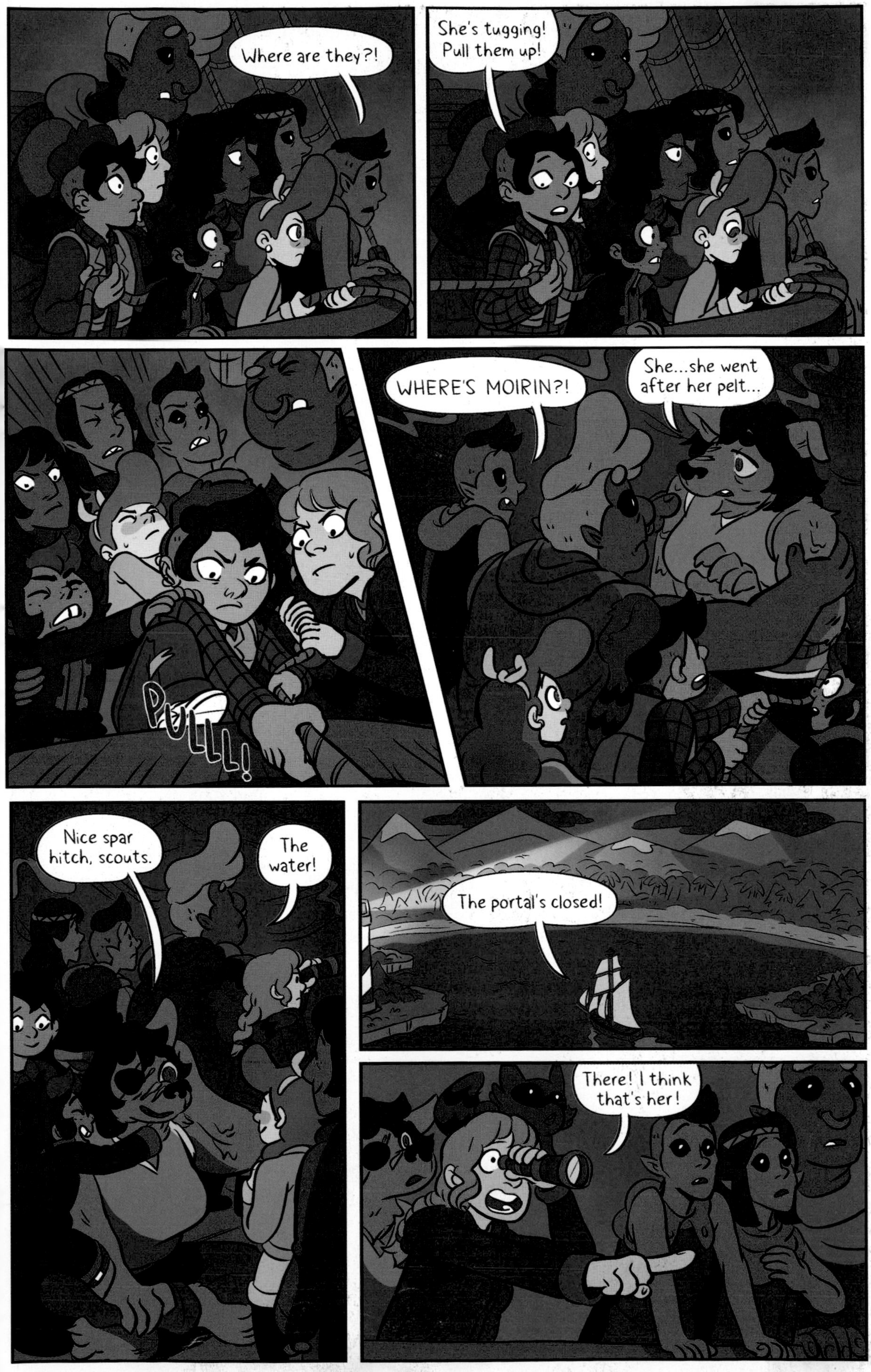
Where are they?!
She's tugging! Pull them up!
PULLL!
WHERE'S MOIRIN?!
She...she went after her pelt...
Nice spar hitch, scouts.
The water!
The portal's closed!
There! I think that's her!

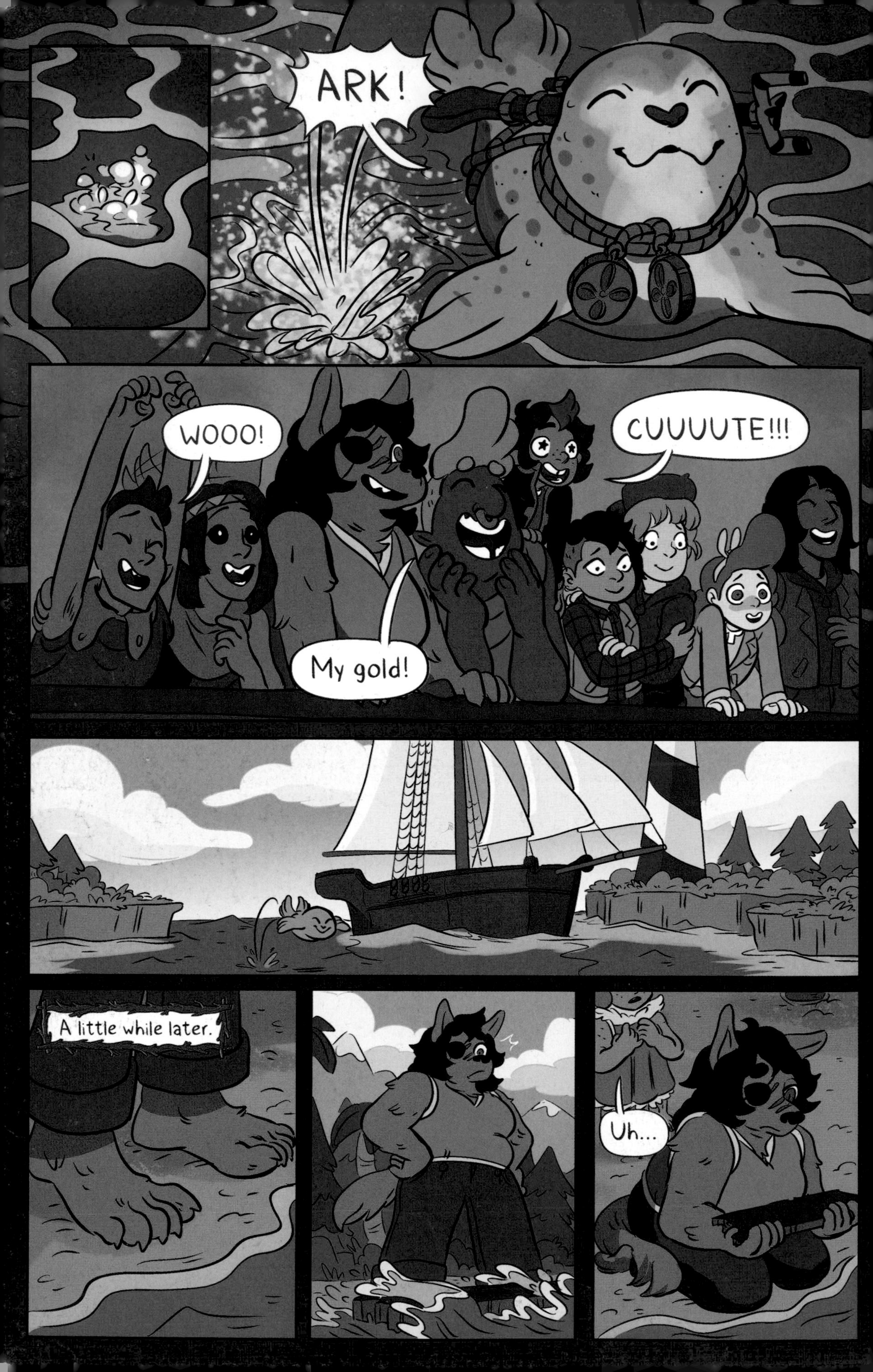
ARK!
WOOO!
My gold!
CUUUUTE!!!
A little while later.
Uh...

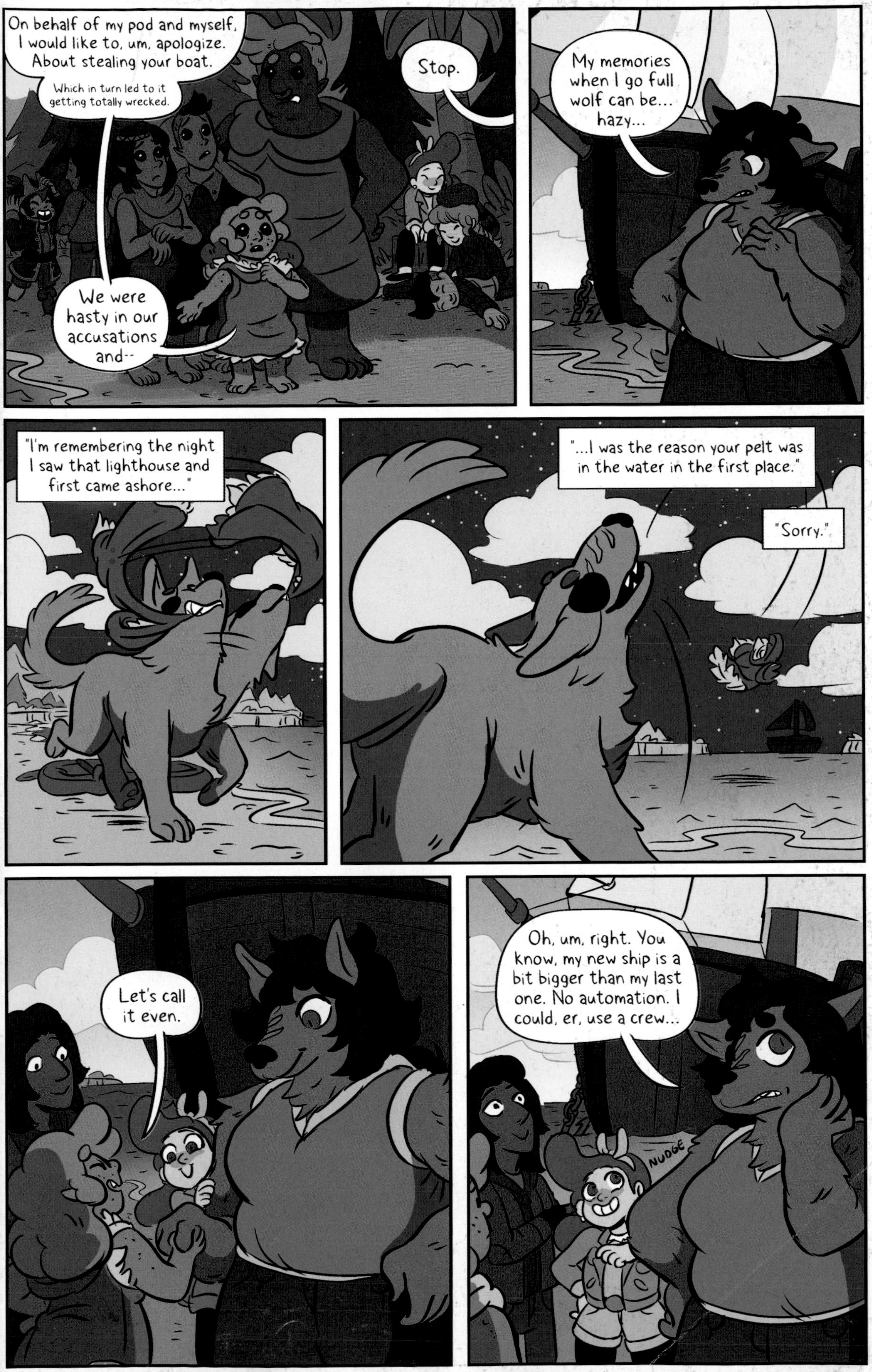

On behalf of my pod and myself, I would like to, um, apologize. About stealing your boat.
Which in turn led to it getting totally wrecked.
We were hasty in our accusations and--
Stop.
My memories when I go full wolf can be... hazy...
"I'm remembering the night I saw that lighthouse and first came ashore..."
"...I was the reason your pelt was in the water in the first place."
"Sorry."
Let's call it even.
NUDGE
Oh, um, right. You know, my new ship is a bit bigger than my last one. No automation. I could, er, use a crew...

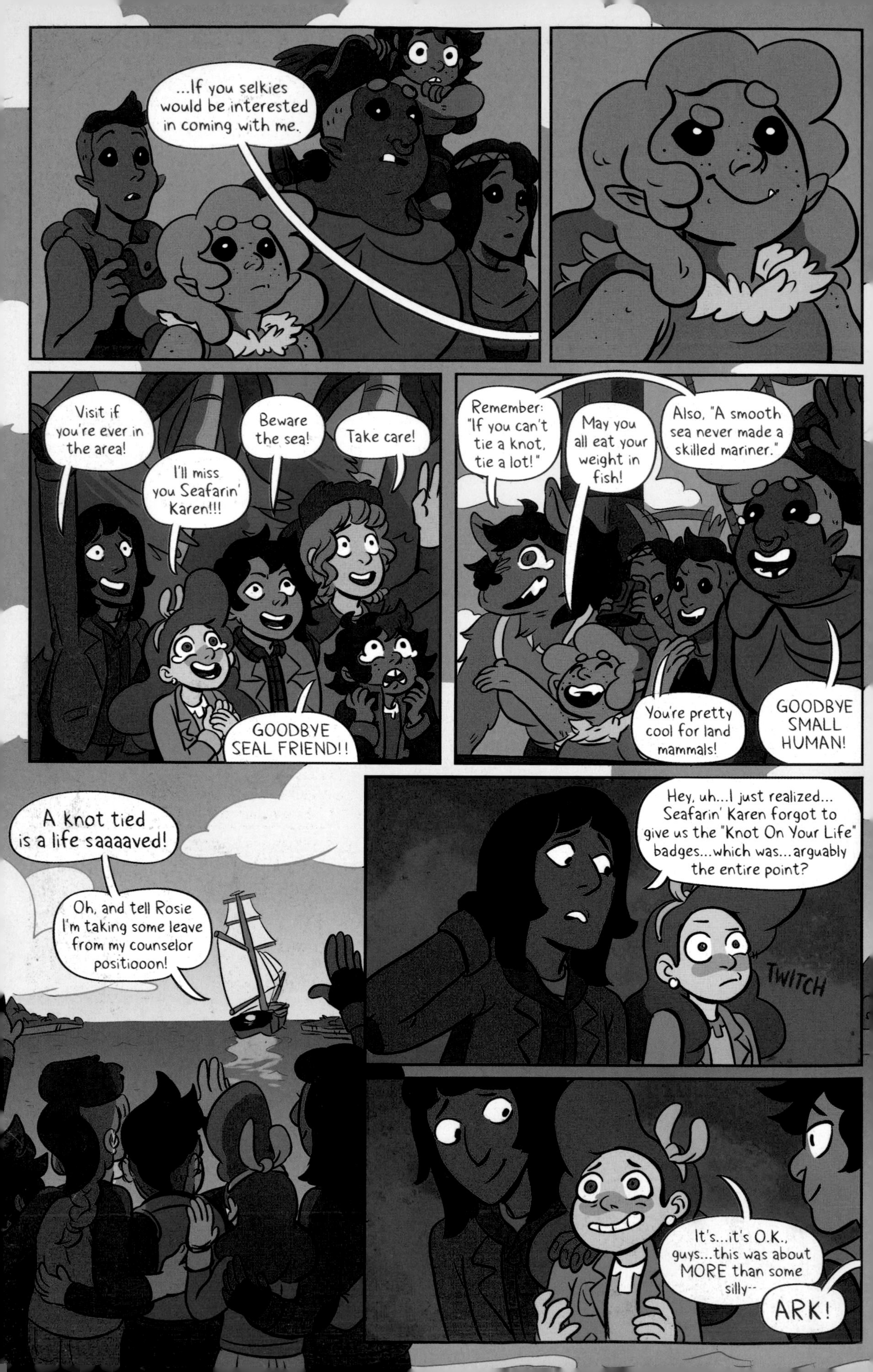

...If you selkies would be interested in coming with me.
Visit if you're ever in the area!
I'll miss you Seafarin' Karen!!!
Beware the sea!
Take care!
GOODBYE SEAL FRIEND!!
Remember: "If you can't tie a knot, tie a lot!"
May you all eat your weight in fish!
Also, "A smooth sea never made a skilled mariner."
You're pretty cool for land mammals!
GOODBYE SMALL HUMAN!
A knot tied is a life saaaaved!
Oh, and tell Rosie I'm taking some leave from my counselor positiooon!
Hey, uh...I just realized... Seafarin' Karen forgot to give us the "Knot On Your Life" badges...which was...arguably the entire point?
TWITCH
It's...it's O.K., guys...this was about MORE than some silly--
ARK!

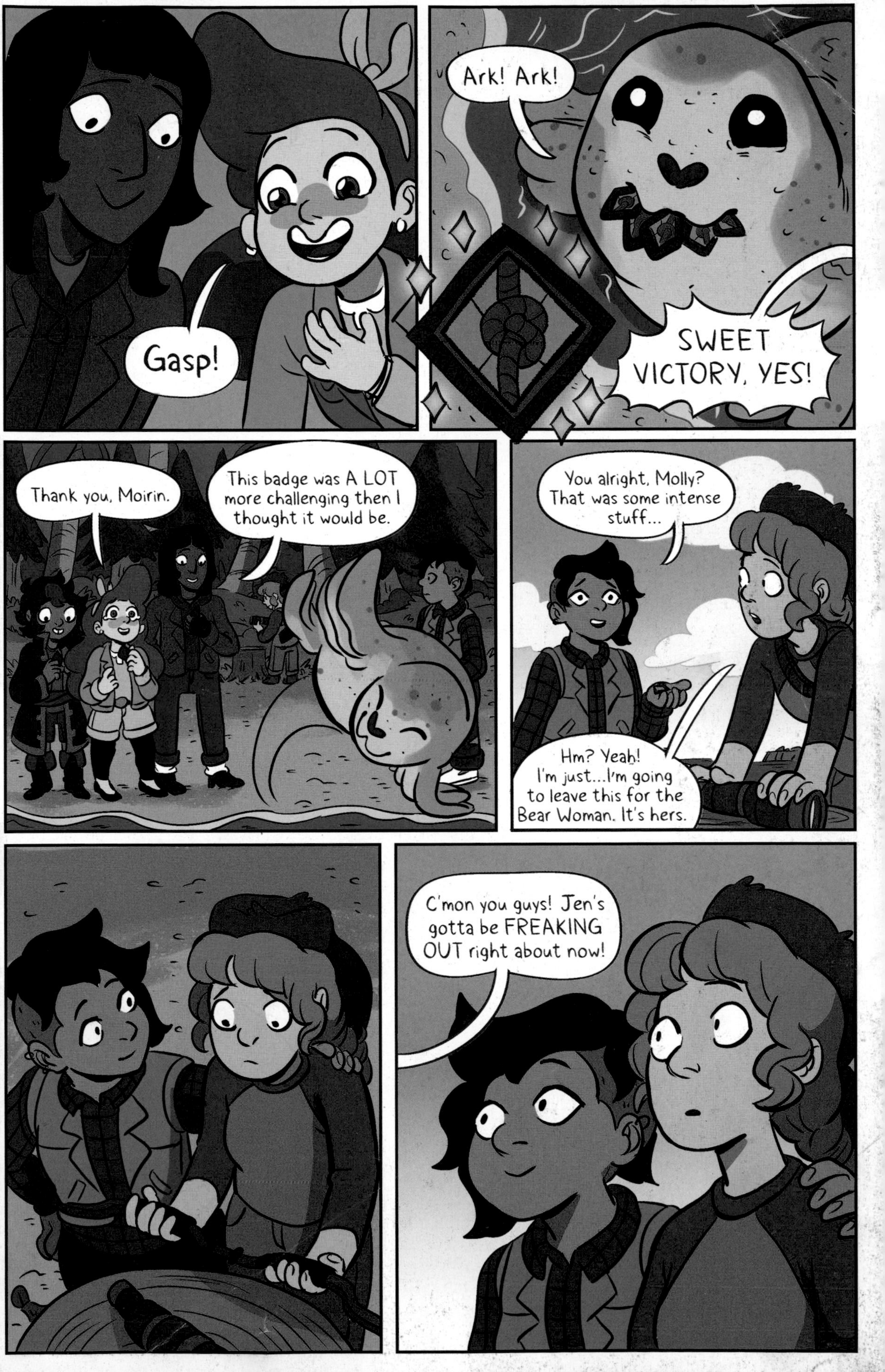
Gasp!
Ark! Ark!
SWEET VICTORY, YES!
Thank you, Moirin.
This badge was A LOT more challenging then I thought it would be.
You alright, Molly? That was some intense stuff...
Hm? Yeah! I'm just...I'm going to leave this for the Bear Woman. It's hers.
C'mon you guys! Jen's gotta be FREAKING OUT right about now!

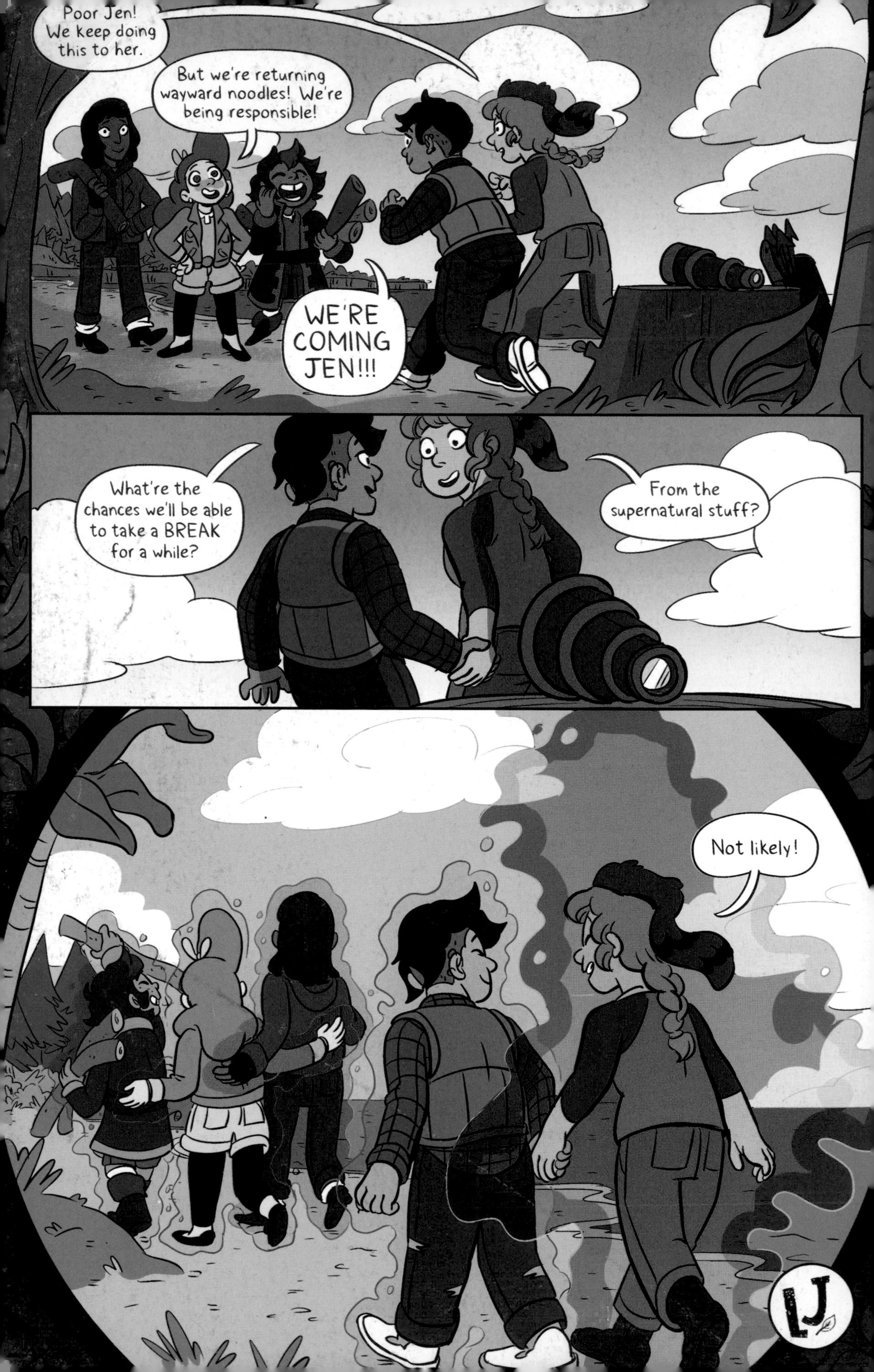
Poor Jen! We keep doing this to her.
But we're returning wayward noodles! We're being responsible!
WE'RE COMING JEN!!!
What're the chances we'll be able to take a BREAK for a while?
From the supernatural stuff?
Not likely!

will co...

The m...
It help...
appearan... ...should be worn at camp
dress ... ...events when Lumberjanes
Further... ...may also be worn at other
Lumber... ...ions. It should be worn as a
to have... ...the uniform dress with
part in... ...rect shoes, and stocking or
Thiskw... ...out grows her uniform or
Hardo... ...ng ...ster Lumberjane.
have... ...a she has
them... ...n her
... ...r her

The... ...CES
yellow, short sl...
emb...
the w...
choos...
slacks, ...
made o...
out-of-do...
green bere...
the colla...
Shoes ma...
heels, rou... ...ngs or
socks shou... ...with the shoes or wi...
the uniform. Ne... ...es, bracelets, or other jewelry do...
belong with a Lumberjane uniform.

WOOHOO!!

TA-DAA!

ANOTHER ADVENTURE DOWN

HOW TO WEAR THE U...

To look well in a uniform dem...
uniform be kept in good con...
pressed. See that the skirt is the r...
height and build, that the belt is...
that your shoes and stockings are...
uniform, that you watch your posture ... ...uniform
with dignity and grace. If the beret is remo... ...helps to cre...
be sure that your hair is neat and kept in place with an in a group. ...
insconspicuous clip or ribbon. When you wear a active life th...
Lumberjane uniform you are identified as a member of another bond...
this organization and you should be doubly careful to future, and pr...
conduct yourself in a way that will show everyone that in order to b...
courtesy and thoughtfullness are part of being a Lumberjane pr...
Lumberjane. People are likely to judge a whole nation by Penniquiqul Thi... ...ore Lady
the selfishness of a few individuals, to criticize a whole Types, but m... ...es will wish to have one. They
family because of the misconduct of one member, and to can either bu... ...s, or make it themselves from
feel unkindly toward and organization because of the materials available at the trading post.

COVER GALLERY

Lumberjanes "Arts and Crafts" Program Field

TREBLE MAKER BADGE

"Some risks are worth the reward."

Music fuels the mind and thus fuels creativity. A creative mind has the ability to make discoveries and create innovations. The greatest minds and thinkers like Hildegard von Bingen, Barbara Strozzi, and Florence Mary Taylor all had something in common in that they were constantly exploring their imagination and creativity. As a Lumberjane it will be vital that we not only enrich our minds, but enrich those around us. Music is just one of the many mediums that can create an empowering environment, it is one of the few mediums that can be enjoyed at any time.

Listening to instrumental music challenges one to listen and tell a story about what one hears. In the same sense, playing a musical instrument gives a Lumberjane the ability to tell a story without words. This will become handy should words escape her, and every Lumberjane understands the importance of not being limited to just words. Listening and telling a story require maximum right brain usage which not only exercises one's creativity but also one's intellect. The strength of all the arts including writing, painting, dance, and theater have the ability to create a similar effect. It is the understanding of that strength that will help the Lumberjane earn their *Treble Maker* badge. This badge is considered a favorite at most camps, and will most likely continue to be one of the most anticipated badges a scout can earn.

To obtain the *Treble Maker* badge a Lumberjane must show off their knowledge in not only musical theory and understanding, but be able to prove that they exemplify creativity in their problem solving. While it is just as important to think inside the box as it is to think outside of it a Lumberjane will need to know not only how to think outside the box, but how to create a new box altogether. It's through the many classes and trials that a Lumberjane will gain these skills as they continue on their path to the amazing future that undoubtedly waits for them.

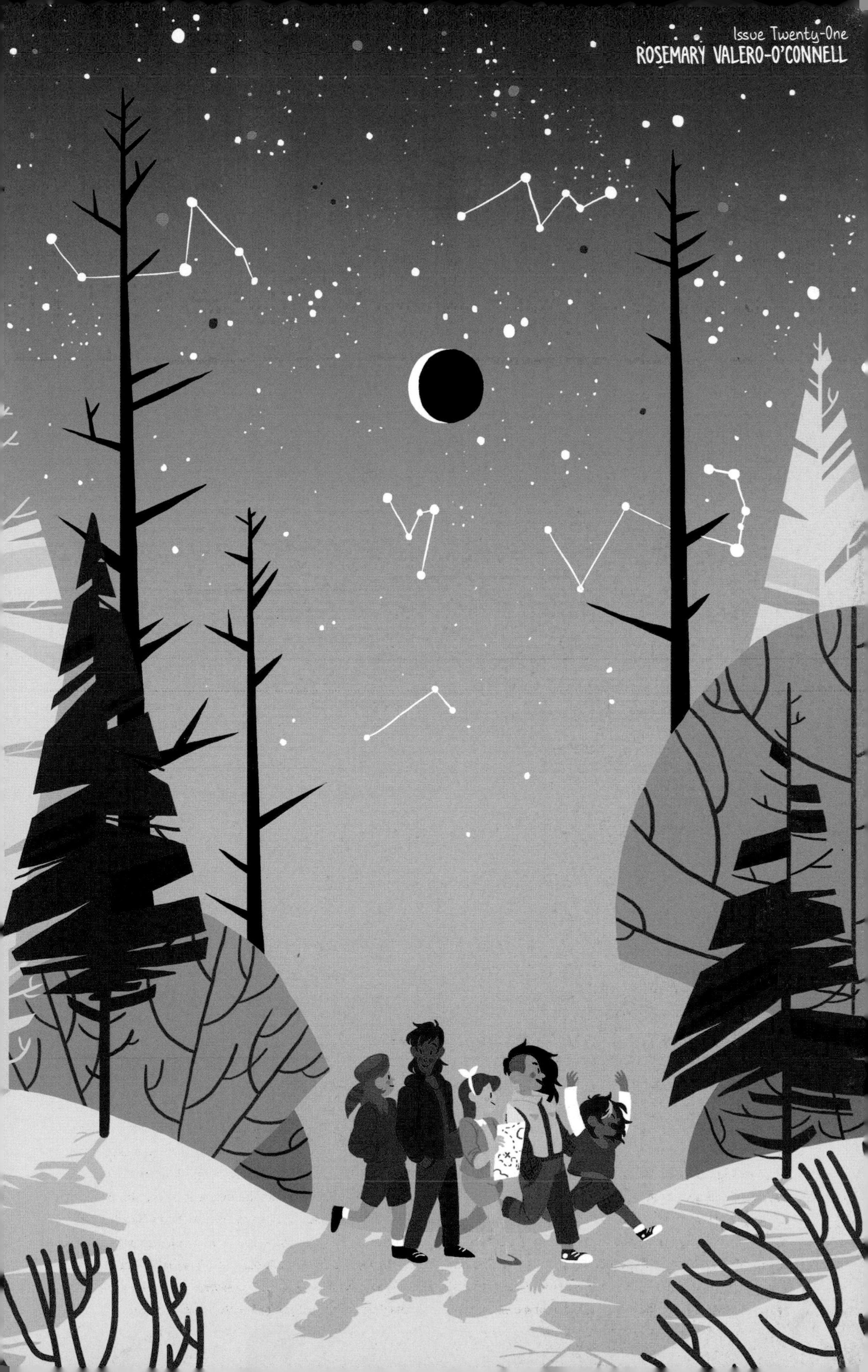
Issue Twenty-One
ROSEMARY VALERO-O'CONNELL

Issue Twenty-One Variant
MELANIE GILLMAN

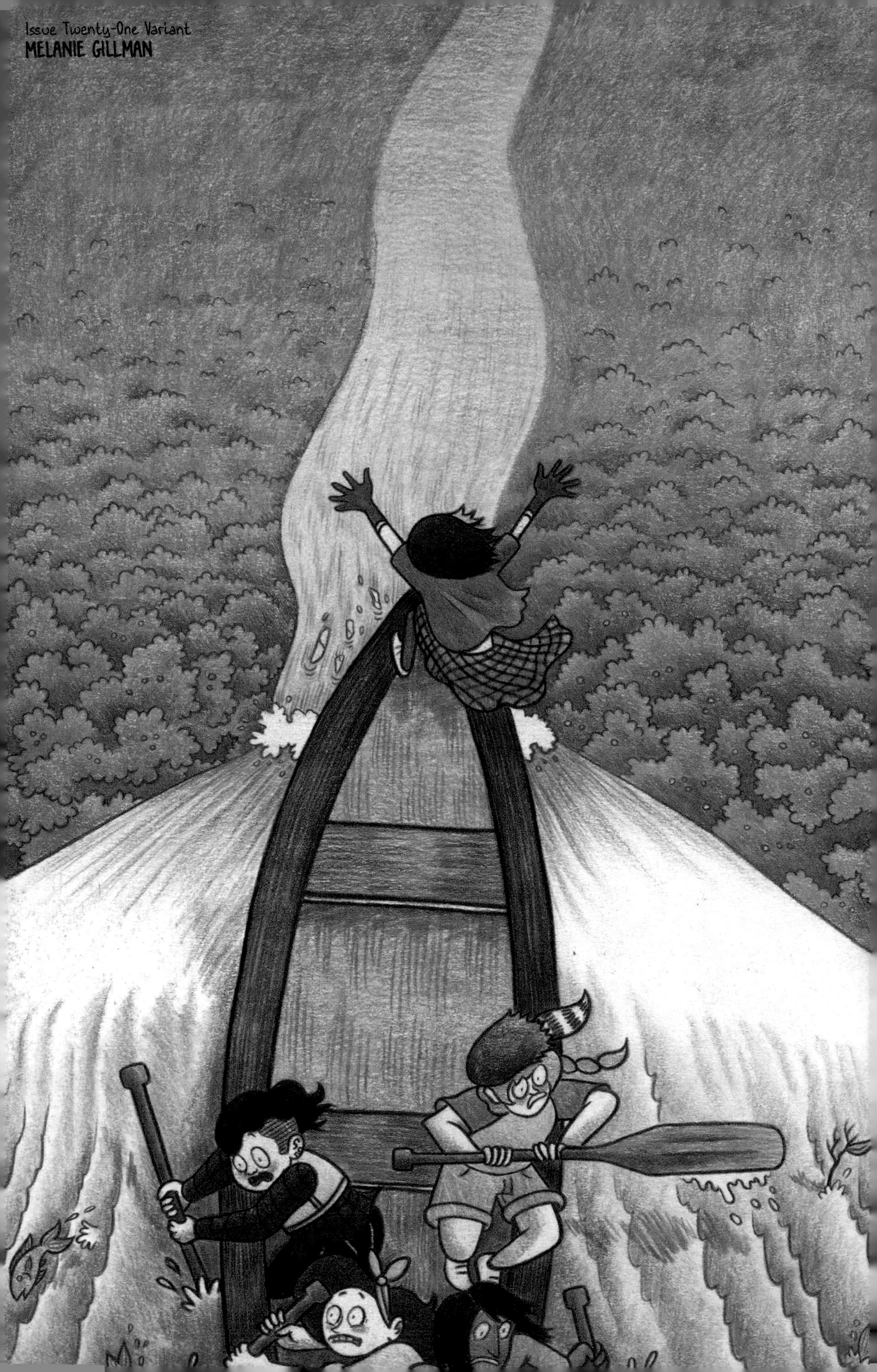

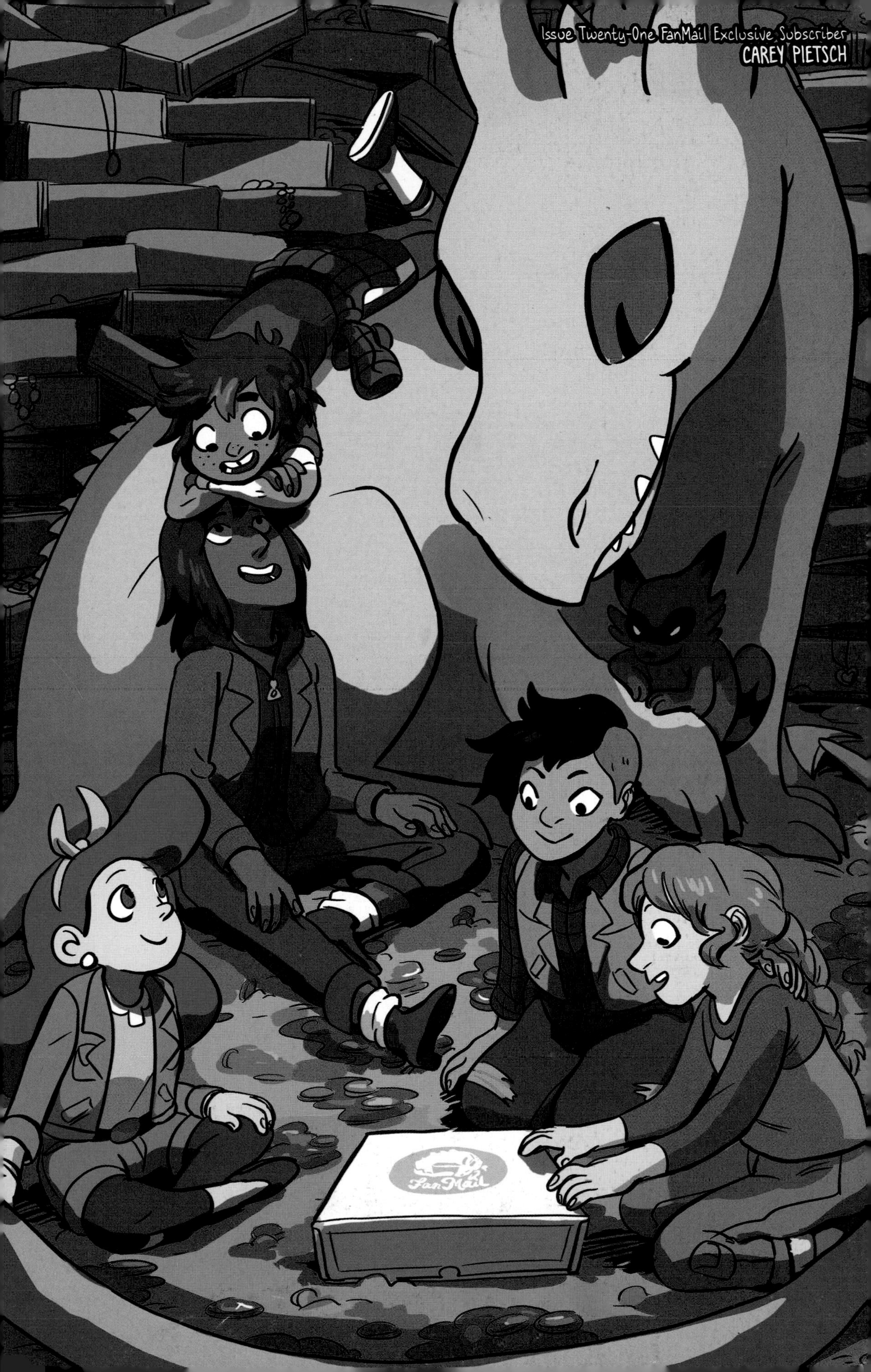
Issue Twenty-One FanMail Exclusive Subscriber
CAREY PIETSCH
FanMail

Issue Twenty-Two
ROSEMARY VALERO-O'CONNELL

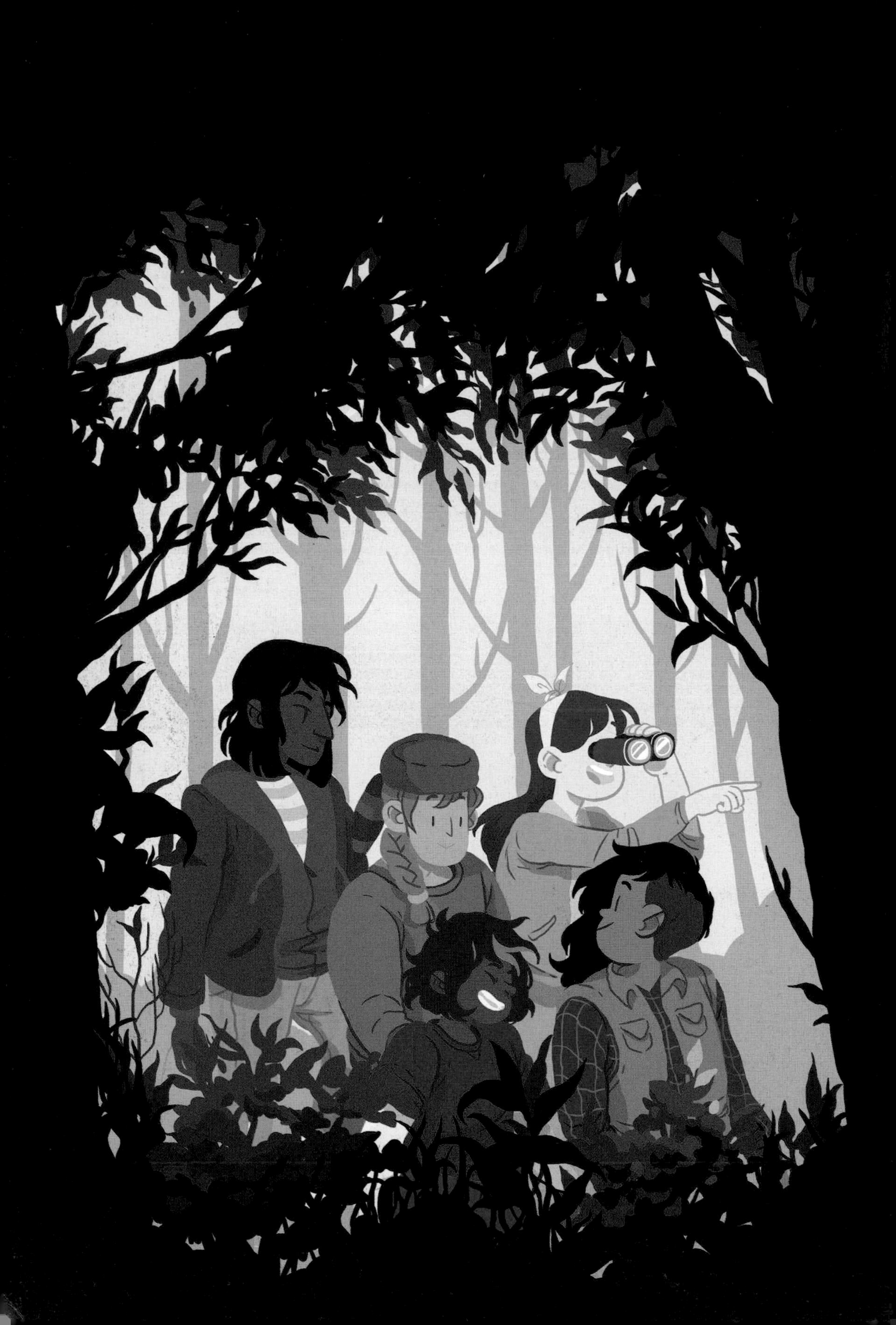

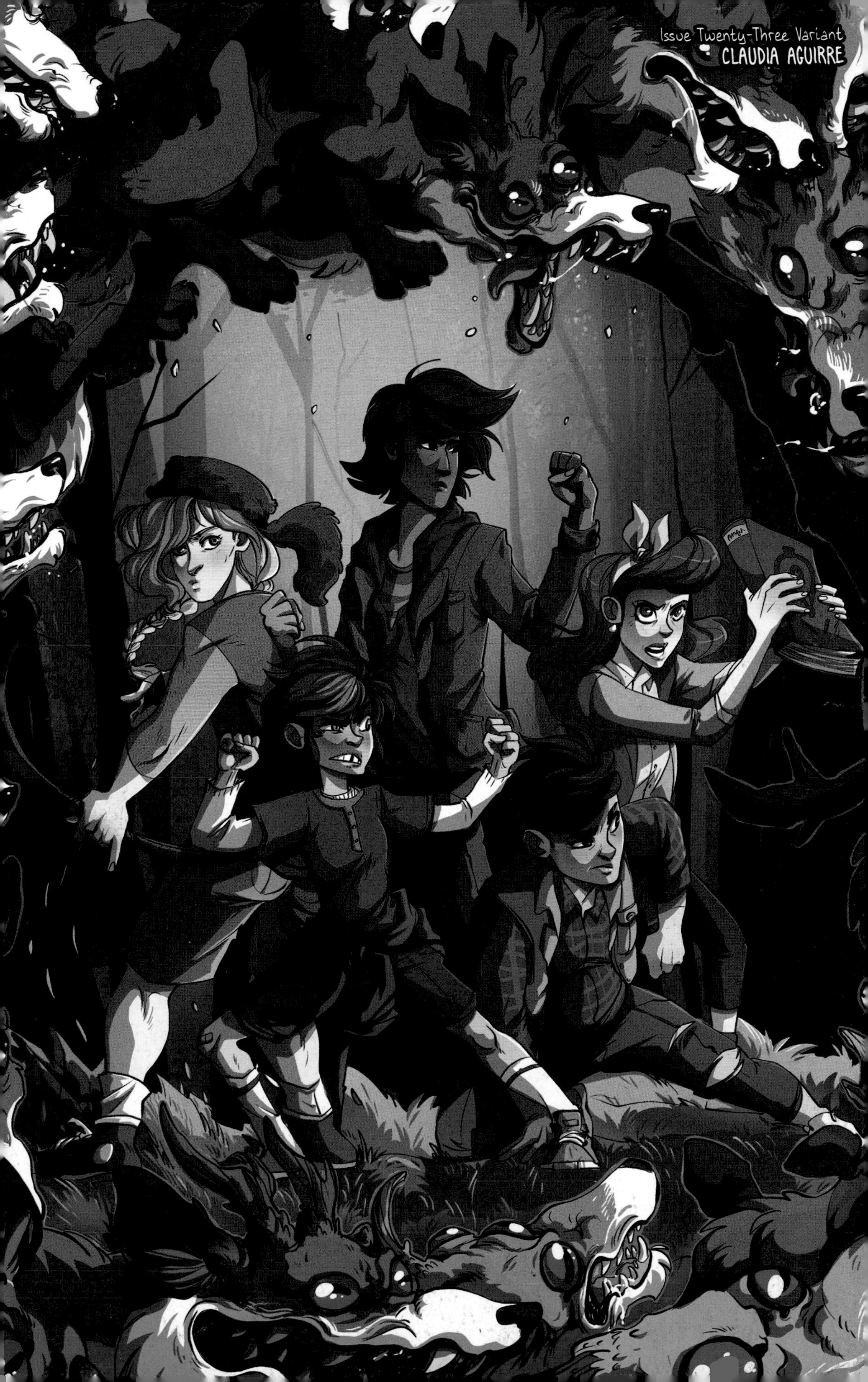
Issue Twenty-Three Variant
CLAUDIA AGUIRRE

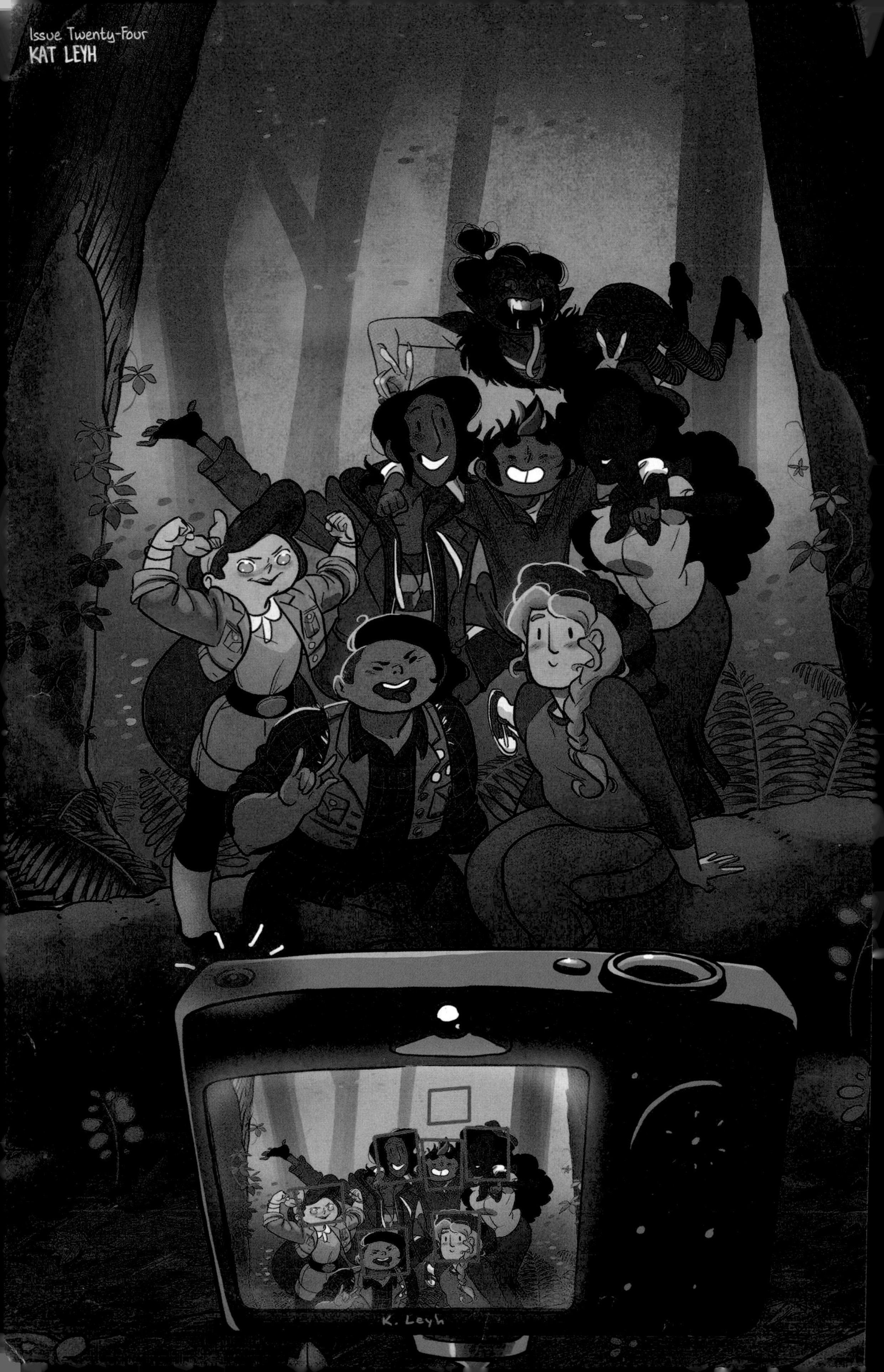
Issue Twenty-Four
KAT LEYH
K. Leyh

Issue Twenty-Three
ROSEMARY VALERO-O'CONNELL

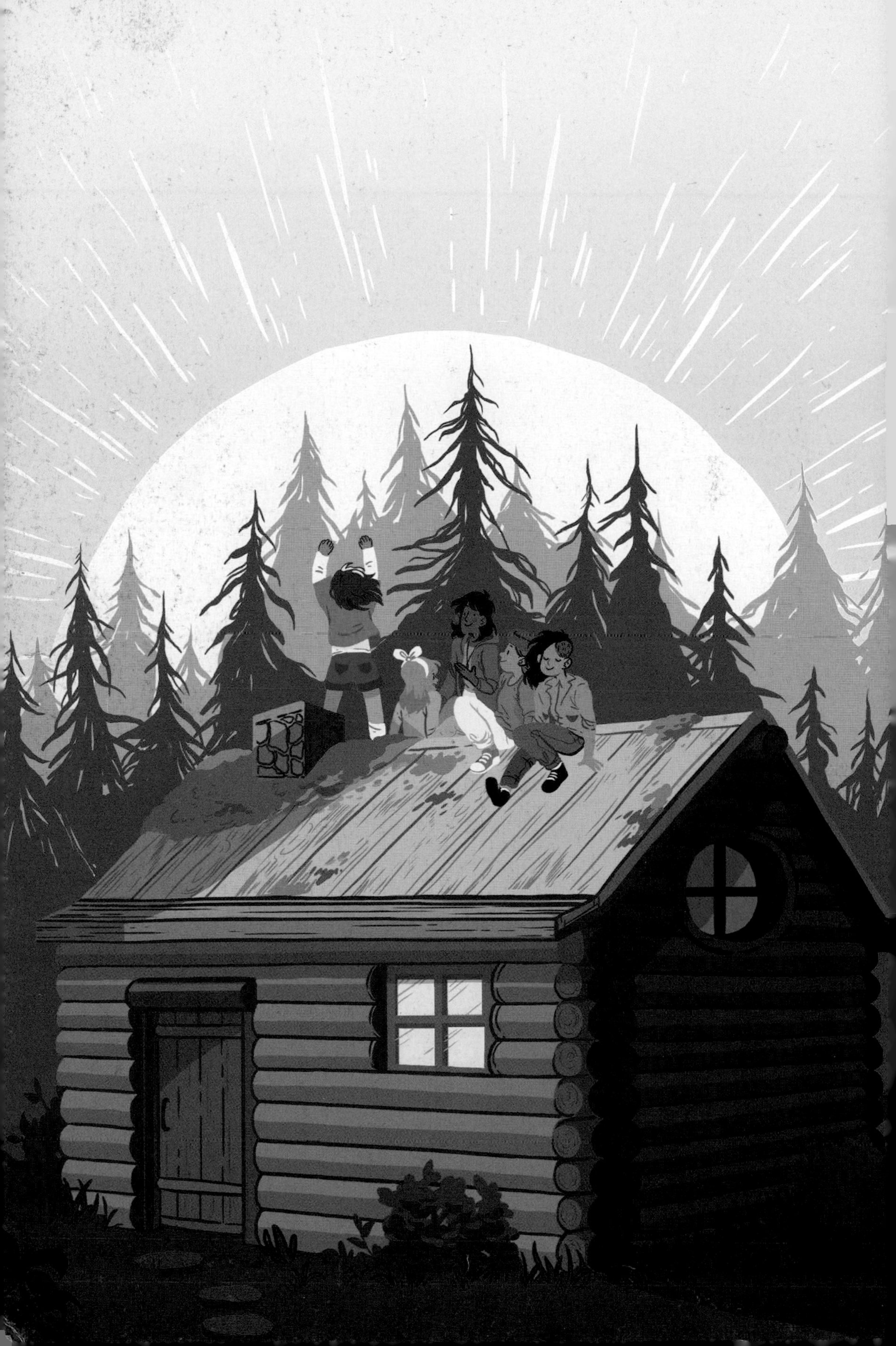

Issue Twenty-Two Variant
EVA CABRERA

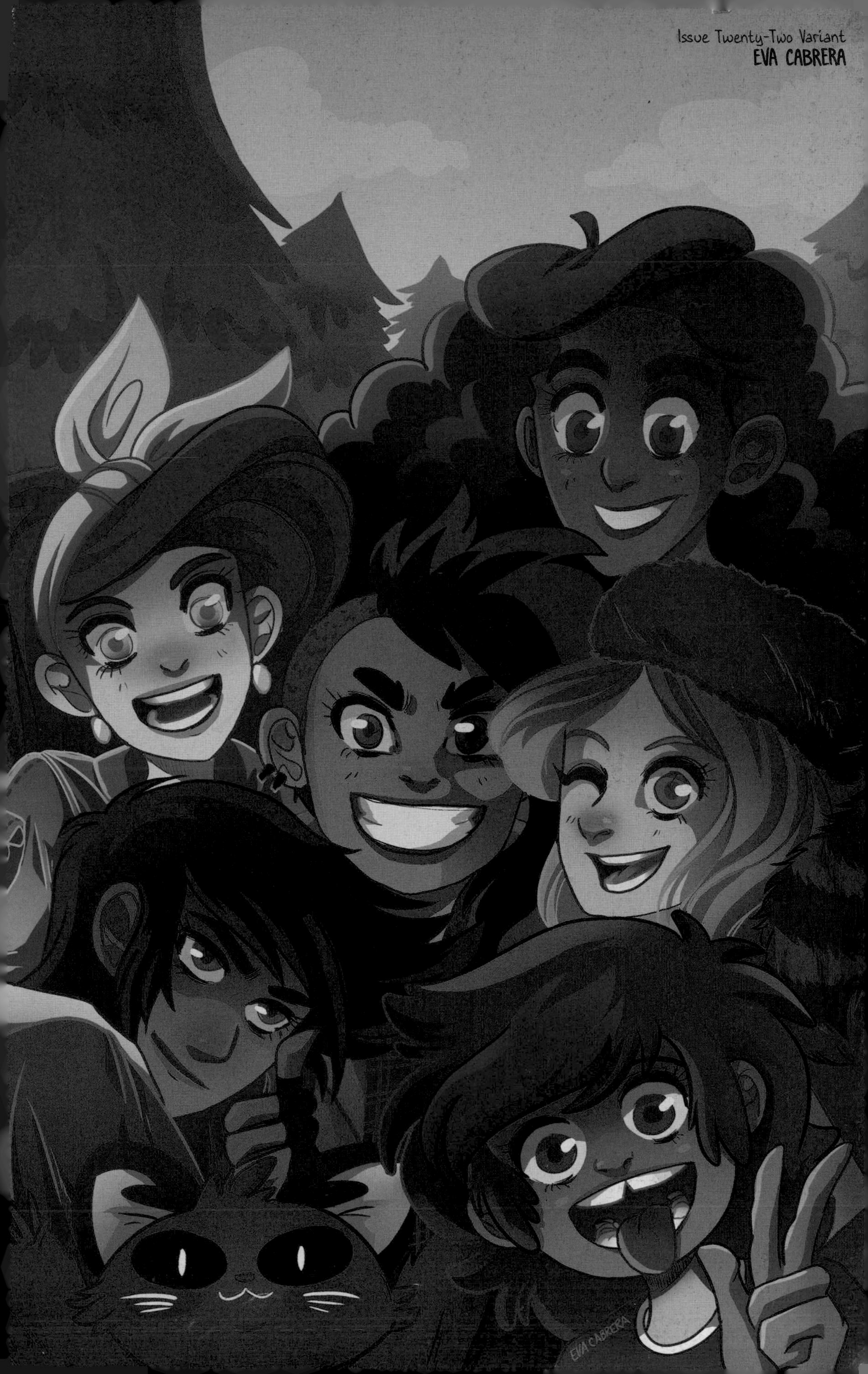
EVA CABRERA

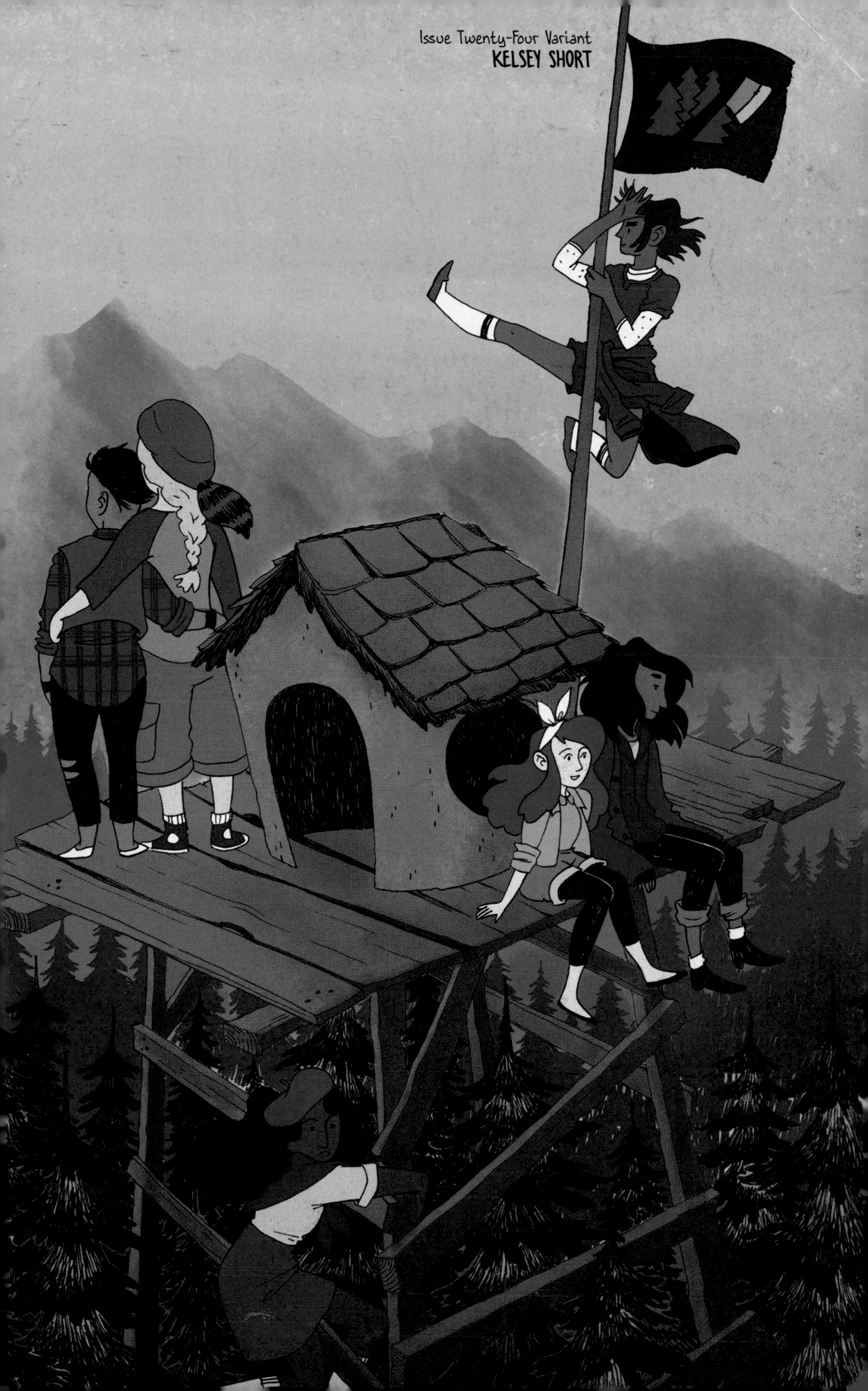

Issue Twenty-Four Variant
KELSEY SHORT

LJ